EVERY BOAT
TURNS SOUTH

EVERY BOAT
TURNS SOUTH

J. P. WHITE

THE PERMANENT PRESS
Sag Harbor, New York 11963

For information, address:
The Permanent Press
4170 Noyac Road
Sag Harbor, NY 11963
www.thepermanentpress.com

Library of Congress Cataloging-in-Publication Data

White, J. P.
    Every boat turns south / J.P. White.
        p. cm.
    ISBN-13: 978-1-57962-188-9 (alk. paper)
    ISBN-10: 1-57962-188-0 (alk. paper)
        1. Charter boat captains—United States—Fiction. 2. Caribbean Area—Fiction. 3. Psychological fiction gsafd I. Title.

PS3573.H4724E94 2009
813'.54—dc22   2009010538
Printed in the United States of America.

In Memory of the Skipper

ACKNOWLEDGMENTS

I'd like to thank all of my stalwart readers and editors who stayed with me over a decade of writing and rewriting including Richard Solly, Jay Peterzell, Ken Freed, Dave Hage, Allan Katz, Bill Tremblay, Joe Gilford, Lois Gilbert, Judith Shepard, and most of all, my wife, Betty Bright. This novel would not have come together without your insights, ideas and honesty.

Every criminal forgives himself in advance of the crime.

— ALBERT CAMUS

I am digging a pit deeper than I need.

— PETER KLAPPERT

There are strange rivers you cannot see.

— JOHN STEWART

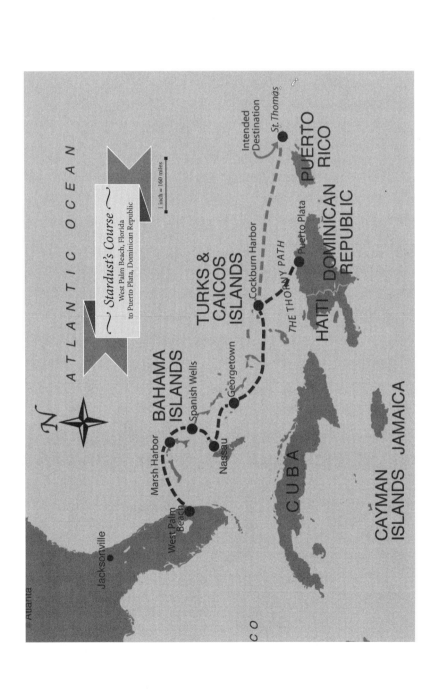

ATLANTIC OCEAN

N

Stardust's Course
West Palm Beach, Florida
to Puerto Plata, Dominican Republic

1 inch = 160 miles

Atlanta

Jacksonville

West Palm Beach

Marsh Harbor

BAHAMA ISLANDS

Spanish Wells

Georgetown

Nassau

TURKS & CAICOS ISLANDS

Cockburn Harbor

THE THORNY PATH

Puerto Plata

Intended Destination

St. Thomas

PUERTO RICO

HAITI DOMINICAN REPUBLIC

CUBA

CAYMAN ISLANDS JAMAICA

CHAPTER I

I slouch at the end of the day on my parents' front steps and smell threads of rain mixed with the musty tang of things growing and rotting in the same catch. I took a train from Ft. Lauderdale to Jacksonville and hitched north carrying two black trash bags of clothes. The wind off the Atlantic tells me I smell worse than day-old fish bait. My legs are so tight and tired from interstate walking I can feel them twitch inside a wobble. A low grade fever wanders my body like a torched and rolling penny. If I had a mirror, I wouldn't greet the man outlined in grit and stubble.

I got lost in a storm at the tail end of the Bahamas in 1980, and now it's 1983 or is it 1984? I couldn't say for sure what the day is, the month or the year. Flung up on my parents' doorstep, I've reached the threshold of as much trouble as I can lay claim to as a thirty-year-old: I'm soaked in sweat with the thunder nickering, hoping my aging parents will take me in because I've got nowhere else to go with my story.

I park my trash bags and stare at their front door. My wrist bones search for any handhold. My body trembles from the taut indecision of what to do next. I lean forward and touch my forehead to the door thinking the termite wood will tell me what to do. It doesn't.

When I do knock, I expect to find my parents mulling a cribbage board on the back porch of this cottage on Amelia Island, Florida; their purple-veined hands flying fast through the pegging of the count. Any harbor, even the harbor of deep-knotted pain, can be weathered with a deck of cards. That's what my mother claims, but she's not telling even half the truth. An only child, and a master of Solitaire, Kings in the Corner, Bridge, Hearts, Poker and just about any other game, she's just as likely to pack a deck as a wallet into her purse. *The cards always conceal as much as they reveal,* I hear her say and I've come to think that phrase could pass as her byline.

My father will be wearing his blue denim work shirt with the sleeves rolled up and his white floppy hat stained with paint and varnish. He might even be wearing his bunched-up blue cardigan even though the room will be damp with heat. My mother will be nattily pressed in white capris, emerald silk blouse with silver dolphin broach. Between them, there will be a scalloped glass bowl brimming with radishes, celery, olives, carrots. He'll be drinking grape juice from a wine glass. She, two fingers of Spanish sherry. I expect to find them neck and neck on Third Street, each playing with the near-telepathic ease that comes with fifty years of hiding inside a two-person game that banks on a secret blind account: the crib. *The crib will save me,* I hear my mother say, but the crib never does. Nothing saves her. Nothing is enough. Not God. Not sherry. Not all the boat travel up and down the Florida coast. Nothing saves her from the long voyage of dark memory unending.

Their doorstep's littered with storm debris. An unexpected rustling makes me jump. Inside a tent of fallen fronds, a chameleon stands as big as a dragon. I stare him down. He doesn't budge. He and I have sized each other up somewhere before. I raise the salt-stained brass door knocker in the shape of a human hand and let it drop hard against the wood. My blood jumps from my ankles to my wrists as I wait for a greeting, an answer, a cracked door, anything.

No footsteps. No voices. I hear only the Atlantic two blocks away jigging up the beach. I cup my hand over the brass hand and let it drop again. I call out, trying to imagine what words will enter my mouth, then I say, "Skip, Mom, it's me."

I lick my lips, twist the doorknob, thinking it's not too late to back away, thumb to the interstate, keep moving north. The door's open. I step gingerly across a gray slate threshold like I'm stepping over stinger jellyfish cast upon the beach. I let myself steal a breath after seeing Skip's favorite print of two sailboats thrashing downwind that hangs on the foyer wall to the left. To the right, I see a vase of wilted flowers and a sprawled stack of unopened mail.

I call out again. No answer.

I see, through the back porch glass, my mother curled in a chaise lounge, her pink knees touching. Her hands hanging slack at her side. A figure of depletion and scattered pulse. I look about the living room and see no newspapers, no magazines, none of my mother's books or needlepoint set about like decorations. The only familiar watermark is a dusty collage of photos on the mantel where my dead brother looks out upon his world after his legendary poolside heroics.

I peer into Skip's room and it too looks vacant. I see one family photo over Skip's bed. The four of us stand on the aft deck of a schooner in Mystic Seaport. My brother Hale and I grip the standing rigging. We are tan and fit and look like the tested working crew that we are. Skip wears his floppy white hat and blue shirt. At fifty-five, he's thin and strong as the edge-nailed cedar he used to build his boat, *Pirate's Penny*. He's taken early retirement from his job with Metropolitan Life Insurance and cashed in his own policies. Mother leans into him with one leg up. We're en route from Ohio to Florida and filled with the promise of an oceanic whisper streaming into us from all the good water ahead. But for this photo, it's as if I've returned to a home fled during the last hurricane that never came, but the owners have not yet straggled back.

The front guest room is closed.

I hear the thin ragged breathing of a child coming from the other side of the door. I push the door open and see him, or rather I see only his pockmarked face and flaky cue ball head sticking out from underneath a white cotton blanket. In a guardrail hospital bed, he looks like a man already cast for his own sarcophagus, and no longer even a distant reflection of his former Montgomery Cliff vigor. Not trusting my eyes, I lift the blanket to see the rest of him and find bleeding lesions over his arms and legs that can't be contained by bandages. His skin is so thin, it looks like it'll tear if I touch him. I jerk back, thinking of the pain he must feel at every pitch and roll of a funky body all used up.

11

I sit down in the rocker beside his bed, then reach out to hold his left hand.

Like my own left hand that's missing the pinkie, his too is damaged. His left hand bears a welted scar that runs the diagonal of his palm, the result of a burn he suffered as a toddler when he saw a distant glow in a dark room and thrust his hand inside a cast-iron stove door to grip the red-eye coals. He blacked out from the pain, but his father owned a fast car and knew a burn surgeon who worked through the night to save his son's hand. My father must feel the weight of my hand in his. He leans up from his pillow and stabs me with a cross-eyed glance as if he's looking at a ghost coming toward him out of a far shipping lane. "Who's there?"

"It's Matt, Skip. It's me."

My father juts out his chin, pouts, gives a little growl.

"You look like something the raccoons forgot to eat."

"That's about how I feel."

He squints hard to look me over from some interior distance I can't fathom.

"Say you don't deserve it?"

"I'm sorry, I wanted to call, but . . ."

"Where in the Sam Hell have you been? Your mother's been sick with worry."

He scrunches his nose, smiles weakly, bites down on his lip in an alternating expression of relief and anger.

"I thought you were sleeping, Skip."

"The Skipper never sleeps when his ship's under way. Merely resting me eyes." His eyes are streaked with blood and fog.

"What's going on here, Skip?"

"What's it look like? I'm dying and it ain't pretty no matter what the preacher says. You picked a damn poor time to vanish off the charts."

"I've come back, Skip."

"Why? You got laundry and no quarters?"

"There are some things I need to tell you."

He ignores me by twisting toward the wall. "Your mother's flat out shot. Money's gone. I can't do anything but flip around here in this fucking contraption like a two-bit sideshow. What are you, between boats? Don't they have phones wherever in the hell you were?"

"It's kind of hard to explain."

"I'm not going anywhere," Skip says, rubbing his eyes as if pinned by a spotlight. "You better start talking before I scatter to the four winds." He shakes his head in disbelief, then pulls the sheet over his head.

I smile at his peek-a-boo ritual and want to laugh, but my cotton mouth won't work right. From under the blanket I hear, "Can't you see I'm a little busy right now. I've got some serious dying to do and you can't do it for me."

My mother leans on the doorframe, her faced pinched by exhaustion. She grabs at her lower back. "Just sit with him," she says. "You don't have to talk. There's morphine when things get bad. He says he won't take it, not ever, but the doctor says he will."

I get up to hug her. She raises her hand, pushes her palm toward me like she's honking for me to slam on my brakes. I try hard to swallow through the scratches in my throat. I sit back down, my shoes digging into the carpet.

"One postcard in three years," she says. "We thought you were dead."

It's not her words that stop me. It's her. The way she looks past me, all blank and sallow and driven far back into a small, hurt place. I don't recognize the thick creases standing over her lips. I can't see her eyes behind her new thick glasses. She's smaller than I remember. Her blouse is skewed because she's missed the bottom button. She turns and leaves almost as quickly as he does by pulling the sheet over his head. So much for finding Jack and Emily Younger pegging the outer banks of Third Street and dipping their radishes in a splash of salt.

I drop my father's hand, the color of stained butcher paper.

I can feel the sweat beading my shirt, my jaw tightening, the air slackening in my chest. One voice pounds my neck veins saying, *Tell what you know, Tell what you know.* Another voice answers, *It's no use, It's no use.* This strangled call and response punches my sternum and shoves me toward the door. I want in. I want out. I want my skipper to look me in the eyes with something other than a burn before he sweeps out to sea. All I have to do is remember to breathe because mostly I want to hold my breath before I have to hurt them more with all I know and am afraid to tell. Then again . . .

I look down at the claw of my hand and think, why should I tell them anything resembling the truth? They've been polishing their dagger scowl toward me for thirteen years. And why not? They believe I caused the death of our family god, my older brother, Hale. Even I believed that story, believed it enough to drop out of high school and ship out for ports unknown, believed it enough to never skulk the long way back and tell them what the hell really happened.

I want a rum, but I suspect my mother has thrown away all the hard stuff years ago. A cold beer at least will start to blur the boundaries between where I've been and this diminishing house with no deck of cards in sight.

What was I thinking before I knocked?

I'll never be able to tell my mother what happened the night Hale died. Mothers never want the whole story. She can't stand to watch the evening news. And the last three years? Why would she want to know about drug running, jail time, and the beautiful liars who made me nuzzle the hem of Jesus on the mountain? Wanting only to lick down the corners of a rum-soaked ice cube, I start to plot the angles of my return, uncertain which legs of my journey to keep secret, which to sketch in for my skipper. I've heard a thousand stories from him. Now he'll have to listen to mine. The dying aren't the only ones greedy for confession.

I slump in the rocking chair beside my father's bed while he curls up in that drowsy, slack-tide netherworld reserved for the dying.

"Where in the Sam Hell have you been?" His words sting my head. I shut my eyes because I dread everything I'm about to see again. I aim to tell my father I've been a long ways gone into one hell of a salvage operation and I'm still waiting to surface.

I want to say there are no calendars where I live. No phones. No postmen. No means to reach back and fix all the broken parts between us. I want to say my nights are stripped of mercy and sweet fruit. I say nothing because now I'm back in Florida, second home of the Confederate flag and the red-headed vulture, boiled peanuts by the bucket, and all seven kinds of poisonous snakes. It's the one place I told myself I couldn't come back to because this is where Hale drowned and I lived. The one place with so many unfinished characters like me who drift out to the last piling on fishing piers, talking in tongues, flashbacks, detours, and sorry-assed reversals of fortune—all of them fishing without enough live bait to catch a snook or drum. This is where great temptation and a world of trouble first got hitched to the ball and chain. Where there's no such thing as hard work just *good luck, bad luck, maybe tomorrow, maybe not, who can say, no way to tell, beats the hell out of me.* I left for good and now I'm back, so what can I do, but tell my shipwright father a sailing story that contains my vanishing and my return and all that skitters in between after the night my god-like brother back-flipped into the Gulf Stream and never rose again. Before my long confession, a shorter one . . .

I've been a shipwrecked sailor for a long time even though I've never stopped moving, never stopped clutching death, fleeing death, seeking work, quitting work, my arrivals and departures more blurred than gasoline on water. If I could drag all my earthly failures into the torn eye of a hurricane, then maybe the slate of who I am would break clean. Maybe. No matter the maelstrom that's certain to one day find me wanting, I also want money, lots of money, so I can get back to the islands with another boat, and I know exactly where my father hides his cash.

CHAPTER II

I drift sideways into the kitchen and flip open all the cupboards for any drink with dark brown, gold, or reddish bite. My mother follows, all swivel-fist and flushed at the throat. Her cheeks, gray hollows. Her mouth thin as a nail. Her eyes blood-shot glazed like those of any refugee from the frozen river of no time.

"Why did you come back here? You need money, right? Well, there isn't any. I've spent most of it looking after your father. There's no booze either. Not even a beer."

Boom, Crack-a, Boom. Welcome to death vigil mother thunder. I don't say anything. My legs have no fight. I can't lift my arms to counterpunch with a woman jacked on grief, not just for her husband's coming death, but for the death of her first and favorite son. And I can't bring myself to get a fix on the contents of the family safe, not yet.

"Just tell me why you've come back?"

"I got into some trouble. I need to catch my breath."

"When haven't you been in trouble?"

"I didn't come here for money or protection. I'm not running from anyone. I came back to tell Skip about Hale." Already, I dish up a half truth I'll have to dispose of later.

"You're thirteen years too late. There's nothing you can say we don't know. We've filled in all the blanks you left empty."

"You don't know the half of it," I snap.

"I know that Hale died a long time ago and you had everything to do with it. That's all I need to know."

My mother pulls at the collar of her blouse with one hand. With the other hand, she digs her index finger into her thumb. I give up looking for a drink and settle for tap water. *Water, water, everywhere*, I say, *and not a drop to drink.*

"You're still living for the next drink, aren't you?

"No, not even close," I say, clenching my jaw, wanting more than anything to blur my exit from her kitchen where she never loses a fight.

"Whatever you need to say to your father, you better make it quick. His doctor can't believe he's held on this long. He says any day now."

"I know what my job is," I say.

"I doubt it," she says, looking in a drawer for nothing she needs. "You don't know how to hold down a job."

"You're more wrong than right," I offer lamely with my head down inside my second half-truth.

"Spoken like a man who knows how to outsmart a judge, but not his mother."

My mother long ago sucked all the violent sob out of bereavement and turned it into blame. I'm no match for her tonight, but soon.

"Let's see how you do as his night nurse. I can't get up anymore when he cries out at two in the morning. Let's see what you can do." She turns away and returns to her bedroom across the living room and closes the door. I hear a second click like the sound of a lock. A lock within a lock within a lock, my mother's cottage. Even though there's at least one ocean and a black Bible between us, we're closer than she knows because my life is a story within a story and beneath that wreckage, there's another story yet. We each have our locks and we each have our keys.

Boom, Crack-a, Boom.

I sit tight that first night in a cottage my father built on a canal, packed with rare alligator turtles and smallmouth bass, and within earshot of the Atlantic—although at this moment the tree frogs are so loud the surf is lost inside their bulging throats. I look up to the window screen and see a pair of these long-legged emerald beauties locked and pulsing. In their frenzy, the lovers scald out of the trees and sizzle above Skip's head. I watch their bellies heaving, their red tongues spiking mesh as he sleeps uneasily and wakes and navigates the slack tide between this life and what comes next. He barely resembles the man I remember. His blood is now more purple than red and erupting from scalp to knuckle, from knee to heel, the vanishing weight of him already approaching something like thick, brackish water working every angle back toward the Atlantic.

Desire everything, I think, watching the lurching and dangling tree frogs, *Get nothing.*

Skip, I know you can hear me, so hear this . . .

Before I travel all the way back to tell you about the night of Hale's death, I need to tell you about my last three years in the islands. I need to show you how far off-course one bad night can take another sailor who, like you, didn't know how to make sense of the repeating heave that Hale's death created in all of us.

Please, let there be time enough to unshackle what I know . . .

In West Palm Beach, in January, 1980, I meet a well-heeled Sam Wells on the docks and convince him to hire me to deliver his boat to Red Hook Bay in St. Thomas. I show him an Honors Certificate from a correspondence school in New Jersey that grants me a captain's license, known in the trade as a six-pack license, meaning I'm eligible to take six passengers. The certificate is as phony as a cubic zirconium diamond ring. I'd bought the certificate from a man in a bar for a hundred bucks and signed my name. What I don't know about sailing ain't worth knowing, I tell Sam Wells. He hires me after the second G&T that tastes more like a two-finger martini.

Before I sign on for the job, I take *Stardust* out for a sea trial in brisk seas off West Palm Beach and she stands up to weather. She slices the water, not as three hulls, but as one, a sturdy craft with no apparent weakness in her various articulating limbs. Skip, I know you have a low opinion of multihulls, but *Stardust* is a nimble forty foot trimaran. Like all multihulls, her stability comes from her impressive twenty-seven foot beam rather than her ballast. She's light and spry like a broad-winged frigate and can easily fly over fifteen knots downwind. She has a fifty-eight horsepower diesel that gives her a motor speed close to eight knots. She has standing headroom in the main cabin with plenty of bins, cubbies, lockers, and nooks, and a real elbow-sized chart table. She's trimmed out in satin-finished mahogany from the galley to the forward V-berth and has a cozy salon with settees port and starboard flanking a fold-up dinette and a fully-enclosed head with shower. I know what you're thinking, the interior finish is just window-dressing. The cockpit's cozy, if not a little cramped, but every control line I need to sail upwind or downwind runs back to the cockpit.

Sam Wells paid $90K for *Stardust* and to tell you the truth Skip, it seems like a bargain because *Stardust* also comes with Anderson self-tailing winches (which you would like using, given your hobbled spine) and a brand-new one-fifty self-furling jib. Sailing her is effortless and fun, quick but stable, high performance with low maintenance. I tell myself she'll do just fine on a long island-hopping run through the Bahamas. Still, what's the old saw? *Appearances are deceiving*. I should have listened to you, but I was eager to leave the land after I got fired from my last job at a marina on Satellite Beach. I got blamed for the fire that ate half the docks, but I had nothing to do with an engine blowing up. It didn't help I was hung over when the first boat went up like a sparkler. I needed to get out from under that sour lemon and make something work out on the water. This is what I'm good at. What you showed me how to do.

Before I leave West Palm Beach for Marsh Harbor in the Abacos, I should tell you about Jesse, my cook, and Philip, my mechanic and first mate. I met Jesse at the same bar where I bought my phony six-pack license. This blonde leans against the bar with two rummies. She could be a hooker, but I don't care. Her two sidekicks are skinny and pale like boys raised on Velveeta and white vinegar. Their faces are both pockmarked and they wear black guayabera shirts with silver embroidery running front and back. When they talk to her, I can hear their teeth sawing. When they turn sideways, they disappear next to her full-bodied, sanguine figure.

She wears a short green dress with a cutaway back and black cane Brazilian sandals and a full fleet of fire-engine toenails. You might like the dress, Skip, but her three tattoos would give you pause. On the top of her right index finger, she's got a black scorpion sprawled between joint and knuckle. When she bends the finger, the scorpion snaps its tail. No kidding. Behind her right ear, a ruby dagger. Her right ankle is wrapped with a rainbow coral snake. *Scorpion, dagger, snake.* That's a lot of venom to burn into your hide. Some women are born to chase down the apocalypse. Others have already held it in their teeth. Sure as sugar, she's from the later school with breasts that perk up inside loose-fitting cotton. In a twangy Southern baritone, Jesse tells me about wanting to get out of Florida for the winter. Think of her, Skip, as the siren in a fogbank and don't bother with putting wax in the ears. She smells like California desert almonds or maybe lilacs itching to bloom, I can't tell which.

"I've dropped the hook in places where no one goes," she says as if she's squeezing the great sword of the horizon line in her hand instead of a beer. Then, the bragging starts. "I can take you to little gunk holes you'll never find on the charts. I can show you lobsters the size of your arm. And beaches no one's set foot on except giant iguanas. If you want to snag a shark, I can show you where the great whites swim at night."

She's worked on shrimp boats since she was eight and claims to know how to read blue water and coral heads better than anyone except her old man. "When you look toward an island, you just see the top of the water. When I look out, I see top and bottom. Just by looking at the color, I can tell you whether the bottom is shoal, sandy, rocks, ledges, or deep water on the edge of a drop-off."

"I bet you can," I say, looking at her from top to bottom like Christmas come early.

She already knows there's a trimaran at the Municipal marina in need of a cook to make a run to St. Thomas. She volunteers two of her favorite recipes, poached grouper with fresh ginger and almonds and grilled shrimp portofino with crushed rosemary, garlic, lemon. Her name is far from plain vanilla—Jesse Dove. She comes on board with a couple of bikinis, one duffel, and a green parrot named Rosie. Any way you size her up, Jesse trolls a lot of bait in the water. I can't say I like her, but it's hard not to linger. It's like looking at a wild animal in a cage with rain-slick fur. You can't quite believe the lips, the legs, the tits, and how she uses your disbelief to get her way.

As for Philip Laforgue, I overhear him talking at the harbor chandler, telling another man he's looking for a sailboat going south. Philip relates how once he'd been caught at an anchorage in Nicaragua by a *chubasco* wind—a storm you can't see or feel coming from any direction.

Imagine, Skip, a storm with no thunder. No lightning. No rain. No swell. No hint of anything bearing down on you, just bang, a sail-ripping sixty-knot wind in the middle of the night. Philip knows about *chubascos* and rushes up on deck, starts the engine on a fifty-foot Kettenburg sloop. He puts the engine into gear to take a load off the anchor line and keep the bow into the wind. Still, the anchor drags, so he instructs another crew member to let out more scope. That *chubasco* does him no harm, he says, and that's all I need to hear. If something fierce and freakish ever finds me, I want this guy on my foredeck or inside my engine room.

Ace mechanic, refrigeration maven, Philip's also a casual student of French and English poetry, the Bible, Shakespeare, French painting, plus he's a master diver. Before Philip started repairing diesels in Ft. Lauderdale, he'd worked for years on cruise ships, teaching men with "tight butts" and women with "intelligent hips" how to dive. During his twenties, Philip had sex with more women than men, but as he slipped into his thirties, he switched to men, and now he says he seldom spends a night out wanting for companionship.

That's my crew, Skip. Dicey and dangerous, but then I've already forged my credentials, so who am I to dig into their résumés? Skip wakes, tries to sit up, can't. He nods, seeing me and not seeing me fully like I'm only a silhouette or a house sound he can't place. I wipe a curlicue of spit from the crease of his chin. The tree frogs will not park their lust till dawn. The rains will start again soon. My father scoops his hand in the thick June air as if beckoning me to come in or go on . . .

I tell Sam Wells I should take *Stardust* on the outside of the Bahamas, then take a straight shot for Red Hook Bay, but he wants me to drift down through the islands and tell him if I see anything he should check out for future gunkholing. Fair enough. We cast off and make good time. Shit, it's all downwind. How can I have problems in a slingshot boat like this? I clock better than ten knots when I hoist the rags.

From Marsh Harbor, we fly over to Spanish Wells on a night run. Jesse and I are on watch between two and six. She tells me she's a shrimper's daughter from Jacksonville, never graduated from high school, never worked anywhere but on her Daddy's boats. Nothing's worked out for her. She says she feels like a refugee between wars, and that's how I feel, Skip, after I quit high school. I just skid along from one job to the next until I start delivering boats up and down the Eastern seaboard and over to the islands.

"Tell me about shrimping," I say, admiring, in the red binnacle light, how her brawny shoulders stack over her tiny waist like a thunderhead.

"Not much to tell. I was a striker, a deck hand. I haul lines that drag the nets. It's knuckle-busting work dragging boards along the bottom in twenty to forty feet of fast current. You're out on the ocean long before dawn. Sometimes it's flat. Other times, she's boiling. Wind, rain, heat, cold, engine problems, winch problems, ice maker problems, too much shrimp, no shrimp, everyone says fuck a lot even though there's a beauty to the haul. If nothing else, you get to know what kind of shit people lose or throw away. I once found a set of false teeth wrapped around a clam shell, a box of shotgun shells, and a used rubber stuffed inside a coil of pantyhose."

"What happens back on land?" I ask, hoping to learn as much as I can about my beautiful cook.

"The usual shit. Drinking and fighting among cunthounds. Nobody says what they know because you don't want another shrimper working your vein of gold. You never tell anyone when you're leaving or when you're coming back. The middle of the night might as well be noon. Secrets save your ass, even though none of us stay more than a couple of miles off the beach."

"How did things go south on your family?" I ask, as she leans against the combing like some blonde goddess, her eyes revealing nothing about what's going on inside so I'm left to make up what she leaves out.

"Bank repossessed our boat, *Miss Edgefield*. Daddy hurt his back real bad," she says. "He fell behind in his payments and that's all she wrote. Fucking credit officer threw a padlock on our wheelhouse."

"He couldn't renegotiate the loan?" I asked, thinking she's more intriguing than the light inside a lemon grove surrounded by alligators.

"You must not know bankers," Jesse says. "Daddy got so mad at the bank, and so mad at himself for hurting his back, he picked a fight with somebody who didn't have nothing to do with him losing his boat. The long and the short is he got himself killed. Stabbed in the ticker with his own filet knife in his favorite watering hole."

"Sorry about your old man."

"Yeah, so am I. The dumb fuck."

"Some things never work out," I say, thinking the dead seldom get a biscuit thrown their way because the living mostly think the sick and dying had it coming.

"Most men want twice as much power as they can use, and they want twice as much woman as they can handle. They don't care how they get it or who get hurts. What happens is just detours and dead-ends, one bad choice after the other. It was pathetic to watch my old man chasing after every pair of jeans, coming home stinking of perfume. I'm tired of men fucking up and getting me caught up in their mess. Tired of men talking whiskey and pussy like it's the promised land. Just flat out tired of men trouble."

"You prefer woman trouble?" I ask.

"Don't know about that," she says. "Actually, Matt, I prefer no trouble, but I suppose that don't exist in this life," she replies, the red light of the binnacle ghosting her face as we make good time in route to Spanish Wells that's fifty miles N.E. of Nassau and two hundred miles east of Miami.

Jesse talks more about her fugitive days since her father's death.

She talks not to me so much as to the sloshing, blue-rimmed darkness. She says her mother took up with another shrimper, another hard drinker who's always late paying his crew and who plays around. She says she moved out of her parents' house before finishing high school and worked instead on boats, doing almost anything to make a buck. Her dream, since she was a girl, has been to own a sailboat, to vanish into the islands south of the Tropic of Cancer, slip through the Panama Canal, and head west along the Equator until she hits Borneo, then round the horn of Africa and back to South America. I listen intently, seeing myself in her wanderlust, and in her need for escape from people and situations gone south. Is it a simpatico leaning me toward her or simple lust?

Everyone in Florida talks about astronauts, she says, but she wants to be an Argonaut, a shaper of voyages, a Magellan. "Why not?" she says. "Just because I was born tearing the assholes out of shrimp, doesn't mean I have to smell poor forever."

She unravels a troll line off a smooth-handled wedge of wood, flips a brightly-colored plumed lure off the stern, and watches it skip along the wake. No more than two minutes later, something hits her line. "Slack the sheets," she shouts to me. "Slow this baby down while I get these groceries on board."

Jesse's line runs a good hundred feet off the transom. When her fish dives, she lets it take more line, bending her body out over the water as she fights to hang onto the spool. When the fish rises, she spins the wedge in her hands to take in slack. How long can she hold on before the whir of line cuts through leather and takes her flesh? Again and again—dive, bend, reel—until fisher and fish move like some frayed, dancing ribbon.

24

"*La sobra fuerza para luchar*," she says.

"What did you say?"

"I've got to get this bitch in before a 'cuda gets it." Jesse swings a gaff over the stern and hooks the twenty-pound Spanish mackerel through the gills. The sullen, silvery fish gulps air, its pectorals stroking, its green-silver belly spots heaving.

As she kneels over the gaffed fish, a wave smacks the stern and drenches the seat of her khaki shorts. I see blood on her hands, the fish thumping its tail against the lazerette, its gills kneading air. Beads of water run down the crease of her ass and fall upon the gasping fish. The roundness of her cheeks shimmers silver, nearly lucid, and I see through the blood, moonlight, and waves swelling behind her, she isn't wearing anything underneath the shorts. I see threads of pubic hair curling outside the cuff. She grips the fish by the gills and slaps it down on a cutting block. With four quick strokes of a filet knife, she draws down the belly of the fish and tosses the guts overboard. I want to peel down her wet shorts, grab her haunches, and become what the dying fish in her hands can't ever be. She sees me watching her and not the silver fish in its death throes.

"Breakfast's gonna be good," Jesse says, running her hand lightly over the saw-tooth ridge behind the dorsal. "*Comida abundante.*"

"Your Spanish is pretty good," I say.

"*Mejor que nada,*" she says, holding the bloodied fish by the jaw and descending into the galley to pack her prize on ice.

Skip, I probably should have known right then she was a pro. What kind of pro? That's a fair question. A professional fisher, you might say. Someone who knows where the sunken piling lies and where the fish nose up into shadow. She knows how to reel in anything and leave no mark upon the waters.

In Nassau, I get drunk on Paradise Island after losing two hundred bucks on blackjack and someone steals our Avon life raft. I figure, at first, it's my fault because I don't remember anything after getting tossed out of the casino. I try to buy another raft in Nassau, but no one's selling. Philip and I hitch a ride back to *Stardust* with another party anchored off Paradise Island. Jesse doesn't return to the boat that night. Stolen Avon. No Jesse. I gloss over any possible chain linkage between the two.

We sail from Nassau to Georgetown in the Exuma islands with the wind holding strong at our back. I call Sam Wells, the owner of *Stardust*, and tell him Georgetown is a sweet harbor with poor protection from the north. We stay there for a week looking for a replacement raft and diving for grouper and lobster. With his skill in diving and dominoes, Philip becomes a local celebrity. Two men fall in love with him. One woman wants to marry him even though he's queer as a two-legged sea horse. She loves the way he talks poetry. Wild promises and tender mornings, that's how he lives his life, even if he has just one night in port.

One night I get Jesse out on a reggae dance floor but after twenty minutes she disappears and I don't see her again until the next morning. She has this gift for appearing and disappearing like a barracuda hanging back from a reef on its ring of hallucination, waiting for the glint of a slow moving, injured fish.

On one screaming downwind run, we leave Georgetown and sail *Stardust* into Cockburn Harbor, the last stop in the Turks & Caicos. I want to ride this wind all the way to Red Hook Bay in St. Thomas but Jesse convinces me to stop. She doesn't like the idea of crossing four hundred miles of open water without a life raft. I don't like the idea either, but a steady wind on my stern is better than gold, maybe even better than a life raft.

Twenty-four hours after our arrival in Cockburn Harbor on April Fool's Day, the blustery northeast Trades we've ridden all the way from Nassau blow themselves out. Imagine that, Skip, on April Fool's Day, the spring Trades flip around and kick out of the southeast with a vengeance. The Trades won't pivot back in my favor until November. I've misjudged the wind by a day. Just one fucking day. I can't believe my bad luck although as you'll see, luck's only one way to describe my unraveling inside the compass rose.

Pinned on a bleached-bone island caught between Africa and the Americas, I'm blind with too much light. The wind punishes. The shape of things trembles and deceives like the scales of a candy bass in coral. South Caicos is a thicket of scrub palm, pastel shanties, and idle men leaning in doorways spent on gossip and petty revenge. Turn too fast on land and you stumble over a strawberry pig or a runaway Haitian. Look out toward the harbor and you see only pelicans stalling and plunging like collapsing umbrellas hit by a thunderclap. But there's no thunder. Only hard sun hits hot nude rock. Three weeks later, I think about telling Sam Wells to find himself another skipper to deliver *Stardust* to St. Thomas, but I hold off.

Jesse spends more time off the boat, than on.

You might think of her, Skip, as a diamond in a drawer. I want to peek but the drawer's always locked. She stays up late, rises early, and escapes the heat of the day by going into town, but where, she never says. At night, at the Salt Shack, the island's one well-stocked rum bar, I see her hanging on the arm of a pilot with a wave of black hair and a glistening set of porcelain teeth. The pilots here are all rumored to be drug pilots waiting out assignments. They look like B-rated movie stars or soccer dads from Missouri. I figure she's talking her way onto his craft, the same way she did mine, by letting her three tattoos not let the sun go down. I notice a burnt pink flush to her nose and wonder if she's snorting coke by the tablespoon. I catch up with her on the docks, hauling in groceries, and ask about her plans now that we've stalled out.

"What's next?" I ask, blocking her path.

"Maybe I'll stay on for a while. Someone's always going north or south," she says. I hear her words mixed with the back-sucking of harbor water caught at slack tide. "If a front doesn't come and hammer down the Trades, I might just as well stay on. I've got lots of practice waiting out weather. I sure ain't going back to Jacksonville."

"Why did you want me to stop? You knew the Trades were about to switch. You knew we would get stuck here. This is what you wanted, isn't it?"

"You're blaming me for the wind? That's a good one, Matt. Do I look like a weather forecaster? I just wanted us to get another Avon before we made the next big hop to St. Thomas."

"I don't believe you. You're a liar. You told me you knew everything about the islands. This is your playground."

She looks past me, Skip, to the blue water jagging the harbor entrance. The whitecaps are thick as handcuffs. She sets down her two canvas bags filled with canned goods, crackers, peanuts, rum. Jesse wears a pair of little beige cut-offs over her bikini. More skin showing than not. It's hard standing there in the blinding sun talking with a woman whose tits spill out of her top. Harder yet to picture this cleavage-rich woman standing on the poop deck of a trawler hauling in shrimp nets, snagging the occasional turtle, throwing the trash fish and seashells overboard so she can shovel her shrimp into an ice tank. Nothing about her adds up to something I can sort out.

"Check it out, Matt," she says, pointing to the blue hills with their tops sliced off. "It's blowing like stink out there. Probably more sharks per nautical mile than anywhere in the world. It's steep water filled with rows of teeth. I would say that's a good enough reason to stop and find another Avon. It's not my problem you can't find one here. Face it, the wind is boss. You just got unlucky."

"Like I did in Nassau," I fire back.

"That was your doing, not mine," she says. "You're the one who tied one on and untied the boat."

"The thing I don't get is," I jump in, "you left the casino before I did. You were the last one to see the Avon."

"Matt, I told you I spent the night with a guy I met at the Blackjack table. I never went anywhere near the Avon."

"I've never lost anything on a boat, not even a winch handle," I protest. "It doesn't add up, and coming into Cockburn doesn't add up."

"Better here than out there to windward getting the shit beat out of us. Remember, there's a reason why an Avon is called a life raft."

It isn't yet noon and I want a rum to soothe the scrape of this jig and jag that won't break in my favor. A pelican hops off a dock pole and flaps within a few feet of her head and catches her eye. In that turn of her head to see the bird, I kiss her mouth hard and catch a strand of her hair in my teeth.

"You're not my type," she says, wiping her mouth.

"What *is* your type?" I say, not feeling the least bit apologetic.

"Latino," she says.

She picks up the two canvas grocery bags, hails the Bahamian boy who runs a taxi service, and returns to the boat. To blur the pull of her bikini, I head to the bar for an afternoon rum. The Trades will not be trumped. Jesse will not be made or broken. No big deal, right? When I might have just waited a little longer or admitted defeat, I make one more mistake. Out of boredom, sexual frustration, or some misbegotten desire to bend back the Trades in my favor, I dig an April Fool's hole into the bright darkness of Cockburn Harbor, a hole that's much deeper than I need.

From a location as remote as a dead man's float, Skip jostles under the cotton blanket, blinks, reaches out to me with his rheumy eyes as if I alone can help him reclaim the oxygen stolen from his lungs. He gasps, sputters: "Is this another one of your boating gone bad stories?"

"Yes and no," I say, touching his face, wanting to soothe his weepy eyes.

"It can't be both," he argues.

"You're right," I offer. "It can't be both."

"Where's your brother?" he says, struggling to lift his head, his mouth kneading air, looking for his glass of water, the straw, the sip, a momentary revival.

"What did you do with Hale?" he asks as I lay his head back down. "Just tell me that."

"Are you hungry, Skip?" I can't remember seeing him eat since I arrived.

"I don't need food, but tell me your story, such as it is," he grumbles, nods, and curls into himself like the long running, unchurched wave he will become.

29

CHAPTER III

My long night nurse ritual has no crest.

There's no end and no beginning, like the June rains that scorch the gutters, then quit, then swing back from a different quarter. From my father's window, I see the rot of fronds bright with long strings of wet shine blister.

His sagging and discolored face says only this: everything stings or shrinks with age except memory and longing. I lift my father's head and guide his blistered lips to the straw. The water dribbles on his chin. "Some nurse you'd make," he says, his eyes skidding over the ceiling as if he's had the wind knocked out of his lungs. I ease his head back on the pillow. His eyes flicker like a doll's eyes built to close when the head falls back. He tries to talk more but his heavy tongue clings to his teeth. It's 3:00 A.M. and my father and I work our passage towards dawn. He sleeps or pretends to sleep and waits for the stalled moment when neither sleep nor waking is required of him.

Though I try to break him loose, my brother Hale is in the dark ether of the cottage with us. He's in my mother's stab. He's in my father's sipping straw. He's in the belly of that tree frog spiking the mesh of the screen over my father's bed. He never leaves. He never fully appears. I never see him except at the base of my skull, swelling there like the ink of the Gulf Stream, the hot black salt sucking him down. I want to grab my brother and thrash from his body an argument for why I should live the rest of my life. And I want to shake him off my arms and never again hear his name caught in my throat like a bite of Sargasso weed. *I want in. I want out. I want to be done with my unsalvageable brother.*

I talk on in spite of the ghost I can't shake, thinking, maybe my first night with my skipper will also be my last . . .

Stuck on a white rock with the wind on the nose, I drink during the day, gamble at night. Like you, Skip, with your whisky and gin, I inhale every kind of rum from the back shelf: white rum, black rum, reddish-brown rum, light and dark gold rums; rums from Jamaica, Cuba, Barbados, Trinidad. The bartender tells me rum always starts clear, then it gains its gold from aging. I tell him to shut up and keep pouring so I don't have to think about the easy bite of a gold spider. The rum blur has become my gimbal friend that keeps me steady no matter how the room tilts or spins. This is just like one drunk rhapsodizing about his poison to another drunk, so forgive me, in advance, but let me for a minute praise the light wrapped inside a rum bottle.

"Ain't no whiskey in this house anymore. I'm clean as a whistle," Skip says in a smoky squawk.

"Hey, you're listening to me," I say, not quite believing that the man with his eyes pinched is really my father.

"What the hell else am I going to do." He turns away from me and pulls the sheet tight under his chin.

Rum always lifts me straight to the roof like a sweet, faithful, flame-throwing rocket. Up high inside the swirl, there comes a point where I'm staring down the throat of an orchid, repulsed and charmed by the gripping tongue of such a swallowing beauty. "Better than a pillow-grabbing orgasm," one woman says to me about the flash found inside Captain Morgan rum, and I nod from my tin roof, thinking she might be working the Salt Shack, but no, like me, she just wants to blunt the knife of the Trades and keep moving south into the chosen pink of her next island destination.

"Two pears and a plum won't do, sailor boy," says the bearded man hooked on my shoulder. Dressed in army fatigues and a gold necklace, the man wears his sunglasses on the top of his head like a second pair of eyes with an ivory toothpick jammed in his lips. The bartender tells me this man and his brother have been mercenaries in Rhodesia. Now, they work at the island's one business, a lobster factory, and check their mail each day hoping to score another mop-up job in the fickle, post-colonial heart of Africa.

"Yeah, I've had enough losing for one night," I say.

Skip, there's no seafaring life raft for sale in Cockburn Harbor, so I give Jesse a thousand bucks and tell her to scoot back to Miami with her flyboy and buy us one. I figure a grand is a small price to pay to be rid of her. I'm not planning on her coming back. Before she leaves, I rifle through her duffel and find six vials of cocaine.

After another three weeks in Cockburn Harbor, I call Sam Wells, the owner of *Stardust*, and tell him we're stuck at the southernmost tip of the Bahamas waiting out the Trades. Wells ain't happy. Tells me I should have known how to avoid this wind shift. He says his wife's health is improving and he wants to fly down to St. Thomas and use his boat. The longer I talk, the madder he gets. He thinks I'm drinking down his money or making up the business about the Trades having switched around. How convenient, he says. I tell him I don't like the prospect of putting his boat into a meat-grinder. I think my meat-grinder line has got him back around in my favor, then he gets whipped up even more and fires me. Says he's going to bring down another crew. Says I can leave or stay with *Stardust* until another captain and crew show up in a week. I tell him he doesn't know the first fucking thing about these winds, how brutal and unforgiving they can be. He hangs up and I think I'll call him the next day and he'll be cooled off enough so I can get my job back. I don't tell Sam Wells the truth of the situation.

With the Trades having switched, no one's leaving Cockburn Harbor going south. Not in a week, not in another month. Columbus called the stretch between the Turks & Caicos and Haiti, the Thorny Path. And the name fits for good reason, Skip. This stretch of water is packed with reefs that broke the spine of the Spanish gold and silver fleets eager to make a swift return. Until they discovered the Gulf Stream hugging Florida, the Spanish thought the shortest distance between two points was a straight line, but straight is flat-out crooked down here with a cyclone current thrown in. And did I mention the wind? There's no rock between Grand Turk and Africa to iron out the waves. No, the sane man would rather shake the slot machines and drink more rum than take the Trades on the nose. Out there in the quick two-step of the Thorny Path, nothing's watertight, nothing lasts forever, nothing is what it seems. That's what the Spanish found out by sucking down an avalanche of salt and losing all they came for. Bob Marley chants over the barroom chatter,

You gonna run to the rocks,
But the rocks will be melting . . .
You gonna run to the sea,
But the sea will be boiling.

"Matt, what are you looking so moony about? Just because you lost $50 to the one-arm bandits and haven't been laid in months? That's no reason to go sour on paradise," Philip says to me while smiling at the male patrons in the bar.

"We're fired," I say. "Shit-canned. Out of work. We need food stamps."

"What?"

"Wells just lowered the boom. He's bringing down a new skipper and crew. Be here in a week. We can either leave or stay until the new skipper shows."

"He thinks we can control the wind?"

"I told him all about the Trades having flopped on us. That didn't buy us any slack."

"What now, brown cow?" Philip asks.

I shrug. Hold up my hands. Offer a stupid smile like this latest setback ain't so bad. Philip looks back at me like he's just been told school has been canceled and he's free to cruise for the men that lovely dreams are crafted of. I'm feeling bent by the phone call with Wells and he's feeling giddy.

Philip carries a wave of thick strawberry-blonde hair brushed off his forehead which makes him look like a slightly carnivorous version of Alan Ladd. I try to ignore or deny it, but a surge of

33

envy for Philip's sensual ease floods my face. You won't approve of his sexual appetites, Skip, but you have to admire his moxy and skill. Like Hale, he's just plain gifted on board a boat, and in the water. The Bahamians love his shambling gait, his throaty laugh, his toothy smile.

I watch dark men take Philip into their houses and feed him rice and peas after he brings them speckled green turtles he's chased down through staghorn coral. On any dusty, one-lane road, Philip pulls up a chair to badger the domino players. Philip masters the telepathic rules, the sidelong whispers, and whistles until he too slams down his pieces, egging on challengers, mixing French with English, winning the hearts of the Haitians who speak a blistering Creole that he responds to with instant affection.

Almost better for Philip than wandering through a Bahamian village in search of a lover is his daily descent into a coral reef, that complex metropolis seething with warriors, queens, elaborate defense structures, marital squabbling. Standing at the bar, he tells how he borrows a skiff, slips on his fins and gloves, grabs his mask, and drops overboard in the lee of Dove Cay with a tickle stick, belt pouch and lobster net clipped to his waist.

As we lean at the bar rail not knowing what to do next because we've just been shit-canned, Philip says he dives twenty feet down. Once at eye-level with the reef's underbelly, he sees the loose-jointed antennae of a spiny lobster poking out from a hole, its two eyes like headlights jacked above the hood. He tickles the creature near the back of its carapace and walks him out of its hole, then gently places the net behind it, and taps it on the right until the lobster backs up left, directly in line with the net. Philip taps him again. The lobster tucks its tail, shoots backwards. He flips the net over with the lobster flailing and rises. After dropping the first lobster in his boat, he descends for more.

Off to his left, Philip sees a hammerhead wagging its double-sided head like a metronome and he watches the ticking of the head disappear behind a school of porkies. He sees a large conch, its foot hooking sand. He dives again, pries the conch off the bottom with both hands. Nearly a foot wide and long, the conch stands out bright purple in a shaft of filtered sunlight. He says it feels like a bowling ball in his hands. He takes out a knife and digs out the snail along with a rare conch pearl.

There in the bar, Philip takes a leather pouch from his pocket and pulls from it the hefty red orb that looks like a miniature planet, so richly does it gleam in the bulb light of the bar. It's perfectly round and streaked with rays of fire.

"That's a beauty," I say. "What's it worth?"

"I've only found one other conch pearl. I sold it for a thousand bucks, but it was teardrop pink without all the flaws this one has."

"Hey, a grand ain't bad. Lucky you, you've got a lucky pearl. Now I need to find a souvenir," I reply, taking another slug of my all-forgiving, all-understanding Captain Morgan rum.

"How does the lowly conch snail make something like this?" I ask, gazing again into Philip's red orb.

"The same way all beautiful things get made: with pain, my man, with pain."

"Come again?"

"The conch gets a bit of irritating sand trapped in the wrong place and entombs it with layer after layer of resin, until the pain goes away."

"You're making this up, right?"

"It's the law of the ocean," Philip says. "If the ocean can't spit out a wreck, the salt encrusts the broken keel and sister ribs and turns that wreck into a paradise for grouper and porkies. The conch does the same thing except usually all the commotion of the snail slipping in and out of its shell knocks any pearl loose. That's why this thing is so rare," he says, turning the red jewel into the bounced light of the slot machines.

"You talk like a man who would rather be a seahorse," I say.

"No two ways about it, there's a lot more beauty below the waves than above."

"At this point, maybe switching from being a delivery boat skipper to sunken treasure hunter might not be a bad move. Wonder what it pays?"

"It's the ultimate long shot," Philip says, "because the ocean has no intention of making salvage easy."

"Ok, how about mercenary work?"

"Consider this, Matt, in your perpetual funk," Philip says. "By one hair holding off a falling sword, you could just as easily not have been born. The odds are astronomically bad. But you made it. Take heart. Rejoice. We're here on this rock, going nowhere south because one night a tiny seed waltzed with an egg. It's nothing short of a miracle."

"You make Cockburn sound like the site of the Immaculate Conception," I say.

"I don't think Cockburn and Immaculate fit in the same sentence."

"Why does your birth or mine give me no comfort?" I ask, slightly annoyed with Philip's latest philosophical take on our over-extended visit in South Caicos that just got much longer.

"Because you take detours and dead-ends personally."

"Don't you hear that wind?" I say, pointing to the salt-smudged window. "I'd call that a slap in the face."

"Maybe it's just a breach birth," Philip says, pulling my hand down as if protecting it. "And the thing we think is kicking us in the teeth is really helping us to smile at the comedy. Remember Eliot's Magi, 'Were we led all that way for Birth or Death? There was a Birth, certainly, we had evidence and no doubt. I had seen birth and death, but had thought they were different; this Birth was hard and bitter agony for us, like Death . . .' "

"If you weren't such a pagan, you could scam as a holy man," I say.

"I already am a holy man. And so are you," Philip says.

"What star system are you from?"

"Brittany. A small fishing village. Where men go out to sea and women wait for them to drown and walk home across the water in their dreams."

"See. There you go again. Making something pretty out of pain. It's a sickness with you."

"Someone has to do it," Philip says, looking up to see if the latest miraculous birth has finally arrived and needs his nurturing company.

Skip, it's the start of another long night at the Salt Shack trashed inside my own miserable brain. I half think about calling Wells back right then and not waiting until the morning to win him back. I order another bottle of five dollar rum to help get my thoughts organized. Philip sips ginger ale with a lime twist.

"I've put out the word to skippers heading north we want to exchange Bahamian money," I say to Philip, slouching against the horseshoe-shaped bar. I add, "It won't do us any good where we're going."

"You still think we're shoving off soon?" Philip asks.

"I can bring Wells back around. You just said as much with your cockeyed birth theory and now we've got a lucky conch pearl to pull us through." Even as I say this, I think, we're burnt toast on a broken plate. Wells is not going to see the wind my way.

The bartender nods and I think he must be looking for my money, so I dig in my pocket for my diminishing roll of bills. He waves me off, nods again. He wants me to see who walked in the door.

"Jimmy Q," he says.

"The very one?" I ask.

"That's him," he adds.

I've heard the name Jimmy Q for years. He's one of the grand wizards of the Bahamian cocaine trade. He's dodged the FBI in Florida, the Coast Guard, bounty hunters, and human sharks of every shape and size. I'm not sure what I expected from a name like Jimmy Q. Maybe someone suave enough to wear a white silk suit and surround himself with a string of island beauties and not look comical. Maybe someone mean enough to make everyone else want to scramble. Or someone smart enough not to be seen in a funky Bahamian rum bar.

I didn't expect Jimmy Q to be a balding stalk of gristle who could pass for an unemployed plumber yanked out of a soup line. He shuffles toward us, nursing a limp. His face, a smudge of old acne collisions. His eyes are smeared red in the white corners. He wears a gray T-shirt with a torn pocket and yellow flip-flops. His mouth turns inward to a pencil-thin gash, then opens to reveal yellow, scraggly teeth showing light. Red-speckled fins

37

cruise under the man's fingernails. As worn and wasted as he is, Jimmy Q still turns every head in the bar. He draws out whispers as everyone gives him a wide berth.

"Looks like a tarantula with headlights," Philip says.

"Need some bread? American for Bahamian. Where you headed? North, south? Name's Jimmy Q," the man says, jamming his phrases together. I lean over to Philip, "What the hell did he say?"

"Something about swapping money."

Jimmy wobbles like a jarred coatrack without any coats.

"Legend or not, I'm bailing on this rummy," Philip says.

"I thought you liked odd ducks?" I say.

"This guy has stepped on one too many landmines," Philip says as he catches the eye of a Bahamian in a key-lime T-shirt. Instead of walking away, I stand at the bar, listless, drunk, curious, and ready to be coaxed by any promise that my luck's about to somersault, flip-flop, or otherwise blow me further south and to hell with Sam Wells. For the next hour or so, I listen to Jimmy Q, who pitches himself as a frontier Florida crop-duster turned cracker-preacher savior of South Caicos. I tell myself he looks so bad, Skip, so weak and wasted, he can't possibly lord anything over anyone.

Jimmy Q hails from Palm Beach, where he says it doesn't take much to pry open the hearts and wallets of civil servants, politicians, and bikini girls who specialize in beach sex. All those terraced lawns, golf courses, and mansions built by the Astors, Goulds, Posts, Woolworths, and Vanderbilts are all paid for with drug cash, tax dodge cash, or cheap-labor-orange-grove cash. Jimmy knows who does what and when, and who pays off the police.

He boasts how he owns Cockburn Harbor, everything on the rock, the airport, customs, the two grouper-finger restaurants, and the Salt Shack. Formerly a get-away for divers and dive photographers, Cockburn Harbor is now his winter wonderland. He performs a public service, he says, that even the fat-assed Queen of England would be proud of. He has turned her island into what she can't—a common wealth. Get it, he says, at least twice, a fucking common wealth.

"How much longer you gonna wait out the Trades?" Jimmy asks, his face now seeming to change from an emaciated oval to something fiercely thin and hardened like a board lit with nail heads. He now looks taller and fuller than when he first strolled over. I look down at his hands. They are thick and calloused. His torn T-shirt bulges with pop-eye muscles. I shake my head, trying to remember how I pictured him when I first saw him. I take another rum and another hoping it will help me track his shape if he changes again.

"You can work your whole piss-ant life and maybe scrimp together a half million bucks, but I can fork over that much jack in a day. Live rich, die fast. That's my motto. How 'bout it?"

Skip, I've got no business talking with Jimmy Q, but the blood pumps in my temples when he talks. I'm going nowhere against the Trades. I've got maybe a thousand bucks in my pocket, but the cash doesn't belong to me. I've just been fired by Wells. I'm just another pickled sailor waiting for lady luck and the winds to switch. What can it hurt to hear him out? That's what I tell myself.

I follow Jimmy back to a room connected to the bar. He says his door's always open. Once inside, Jimmy twitches from the waist up like a palmetto bug is gobbling sugar in his sleeve. He runs his hands over a vanishing lock of hair and slumps on the end of an unmade bed.

"Last night," Jimmy says, "some new commissioner over in Provo named Dwight Stone busts my Johnny cracker ass. Tells me over the radio to dump my cargo on his fucking rock. This black prick wants me to pay him a hundred-fifty thousand on some kind of regular basis. Problem is, if I want to do business here, I have to keep these people with happy feet."

Jimmy jerks upright, peels off a crisp $100 bill from a gold money clip, and slips off to the bathroom. He returns holding a large paper cup brimming with white powder, and his $100 bill rolled up tight as a pea-shooter.

"Take a hit," Jimmy says. "See for yourself the kind of candy I run. It's the best 99% pure Colombian shit on the whole fucking planet. It's not cut with baking soda, crushed aspirin, powdered sugar, or baby laxative. You'll like the taste of my trouble."

"No thanks," I say. I turn to leave, but want to stay because where else can I go except back to the Salt Shack where Captain Morgan promises to pickle another chunk of my three-pound liver.

"What do you want me to do?" I ask, and as soon as I say it I know he's got me snagged on a deep-running troll line. The coat rack, the tarantula, the crop-duster—whoever this guy is, he's also a fisher of men, and I don't have the common sense of a horsefly to pull back from him and seek my diversions back at the bar. No matter how the rum scrambles my brain, this is the truth, Skip: As much as I want to sail further south, some hungry, lost part of me also wants what Jimmy Q has—that mystical power to call the shots no matter what the hell the wind says.

"The drop's on Provo." Jimmy says. "Worth about two million. You pick it up. Make a delivery. Clean. Simple. I'll pay you a half million cash or twelve kilos, whatever you like. Plus, I'll give you a free bundle of candy for the road."

Jimmy opens a suitcase and pulls out a kilo wrapped in brown manila and twine and tosses it over to me.

"Where's this drop?" I ask.

"On the southwest bluffs of Provo. Near a creek. Next to a stand of royal palms. Got to be over a hundred pounds. You can't miss that much candy on the vine."

"These islanders don't miss a flea falling out of the sky," I say.

"You don't know that corner of Provo. There's nothing there. No houses. No harbors. Just rock and scrub palm. It's a plum waiting to be picked."

"If I find it, what then?"

"Sail over to Curly Cut Cay, off the southern tip of Andros."

"That's a hike across the Bank," I tell him.

"With the wind behind you in that flying machine of yours, you can make it in three days or less."

"I don't get it," I argue. "Why don't you pick it up on Provo?"

"Bad luck for a pilot to walk upon the land," Jimmy says quickly, as if he's said this line a hundred times before.

"I need to talk it over with my partner," I say.

"Pony up, sailor. I'm giving you a half million bucks for a few days' work. Only catch is, I'm flying out of here tomorrow morning. I need an answer now."

"I'll give you an answer before you go," I say, tucking the kilo of cocaine under my arm.

"Don't fuck with me, sailor." Jimmy says, "The ocean's a long way down."

"You've got nothing to worry about," I say. "Nothing at all."

Skip, how can I say this: one voice says, "Stop." Another voice says, "Go." The Trade winds have switched on me like a scorpion's tail. I can't sail further south. Wells wants me off his boat and my chances of persuading him in another call are next to none. I'm not ready to turn back north. I want to be in the south. I want to reach the Sir Francis Drake Channel of the British Virgin Islands and make a new name for myself there.

After leaving Jimmy Q, I return to the bar and kill another half a bottle of Captain Morgan and there, with the gold fire scrambling my brain and sense of direction, I decide I can turn murk into magic. I can feel the failure of my delivery collapsing over me, but the rum tells me I can salvage this failure by trying to outfox a fox. I, alone, can deceive a man who makes his living flying at high speed below radar, and make all the cherries on my slot machine pop into view. My ship can come in, I tell myself, even if I never sail one more mile further south.

CHAPTER IV

My mother sleeps in her room on the other side of the cottage. In the morning, we shuffle past each other in the kitchen like people who've survived an open boat voyage with too little water to drink. We're both parched. The color of our skin is a mix of blood and sand. At night, our lips turn moist. Our eyes glisten. Some hunger far down in our marrow stirs. We become like hawks in a hall, our talons harnessed in leather, our prey not yet released from its dovecote.

"Why did you get Hale into drugs?" she says, biting down on the lip of a coffee cup.

"It wasn't my doing," I say.

"You're lying. He was an honors student, a world class swimmer. He had no time for trouble until you found it for him."

"He was not the boy you thought he was."

"You're saying the newspapers, the magazines, the Naval Academy in Annapolis, the Olympic swim coach, they all had him pegged wrong. That he wasn't destined for great things. Who was he, then?"

"I don't know. I honestly don't know."

"What happened out there in the Gulf Stream the night he never came back?"

In her eyes, I see a large and menacing ship. There, in her blood gaze, I never stop violating the oldest law of the sea: *Never turn your back on a boat in distress or a man in the drink because you never know when your own time comes.*

"It's a little fuzzy, Mom, but I'm trying to make it clear."

Nothing was fuzzy except I couldn't bring myself to destroy my mother's image of her favorite son. The rock in my gut won't split in half. I want to protect her from knowing the true nature of our family god and I want to punish her with the truth. Protect or punish? If only my dead brother could advise me. If only I could see him again across the steep waves, reaching up with his arms to scoop power from the salt and be sure it was he inside the glare of one lost night. What now? I want to ask him. What do I say to our mother now?

"Fuzzy is the best you can do? What are you hiding?"

"I'm not hiding anything." But then I catch a glimpse of the Gulf Stream, the waves steep enough to blot out the moon, a freighter churning its thousand-pound steel props, the backwash swelling beneath us, the cargo doors sliding open, my brother and I side by side in the accursed dark of a brief unloading, our voices mingling, then torn from one another.

"Why did he have to be the one to die that night?"

The swipe and fury of her grief. The rattle in her chest. The night prayers I can hear from behind her closed door. All of her wrangle lit under my skin like a fuse I have to snuff out before my life explodes and I never find all the pieces.

"What should I call my last boat?" Skip says, slapping the stanchion of his hospital bed. I shake my head.

"How about *Out of Jack*?" he says. The old shipwright sneers and sticks out his tongue at his own name. Then, it comes to him. When he's eight, he called his first boat *Ink Eraser*. He built that first boat from a garage door washed up on Rye Beach on Lake Erie. The found door is gashed and bearded in slime but there's enough good wood left for him to resize and shape it into something that stands up to weather. His last bed will be his last boat because it comes with its own steel handrail designed to prevent him from falling overboard.

"*Ink Well*. That's it. My last boat is *Ink Well*."

"I like it," I say, both amused and saddened by his turn of phrase.

"Only problem," he says with a lemon-sour face, "*Ink Well*'s anchored in the front guest room. What damn sense does that make? Can you tell me?"

Skip hates the front guestroom where he now lives. He wants to be in his old bedroom, in his old single bed, but the walls of his former quarters don't reach the ceiling and so whatever sounds he makes are heard in the rest of the house. My parents stopped sleeping together years ago because Skip has a wicked snore that could keep a tree frog on edge. He wants his old bedside table stashed with dates, sailing photos, Hershey's kisses. He wants his old room where he can easily grab the pull cord to the fan. In the guestroom the fan cord is just out of his reach. That stupid fucking fan nearly breaks me. Several times a day he asks me to please pull the cord and slow the fan down. It's too cool at the current speed. I tell him that the next slowest speed is OFF. It doesn't matter. He wants proof, so I yank the cord. After the fan stops, he wants it re-started to the slowest speed. I say, "Skip, this is the last time. When I pull it, the fan will turn off and I'm not going to re-start it. Stop all this whining and go to sleep."

I slip into the bathroom just outside the guest room, feeling sheepish for talking to Skip the way he must have talked to me when I was four. After pretending to brush my teeth, the wheeze of his voice finds me staring down the bathroom mirror. "You win," he says, drawing out his words into an even longer sigh. "How come an old man doesn't know anything?" I too sigh, thinking I've won something that'll grant me peace from the negotiations of the fan, then I feel guilty about hoarding my spoils. I think he could be asleep, but no, not yet.

"Matt, if you could grant a dying man a last request, would you do it?" he asks. "No," I fire back. "If you say one more thing about the fan, I'm going to tear it out of the god damn ceiling and throw it in the trash."

"I always knew you had a mean streak," he says. "How do you live with yourself?"

"At least I don't change my mind every two seconds," I say, realizing I'm arguing with a man who can't fully track the logic of one sentence to the next.

"You know what death is?" he asks.

"I give up," I reply, tired of sorting out his frayed sentences.

"A pajama party with no butter on the popcorn. I'm never going to get out of these pajamas, am I? Why won't you take me to my old room? How would you like it if someone said your room was off-limits?"

I return to his side and look into his two eye-pit shadows barely holding the room in focus. There, in the blur of a dying man, I can still detect the eyes of a lover, the eyes of a father, the eyes of a failing sailor. Then, I feel the shiver behind his grievance.

It's the wind he wants from the overhead fan. He wants the new wind that you see skittering across the water's surface; that faint ripple gathering in the distance while you sit becalmed outside that breath of air with your sails flapping against the boom, praying that the dimple will break and lift your craft forward. Even without the wind from the fan, my father returns to the pluck of the defeated who seek consolation from old songs and new rhymes.

"*Between the devil and the deep blue sea,*
that's where I'll be, he says before he closes his eyes.
I think he's sleeping, but he takes another run at the devil.
"*Between the devil and you and me,*
I'll find the deep blue sea.
Between the devil and you,
I'm not telling on me.
Between the devil and the deep blue sea,
that's where I'll be.
Give me the sea and
I'll show you a devil in blue."

"When's your brother coming home? When can I see him? When you were both young, we had such fun on the boat. Why don't you tell Hale it's time to come home, then we can all go out on the boat together."

How can I go on with my story, I think, when Hale is the only son my father longs to see again? How can I not go on? I invent my own song:

"*Push on.*
Turn back.
Find another boat.
I'm out of jack."

I push on because I need Skip to witness the full length of my crime, so I can unload all of it for good. *Give me the sea and I'll show you a devil in blue.* His song is all the opening I need to return to Cockburn Harbor. I sit on the edge of my father's rocker and remember that every tenth wave is a breaking wave. If I count to ten, will his dying world break open and breathe again? The ocean of his papery skin shrinks on his bones. The thunder approaches from far out in the Atlantic like a bandage lifted slowly from a wound. The tenth wave arrives. My skipper stirs in his last boat.

For once Philip is on board *Stardust* before I am.

He's curled in the main cabin bunk with a sheet half covering his nude body. Without turning on the light, I wake him by shaking one of his ankles. I whisper into the dark, "Jimmy's got a deal."

"You're higher than a satellite," Philip says, with a squint.

"I have a kilo here of 99% pure cocaine," I say, showing him the bundle tucked under my arm.

"A kilo? What time is it?"

"Time has stopped, my friend. From now on, we make our own time."

"You're talking like one of those rummies from Rhodesia after they oil up their machine guns," Philip says.

"That deadbeat we saw really is Jimmy Q. He owns the whole damn rock—the Salt Shack, the airport, the Customs & Immigration people. That scrawny sleazebag is the man."

"So what?" Philip says with a groan. "Your new best friend Jimmy can't make the wind change direction."

"Jimmy wants us to pick up a cocaine drop on Provo. He'll pay us a half million bucks to take it over to Andros." I switch on a galley light, pop open a beer and tell him how much coke is involved, what Jimmy says it's worth, where it's located.

"You know, Matt," Philip says with a rare note of priestly concern, "Everywhere I go in Cockburn Harbor I see posters saying, *Captain Missing, Boat Missing, Pilot Missing.* This island is hazardous to your health. These drug pilots fly without lights, below radar, and they crash a lot. I've met some of these characters before. They think nothing of killing each other over a twenty-dollar bill. I don't know why Jimmy gave you a kilo, but it feels like there's a loaded gun somewhere. You don't think a welcome wagon will be waiting for us in Andros?"

"I've got no plans to sail to Andros," I say, splashing myself on the chin with a swig of beer. "I'm gonna fly over to Provo, find that drop, and bring it back. Then, you and I are going to head out across the Thorny Path, at night."

"You're going to steal the coke and Wells' boat ? How many quarts of oil is your brain pan missing?"

"Jimmy will never expect me to show up on foot. If it's not where he says it is, no big deal. I'll get a little extra tour of the Caicos."

"I thought you wanted to deliver this boat to St Thomas? I thought you were going to call Wells again and bend his ear, convince him we should stay on. I thought that's what you wanted."

"I don't know," I say, pausing long enough to consider the potential cost of my drug excursion.

Philip says, "You're bored in paradise. You need something to do. You think this is a game. You think people don't get killed over this shit."

"Back in two days or less," I say, opening the hanging locker where Jesse kept her things. I dig out my backpack, find my hand-held compass and binoculars as well as a climbing rope. Here's what happens, Skip. I grab a cab sitting outside the Salt Shack and head for the airport. I buy a round-trip ticket on board an Island Cessna and leave on a 6:30 A.M. flight for Providenciales which the locals call, Provo. The smooth take-off on a packed dirt runway is offset by the drumming rattle of the plane's cargo lockers. I'm the only passenger so I sit next to the pilot who makes flying look as casual as pointing a car down a highway.

Near shore, a mottled green gives way to a marl-brown. In between shallow turquoise bays, I see where fishermen have dredged channels through the coral-limestone shelves. Everywhere I see remnants of the once flourishing salt trade. When the colonists needed salt to cure their meats, they hired ships to come here where slave labor made salt collection cheap. I see the outlines of abandoned salt ponds, collapsed windmills, crumbling salt mounds, and I see a string of wrecked planes bleaching in the sun like dinosaurs. Their wings are ripped off. The fuselages gutted. Each wreckage, a witness to the high tariff levied against the running of cocaine. In North Caicos, a family cuts their home out of a wrecked DC-3. A front door and porch steps lead down from the emergency hatch. Flowering vines climb over burnt silver portholes, making no human exit easy.

Ignoring all this blood-on-the-wing, Skip, I'm eager to start the hunt, but even as I grasp this, I imagine you there on the plane, looking cross-eyed, shaking your head, thinking I'm a long way from Tipperary and I don't even know where that is. I tell myself what can it hurt to have a look around?

I land in Provo around 7:30 A.M., take a cab to South Harbor, and rent a Boston Whaler. I want to hike the five miles out along the coast to the bluffs, but I don't like the idea of lugging a hundred plus pounds if I find the drop. The harbormaster looks warily at my backpack and the coil of rope around my neck. He doesn't like my request for twenty gallons of extra fuel.

"Where you be fetchin'?" the white-haired black man says while rubbing the bridge of his nose.

"I want to check out dive sites out near the bluffs."

"You be no diver," he says, glumly.

I turn over the ignition on the Boston Whaler and cast off. Once out of the harbor, I fire up the hundred-horse Mercury and swing west at high speed, the boat skipping over one-foot waves, past big shallow salt marshes cut into jagged coastline. I find a cove near the bluffs where I run the flat-bottomed Whaler up into turtle grass. I figure I'm less than a mile away, an easy hike, but there's nothing easy about it. The island's volcanic rock runs in razor-sharp ridges. I tear holes in both tennis shoes and nearly fall into a cistern-like hole that drops to the sea. It takes two hours to reach the bluffs. The last hundred yards are a jerky, shambling climb through the serrated leaves of scrub palm that claw my legs. At the bluffs, I slip off the pack, take out my binoculars. I hear waves crashing on the rock slabs. Gulls loop overhead. The sun throws down a kiln-like heat that makes my wrists sweat. I can barely feel the Trades roaring from the south.

I scan north and see miles of glistening white sand and unending clumps of sea grass and scrub palm. I see a shallow creek leading to the beach with one royal palm rattling. Jimmy said the drop is near this spot. I realize then, I should circle round the bluffs in the boat and come up on the beach. I think about going back, but instead decide to rappel the wall to the beach.

I drive a piton into the rock, thread the line through the head of it, and lean my weight against the rope to test for holding strength. I step out over air and kick out from the rock, keeping my legs locked at right angles to the changing contour of the rock face. Sixty feet later, I hit a two-foot ledge and see the waves below. On the second rappel, a gull swoops near my face. I swat at it as I kick out. My legs buckle. I slam into the wall as the bird nips my head. I jam the four remaining fingers on my left hand into the rock face, tearing skin off the knuckles. I lose the lowering grip of the rope with my right hand and fall with the gull circling above. I grab the spiraling rope after falling twenty feet and hang on, jerking upwards.

My knuckles bleed, but my fingers aren't broken. I touch down on sand and figure the creek can't be more than a half-mile off. I want to run hard to take my mind off the throb of my hand, but instead I survey the beachhead. Every plant crouches into the sun-bleached rock and makes it damn hard to spot a landmark. I walk on, stopping behind one royal palm to finger-taste the creek cut with sand and brine. I push up the creek until I stand in a narrow arbor looking out on a rise where I see three bags tangled inside the serrated skirt of a large scrub palm. I run again until I'm tucked inside the circle of shade thrown by the palm. Each of the burlap bags is the size of a sack of onions and weighs near thirty pounds. Each is cinched with lumber twine. And each one makes me swallow hard and fast. I slip the knife under the strands and welcome the rip of the blade. With each slash of my knife, I know only this: I better move fast, faster than Jimmy Q.

Inside the burlap, Jimmy's cocaine is stored in double zip-locked bags, each duct-taped at the top. I retie the bag and drag all three away from the creek and up a sloping hill toward the bluff. When I stop to load the cocaine into my backpack, I hear the muffled echo of an engine. I cut the remaining bags and stuff the zip-locked bags into my pack, swing it around on my knee, and hoist it on my back. It must weigh all of a hundred pounds. There's no room for any of my extra gear so I toss it into scrub. I pick phrases out of the chatter below, maybe a hundred yards away, and freeze.

"There's footprints all over the beach," I hear.

I push up toward the bluffs. Any good sense I have left, Skip, tells me to ditch the pack and run deep into scrub, but fifty yards from the upper ridge, I spot a cistern hole with a wide ledge six feet down. I back down inside the hole until my toes grab the ledge. I reach up, find a foothold, and pull fallen palm fronds over the top. I wedge myself and the pack inside the echoing tunnel. I hear only the suck and hiss of water below and nothing of the human threat above.

I park the pack on a ledge and inch again up the hole. I see two men squatting fifty yards away. I reverse the pack, hold it to my chest, and chimney down into this blind sea hole. As I wedge the pack through a narrow turn, then climb after it, a splash of light spills down the hole but doesn't catch my back. I look down into this fissure and think, this is it: I must slither on my belly, down, down, and further down into the swollen length of a black sea snake.

I expect to slip and fall, but the twists of the sea hole help to slow my descent. I straddle the hole in a crouch, my knees and hands bleeding from my grip on the volcanic edges. I kick the pack ahead of me as the fissure winds through porous rock, then I turn upside down to lever myself around a right angle. I'm not afraid of getting stuck, Skip, but of having the fissure simply stop so I'll have to retrace my climb. I push those thoughts aside when I see barnacles and slimy wetness staining the rock below me.

I emerge on a narrow sea ledge, somewhere south of the bluffs and in the direction of my boat. I stand in the sun warming my face and bleeding hands, pleased with my underground maneuvering, neglecting at first to see how wet and treacherous my new ledge is. I want to bask there in the heat and not face my two options: I can jump in the water and risk losing the pack or traverse twenty-five feet of seaweed-covered rock face to a ledge, then down again to the water. I choose the slippery traverse.

I take mincing steps, halting to watch the water crashing below, my breath running in short waves inside my chest. I hang there studying the rock, looking for a way up that won't involve a trip down. I see a dry crack running straight up and over the top. I swing the pack over my shoulders and wedge my hands and feet on either side of the crack and pull up. The weight of the pack drags back while I lean in and inch up until I reach the top of another ledge and roll the pack off my body.

As I hobble toward the Boston Whaler I'd left nose up in the turtle grass, a little jigsaw of panic cuts out a hole where my heart flaps. I realize I'll have to steal the boat and take it another fifty miles across the banks to Cockburn Harbor. It seems unlikely I can shuffle through the airport with a heavy pack and not be stopped and searched, but I don't like the idea of pounding south across open water in a twenty-foot Boston Whaler. What to do? I'll have to swing north around Jubber Point before turning southeast and hope the shallow water will eliminate chop. The sun has already shifted west. I have just enough time to get back to the safety of *Stardust* before the sandbars and shoals catch me in darkness.

Skip ducks and rolls under the covers and says, "Does this sailing story of yours have a happy ending?"

"I'm not sure happy is the right word, but it will have an ending, all stories do."

"Why don't you and Hale get the boat ready and we'll go out for a sail. Just the three of us. We'll go over to Put-in-Bay for the day and have it our way."

51

"Okay, Skip, you get whatever you want, but I need to go on. I need to keep talking this out. I need for you to hear me."

"Did you put Hale in your story?"

"Yeah, Skip. He's in my story."

"Have it your way," he says. "You always do anyway."

I secure the three bags by placing them inside a large trash bag and snug it at my feet so it won't flop and bounce overboard. I turn the Whaler around and punch the throttle. After skipping at high speed across the banks for two hours, I swing into Cockburn Harbor just as the last swirls of sunset fade into blue water ridges. I douse the running lights as I idle past a rusted freighter anchored off the lobster factory. As I step on board *Stardust*, my legs roll and my hands shake from the pounding of the wheel. I look down and see my knuckles crusted with blood and oil. I shove the pack through the lifeline and knock it into the cockpit, wondering what I've done and what it means. I climb up and sit there in the windy dark, thinking it through.

Some childish part of me, Skip, thinks this is a game, just as Philip says, and now I'm clearly the winner. I found the treasure, stole it, and got away, undiscovered. Now, clever me, all I have to do is sail across the Thorny Path, sell something I know nothing about for a high price to dealers who would rather slit my throat than pay, then change my name, my hair color, and vanish forever into some Latin American backwater where Jimmy and his planes never land. I'm screwed, Skip, because if my mind tells me I'm rich as the pope, my body tells me I'm forever bankrupt because I've unleashed a pack of hellhounds that'll sniff out my wake, even if I dump the cocaine overboard and pretend to know nothing about it. Believe it or not, my skipper, this is a story that Hale could tell better than I if he were still alive.

CHAPTER V

I sleep fast in Skip's old room and wake close to noon with a memory about a trip on board the *Pirate's Penny*, the forty-foot sloop he built by hand out of white oak, Virginia white cedar, and Honduras mahogany. Hale's still alive. We're living then in Ohio on Lake Erie. We will leave Ohio in August 1969 and take *Pirate's Penny* to Florida. That first big trip south is all glory and beer and gives me the idea of delivering boats for a living. But in my dream memory, we're still on Lake Erie. It's a hot, muggy, relentless July afternoon. Four days before, twenty parachutists plummeted into the waters off Vermilion near Cleveland. Four of them were scooped out of the drink by fishermen anchored near the spot where the skydivers smacked water. The rest of the skydivers drowned. The Coast Guard recovered all but one of the bodies. This is what happened:

The *Vermilion Photo Journal* says the jump is supposed to be nothing more than a routine, low-altitude exercise on a windless day, but the pilot reads his coordinates wrong without visual confirmation. A cloud bank holds the skydivers safe until a peephole reveals the enormous lake, a cornfield with whitecaps. The anticipated beauty of the jump becomes the cruel terror of the jump. The skydivers tear at their boot laces. Sky, sky everywhere above and nothing but water below. When the divers hit the water, their chutes wrap around each of them like a giant squid. Their heavy black boots fluke toward the lake bottom like anchors. Only Navy Seals train for such a perilous mishap. No other skydiving maneuver comes even close to this level of danger and the skill required to survive it.

We're bound for our annual trip to Cedar Point, the great Ohio amusement park located not far from where my father was born in Sandusky. It's a happy time for our family, but I can't help but think about the doomed skydivers. Just north of our heading, Hale and I spot a large log with gulls perched on top, but gulls don't sit on logs, Hale and I say to each other. We circle closer and find the last dead parachutist, face down. Skip says to Hale and me, "Get the boat hook, boys, and let's fish that poor bastard out of there." My stomach slides to my feet. There's no sign of his chute. His left boot's gone. His red jumping suit is stained with Erie's slime. The hair on his head is as stiff as tar. I lean off the stern and snag the body with a boat hook. Hale and I get down on our bellies and lift the body onto the transom. The face of the dead skydiver is a gray bloated mask with two black holes where the eyes should be. Hale stares into the cavity of the face. I heave. Skip turns me away, saying, "The dead can't hurt you," but even then I sense the dead look hard into our souls long after the blood drains from their faces and want answers we can't give them. They can, indeed, hurt you.

With the bloated parachutist in my arms, I wake and remember my father hungers for his ashes to be scattered out in the Gulf Stream where the lost illegal aliens, capsized fishermen, and dead sons are lost. I may have failed as my brother's keeper, but I'm sure as hell not going to fail my failing shipwright.

I get up to see if he's still alive.

"Are you my bodyguard at the bone-yard?" he barks with his eyes still closed. "Don't you dare put me in that chair. Build me an ark to get out of the dumb dark."

"That's exactly what I want to do, Skip. Build us an ark that'll help us both get out of the fucking dark."

"Would you tell Hale I need to see him?" he says not to me, but to the wall.

Skip cooperates with the hospice women, but he resists my mother and me when we lift him out of bed and into his wheel-chair. The chair is a loaner from a neighbor who lost her hus-band to a heart attack the year before, and every time Skip sees the cracked leather seat he puckers up as if he's just bitten down on a varnish brush. He hates the wheelchair but I've grown to love his wheels because they allow me to give him movement and thus, the illusion of a life still in motion. It's hard to figure how a skeletal man can be so cumbersome, but with no leverage in his arms and legs, no muscle to press with, he's as unwieldy as a lead keel. I scoot him over to the edge of his bed, half-afraid he'll slip off and land on his butt, then I slip my arms under his arms so my face is pressed against his chest. He smells like prison laundry that reeks of fear and regret. To hold myself steady, I lean against the stanchion of his hospital bed as I lower him into the wheelchair. Once down, he looks at me with this puzzled frown like he did when I was ten and floundering in the bow pulpit with a wrapped spinnaker halyard, and said then, "What was so god damn hard about that?"

I wheel him out to the back porch where my mother is waiting lunch which he calls a *dog's breakfast*. He won't eat, so I wheel him over in front of the TV for an hour, then back to bed and a change of his diaper. He wags his head, coughs, and arrives at that familiar thin place marked by a thickness of breath. My selfish desire for him to stay so I can finish my story is balanced by my desire for him to get on with dying. Skip works on a wheelchair riff cooked up in some wild broth fissuring his brain:

What I'd do for a girl instead of this string of pearls not long for this world.

Skip has more one-liners than a repo man.

Maybe his riffs come from his days selling insurance door-to-door or maybe from birth he was a singer of old tales laced with rhyme. When I ask him how he's feeling, he looks at me droopy-eyed from an uncharted island and says, *Like a man who should know better.* Yesterday, he says, to the same question, *I could lick the ocean dry with a spoon.* My favorites are *Not as good as a blind, three-legged dog. Better than two tons of shit in a two-pound bag. Better than I deserve, not as good as I expect. I'm in the doghouse, but I'm pulling on the chain.*

He adds: "It's a strange world, Master Jack. It's a strange world and there's no coming back. There's no coming back to this strange world. Is there, Master Jack?" I figure he's talking about Hale, but he could be talking about me or himself or all three of us in the same boat that eventually goes down with all hands lost. All his lines, arguably, are variations on "better than a sharp stick in the eye," or "all dressed up and nowhere to go," but they pour out of him so easily that it always seems like he could be the original manufacturer of these off-the-cuff jabs at a life unraveling faster than he can sew it up. Morning, noon, and night, his door-to-door riffs are infused with a pagan glee and an allegiance to pain itself, a reminder that, if nothing else, he's still alive and banking on a last-minute wind shift.

My mother hunkers over the kitchen counter cradling a phone between her neck and shoulder. She digs the head of her pen into paper. She takes a call from one caregiver, but needs to schedule another person at the same time. She kicks her foot against the base of the counter. She throws the pen down, reaches for another.

"Blue, can you come at ten in the morning? Good. Gotta go."

She flips through a notepad, forward, then back, finds another number, dials.

"Hi, Cheryl, I need Friday next week, the night shift, you know, 10:00 P.M. to 6:00 A.M. and also Tuesday and Thursday. Can I put you down?"

Skip requires three caregiving shifts starting at 10:00 A.M. and running through each night, seven days a week. That's over twenty shifts a week she needs to fill, so now she sleeps with a cordless phone within arm's reach. I call out to my mother. "I'm here now, you don't need to schedule all these caregivers."

She takes me for a short-timer, waves me off, her look a mix of glare and disbelief. Her anger and pride want me to know she can lift the weight of a dying man. She doesn't want me there or, rather, she wants someone like me, but not me.

I go to the beach and hunt for shark's teeth, but after no success I fall asleep with a towel over my head. I return in the late afternoon when my mother sleeps. I call all the nursing homes within one hour of Amelia Island. I learn from the nursing homes that if my mother keeps hiring "sitters" she could easily shell out five thousand a month. I find her ledger and see fifty thousand left.

Ever since the Depression, Skip has never trusted banks. Never kept the bulk of his money in a vault. Never liked to do business with them. Never thought of a bank as a partner he could trust. Instead, wherever he's lived, he's bolted a safe to the floor of a closet and kept his father's gold watch, his gold coins, and his cash there. If my mother would listen to me, I'd tell her to shift all those valuables over to the Barnett Bank in Fernandina Beach. I'd tell her the cash is no longer safe in the safe, now that Skip can't lord over his nest egg. If I were a good and faithful son, I would tell her all this instead of imagining how I might break into that safe and take enough money to get another boat so I can return to the sea for good.

Night comes with a thunder bang, light skitter, and rain flooding gutters.

Skip looks like a man laid out on a slab with no more secrets. His head thrown back. Spit on his chin. His cotton blanket askew.

I want my father to know who I am.

I'd love it if he'd look me in the eye with something other than confusion or disappointment, but even that I don't need. I just want him to listen to my tale and tell me I'm not an unwanted ghost scraped off the ocean floor. That's all. No hugs, no handshakes, no winks, no tender mercies, no fare-thee-wells. Just hear me out . . .

In my exhaustion and relief to motor back into Cockburn Harbor, I almost don't hear the grunting coming from below decks. Philip has brought a local on board and the two of them tear up the floorboards with their lust. After fifteen hours of clutching two million dollars in cocaine, I never expect to return to a boarded-up love boat. I try to stomp my feet, but they're too sore. I want to rap my knuckles on the cabin top, but my hands are a pulpy mess. Instead, I grab a screwdriver from the stern lazerette and tap on the companionway slats. In his own sweet time, Philip and another man emerge from below, half dressed and painted with a sweat sheen.

"You look terrible," Philip says, and in the same breath, "Matt Younger, I'd like you to meet Jeremy Higgs." Like most Bahamian men, Jeremy wears pants instead of shorts. His red pants, black belt, and a matching red T-shirt stand out in stark contrast to his plum-tinted black skin. I lean down to Philip as Jeremy ambles toward the bow.

"We're shipping out now," I say, turning away from Jeremy.

"For where?"

"St. Thomas."

"Against the Trades?"

"To hell with the Trades," I say, pointing with my mangled right tennis shoe at the swollen backpack.

"You found it?" Philip asks.

"You in?" I reply, looking at my hands, shaking. "I'll give you half of what this stuff is worth if you see *Stardust* across the Thorny Path."

I see in Philip's squinted eyes the tiny wheels of hesitation braking.

"I need you," I add. "I can't sail this rig alone."

"It'll be ugly if we get caught," Philip advises. "In the DR they shoot you for possession. In Puerto Rico we'll get sentenced according to U.S. law. In St. Thomas we'll get swallowed by the Brits. If Jimmy catches up with us, the sharks won't even be able to find us. Not to mention we're now stealing Sam's boat. Remember we got fired from this gig?"

"Wells will come around," I say. "I'll call him from St. Thomas. He'll be thrilled we arrived."

"And Jimmy Q?"

"This is penny-ante stuff for him. He's not going to care about it. We're not going to get caught," I say softly as I watch Jeremy at the bow, cupping a cigarette from the wind, probably thinking we're fighting over him.

"Believe me," I continue, "the hard part's over. We're going to be very rich, very soon." I tell Jeremy to get in his skiff. He looks hurt, jilted, peeved. I shrug and shove him off.

"It's crazy. It's dangerous," Philip says. "But why not? I guess I'm more than ready to leave this place, now that I've got my good luck charm."

"What's that?" I ask, forgetting everything else that's already happened in South Caicos.

"My pink pearl." He cups the large pearl in his palm for me to see again.

"She's a beauty alright," I say, digging out a spare anchor so I can leave the stolen Boston Whaler behind.

"Are we taking a shortcut to Davy Jones's locker?" Philip asks, now quickly dressing.

"What's going to stop us now?" I reply.

"How about that wind blowing straight away from Africa at about twenty-five knots."

"Fuck the wind," I say.

"By the way," Philip says, "We're missing our extra set of engine keys."

"They won't do Jesse any good in Florida," I say, watching a train of clouds scudding over the Thorny Path.

I need an hour to stow the cocaine in a forward compartment inside the starboard hull. I take each sealed bag, wrap it in aluminum foil, and hide them all inside a panel tightened down with four hefty screws. Philip prowls the engine, checking oil, injectors, fuel line, batteries. We each take on necessary jobs with the speed and efficiency of the hunted. After each completed task, we give the thumbs-up sign and move on to the next. Around 11:00 P.M., we weigh anchor.

The only other boat in the harbor besides the rusting freighter is a sixty-foot cruiser named *Citadel*. I see her lights showing. I hear the low growl of her diesels. She's a fancy craft for such a remote harbor. I hope her crew thinks I'm headed toward Provo to the north, rather than, foolishly, south. We slip out of Cockburn Harbor with the wind freshening to thirty knots, out of the southeast. On a 130 degree heading, I aim to round the tip of the DR and make good for Puerto Rico three hundred miles to the southeast, every mile of this heading running straight into the crooked teeth of the southeast Trades.

Stardust handles the two-hour windward leg to Salt Cay with surprising finesse. Our big trimaran flies into the darkness like a three-hulled dragonfly born of some ancient earthly violence. More wind. More waves with their heads torn off. More darkness flashing like the swish of a long tail. The night terrifies me and that terror tells me Jimmy's hellhounds have been unleashed. I can't see them, but I can hear their panting. Once below Grand Turk, the seas run at us from the southeast and throw down a black, inky sheen backlit by the moon.

"Let's reef this puppy down and fall off," Philip shouts below where I wedge myself against the navigation table working out alternative headings in case we get knocked down.

I jump topsides as Philip brings *Stardust* into the wind. The jib whips against itself. The boat heaves in the groundswell like a panting beast. Oncoming waves crash through her bow netting and break in giant sheets on the foredeck. I lower the mainsail on the hoist and hurry to secure the first set of jiffy reef lines to the boom.

"Easy twenty footers," I yell into the spray of a breaking wave. "This is gonna be one hell of a ride." I start to sing one of your rhymes, Skip, that you always sing when the gray teeth of the sea turn white:

> *"Hold her down McCarty cried,*
> *Stop her said McGue.*
> *The devil's in the wheels behind,*
> *As over the road we flew."*

Skip stirs, kicks at his sheets, and looks at me, flummoxed seemingly, not so much by my story, as by the fact he's not in this storm. "When are you going to make good with your mother and tell her where you've been?" he asks, looking at the unmoving fan overhead. "I wish you would tell your brother I want to talk. We have some catching up to do."

Skip returns to his zone of unmeasured fog, half listening, half sleeping like a bell buoy tethered to a chain at the mouth of a river with no name. As I finish tying the last reef point on the main, a rogue wave rides underneath and whips *Stardust* sideways. I lose footing, skid on one knee across the cabin top, catch myself at the lifelines, and claw back to the cockpit.

By 1:30 A.M., *Stardust* stalls in steep chop. To go below is a cruel, taxing punishment. The flexing of the fiberglass in the forward berth sounds like the ripping of tin foil. With each rise and reverberating plunge, it feels, Skip, like *Stardust* will topple over the earth's edge and somersault into some other more distant ocean no man or god has ever known, and I'll deserve my fate without a last glimpse of the Great Perhaps.

"No way we can hold this course," I shout to Philip who leans against the cabin. "We've got to head for the DR."

"That's where they shoot druggies first, hold the trial later," Philip calls out.

"We don't have a choice," I say. "She simply can't take these seas. I'll get us a new heading."

"I'd rather take our chances out here," Philip mutters when he takes the wheel and I go below to seek the thin blue light of the navigation table.

The once Bristol-fashion *Stardust* is now in shambles. Nearly every stowed book, chart, pencil, and cup lies scattered over the cabin sole. A netting of fruit has broken loose from its eyehook. A smashed banana clings to the cabin top. I sweep off the debris and spread out my chart of the Caicos Islands and Adjacent Passages and combine it with a chart covering Haiti, the Dominican Republic, and Puerto Rico. I step off with the dividers the distance we'd come, based on time and speed. I put us roughly sixty-five miles off the DR, or a little over half-way across the Thorny Path. If we lay off another twenty degrees, we'll arrive off Puerto Plata on the north coast of the DR near dawn. I only hope we're well south of the Mouchoir Bank and its spike of exposed coral heads. I climb up the companionway feeling queasy, worried at the kick of steeper seas bearing down.

"How 'bout some relief?" I say to Philip whose hands are locked on the wheel.

"It's all yours."

"I've got a new heading for Puerto Plata," I say.

"Are you sure you want to go there?"

"Don't see how we can stay out," I say, not fully recognizing the consequences of entering the Dominican Republic loaded with cocaine.

"You're the skipper, but I would stay out, rather than make a landfall, anywhere."

Philip has a point.

Just like you always say, Skip, staying out in a gale is better than trying to fetch a harbor, but I don't think *Stardust* can push through the steep oncoming seas without breaking up. I can hear you talking to Hale and me saying once a ship gets caught out in a blow, she needs to hove to under a spitfire jib and not try to outsmart the pitch and roll.

Stardust ain't your *Pirate's Penny*.

She can't take this pounding to windward all night. As it is, I feel her tearing apart. I grab the wheel and swerve *Stardust* to the south. I look over my shoulder at the wake of *Stardust's* three hulls, stunned at their ten-foot height standing over us like a mountain falling away and racing toward us simultaneously. Down below, I hear a crash like a rock tumbling down a mountain. I stick my head down the hatch and see our dining table sheared from its bulkhead hinges. As clouds draw down the moon, the first sheet of rain rakes our decks. For all my looking into the maw of this wet ride, I don't see the full brunt of the storm breaking loose from the darkness. What I do see is a round light shooting off into the sky. The light plunges down, rises up, crisscrosses, disappears, rises again like the headlight on a runaway train, its hot brakes throwing sparks off its wheels.

"Do you see that light?" I shout. Philip doesn't hear me as he checks the automatic bilge pump.

"There's another boat out here," I yell. "It's following us."

"What?" Philip shouts over the rain.

"Kill the running lights," I tell him.

The swerving dial of light spins around the darkened *Stardust.* As we skid into a trough, a voice booms over a megaphone.

"*Stardust,* prepare for boarding."

At first, I think this unseen warning springs from the omnidirectional voice of the Coast Guard. My spine stiffens for more instruction. Nothing comes. My body uncoils. I remember the only law in the Turks & Caicos is owned and operated by Jimmy Q. Through heavy plumes of rain, I take a long look and see the cruiser from Cockburn Harbor. I alter course to the east for what I hope is the northeast breaker of the Mouchoir Bank. The water there drops from a hundred fathoms to two. I hope *Stardust,* with her shallow draft, can surf the edge of the shoals, where the cruiser will turn back or capsize. The best I can bargain for is a game of hide-and-seek, where one boat races down slanted crags, while the other rises on the crests. The blood pounding a hole in my chest tells me this is madness, but the hounds are near, Skip, and I have one chance to shake them before they shake me with a fury even greater than this storm.

"Get me the gun," I whisper to Philip.

"What are you going to do?"

"Pray for a lucky shot," I say.

"What's that supposed to mean?"

"I'm going to try to hit their radar," I say, my tongue clicking hard, my hands prickly hot.

Philip grabs the gun from its holster, hands it to me, and takes the wheel. I lock my arms against the combing. As the light tracks behind *Stardust,* I catch a second sketchy profile of the *Citadel* and fire six bullets. I re-load and fire again, trying to hit both the searchlight and the radar, but I'll settle for either one. A moment later, the light once again washes over the waves, no closer, no farther away.

"I think this is where trouble begins," Philip says, forcing a laugh.

"Not necessarily," I reply, still looking behind at the cruiser tracking us through the jag of colliding spray. Ahead, Philip sees a crooked chain of enormous white spokes throwing off buckets of foam as water pours over rocks and sucks back into blind holes the size of houses.

"You got a plan for negotiating this shoal?" Philip asks.

"Yeah," I say. "We're going to aim right for the reef, then slack off and run downwind. And you're going to stand on the bow and direct me, port or starboard."

"You mean you're turning us into shark bait."

The cruiser pulls back from the first breaking waters of the Mouchoir reef. It's dwarfed by the waves as it bobs over crests, then yaws east, north, then shoots west behind the next wall of rain. I lose sight of the cruiser's searchlight. Instead, I stare into the swirling cascade ahead. The white water backslides around our hulls, pulling us toward the shoal. Philip clings to the lifeline as we stagger sideways, draw back, claw forward through spray. For one moment, with the blue-gray waves breaking over his head, Philip looks like a painted figurehead pegged to the bow— an apple green face with tourmaline eyes. If he pops overboard, I think, I'll never find him in these seas.

"The hatch on the starboard hull just blew off. It's totally awash." Philip bellows, gyrating his arms like a windmill.

"Left or right?" I shout, forgetting the nautical terms.

He thumbs me to the right.

I swing the boat to the south as we swoop down beside the ghostly heads of foam and leave them to port, nearly capsizing inside a wall of water.

"We did it," I shout. "I don't see them behind us."

My elation is short-lived, Skip. As the sea's white stub melts into gray, I see *Stardust* listing to starboard. Even off the wind, she hobbles. Philip clambers back to the cockpit and opens the stern lazerette for the manual bilge pump. Fifteen-footers break over us. There's no way to stay even against such a mountain of water. Already, there have to be a thousand pounds of drag on the starboard hull. Philip stays forward for at least thirty minutes, pumping out the compartment, his harness snapped into the life lines, a flashlight in his teeth.

I fire up the engine and change course for Puerto Plata, but the new heading is nearly as brutal and unforgiving as the old one. With each broadside slammer, *Stardust* lifts her port hull out of water and the wind slaps hard and hobbles us like some red-eyed stray born of a deep scar. A random combination of pitching and rolling threatens to flip us over. Philip returns to the cockpit, drenched, woozy, frightened.

"What about the coke?" I ask. "Go check on it."

"What does it matter," Philip says. "We're sinking, if you hadn't noticed."

"Go check it."

Philip disappears again for what seems like an hour. When he returns, he's too exhausted to stand. "It's gone," he says.

"What do you mean? Take the wheel."

I rush forward without a harness and jump into the starboard hull with the hatch blown off. I stand up to my thighs in seawater and fumble with a flashlight to find the sealed compartment. I don't trust what my eyes tell me. I feel with my fingers for the panel, but it's gone and so are the taped bags of cocaine. They should be floating inside the hull, safe and dry, but they aren't there. All of them gone. Washed out with a wave. How could it happen so fast? I crawl back to the cockpit, baffled by the loss.

"Listen, we'll be lucky to get back to land in one piece," Philip says consolingly. "Besides, that coke was a death sentence if we got busted in the DR."

"Two million dollars' worth. Poof. So much for my retirement in St. Thomas."

"At least we're not floating face down in the soup," Philip says, a slow smile breaking.

I smile back until I hear a knock scraping against the hull.

"Did you hear that thud?" Philip asks cautiously. "It sounds like we hit bottom. But that's impossible. Right?"

"It's all good water here," I say, tasting the sweat running off my lips.

"Oh Christ, the engine just conked out," Philip says. He turns over the ignition, but the gears won't engage. In the abrupt quiet of the boat's failed RPM, Philip rips up the engine hatch to find water seeping around the stuffing box. "We must have hit something," Philip says.

"No way," I reply. I look over the transom.

"God damn it," I shout, "the anchor line is wrapped around the prop."

I look forward and see that the safety nets between the two outer hulls, where the anchor line has been tied off, have ripped away. One of us has to go overboard and cut the heavy-braid nylon anchor line tangled around the shaft and prop. With luck neither are bent, and Philip can re-engage the engine. With one hull sloshed full, *Stardust* doesn't have enough steam to sail up and out of the troughs. The waves are stacked too close together. Trying to cut a line underneath a moving boat in murderous seas is at best crazy. Philip's a master diver, but how can I ask him to volunteer for such a dive? How can I afford not to? I slide off the hatch and bathe every inch of the engine with my flashlight. I see water trickling through the stuffing box, but I also see something Philip doesn't see: one of the engine mounts has busted loose.

"It's no use going overboard," I say to Philip, my throat cinched down so tight I can hardly breathe. "When the anchor line wrapped around the prop, it must have sheared the engine off her mounts. She's out of alignment. No way she's gonna run. All we can do is get the bilge pump down there. Try to stay even."

"Let me see," Philip says, taking a long look inside the engine's cavity while *Stardust* rolls down the waves, some charging toward her, some boiling beneath, others smacking her abeam. With a listing starboard hull, no engine, and the wind tearing the head off every wave, we list on a very slim margin, but we have to make ground, Skip, or I know we're gonna die out there. I close the engine hatch and take the wheel while Philip goes forward, hand over hand, to raise the mainsail all the way up on the hoist. I spin the wheel and bring her up into the wind. From the cabin top, I winch the furl out of the jib and swing the boat off-wind. *Stardust* slams through the next wave with more muscle, but still, with all rags flying, the starboard hull drags us farther south than east.

Three hours later, the walls of rain close down around us, still running with lights off. I worry about broaching from a cross-hit rogue wave. I figure we're thirty-five miles off the DR, between Puerto Plata and Haiti, with no good ports of entry, and no way to sail upwind. I slow every movement down to make sure I don't lose grip. Philip delivers the less-than-cheering news that the batteries are nearly flat. Soon, none of *Stardust's* navigational equipment, lights, or refrigeration will work. In a few more hours, she'll be without any power, just a flagon of floating dark, with two sailors, eyeball to eyeball with the thorns of this ticklish, Spanish place.

Any way I filet the fish, we're screwed and tattooed, Skip, and I have no one to blame but myself for this long night. *Stardust* can't go forward. She can't go back. The wind's blowing barrels at us. Our engine's dead. If you'd been there, Skip, maybe you could have figured something out, but I don't even know how to stop the drumbeat pounding my head telling me I'm the king of all sailing fools for setting out against the Trades.

Then, something curious and unreachable happens.

I feel this lightness pouring into my face. I hear Hale saying this night will pass, and my boat will arrive in one piece. As bad as things are, *Stardust* will not crack up. She will not sink and I won't chum the waters of the Thorny Path. I'm not going to die under a mountain of back swirling water. Do I imagine my brother's voice or do I really hear him say, "You won't die tonight"? Do I conjure him up out of Thorny Path or do I only crave him? I can't say for sure, but after his invisible message, I sense a very different outcome. I lean into the ragged seas. I merge with my listing trimaran until I see the whole night folded around us as well as the next day. There's no other way to say this, Skip, but the dark and light of this crossing, not fit for man nor beast, blends into some kind of homecoming where there's no home except to go farther into the salt blur of my own wreckage.

Just like now, with you in your bed, when the night could be day and the day night, *Stardust* crabs toward the DR like a man side-stroking out of a riptide. Slowly, impossibly, mercifully, our damaged boat is drawn out of her misery by the mountain air lifting the easterly crush of the Trades off the island's coast and off our bow. We feel too exhausted to nibble from the wet box of saltines lying between us and yet Philip lifts his nose and catalogues the island smells—black earth, rotting mangoes, cows, charcoal, vanilla bean, cane standing in the field.

Even with Hale's help out there, I'm still afraid our headsail will tear off the drum, not from a gust of wind, but from scooping water in its belly when the boat drops into a trough. I'm ready to cut it down should it falter and drag in the water, though if it comes to that I can't imagine how *Stardust* can maintain any headway with just the mainsail. At 6:00 A.M. the first light pricks swatches in the east, and we look there instead of toward the three silver sharks trailing aft like half-moons.

"Jesus Maria, we made it to the DR. Would you look at that mountain," Philip shouts like one of Columbus's men squirreled in a crow's nest. The coast looms up like the silhouette of a woman's body, a high scrim of rock floating behind a feather-brush swirl of clouds, the bights and headlands wrapped by a splice of surf and sand. After our detour in flat, heat-soaked Cockburn Harbor, I love the sight of so much mountain rising out of the torn, blue water.

"Now, all we have to do is figure out how to get off these seas," I say. I radio into the Dominican Republic, but no one, not even the military coast patrol, will come out in such high seas to lead us in, even though a double rainbow, wide enough for an armada, flumes a gateway. By mid-morning, we know Puerto Plata is still too far east, so we get radio directions for entering Luperón to the west where the surf gushing between shoals looks like puffs of smoke fired from a cannon. We hug the beach in order to spot the entrance, the sharks still in tow, then we shoot down between reefs. Once in the channel's lee, dark blue water glasses over. Men and women in skiffs paddle out to greet us. As we limp in under sail, one man throws me a bottle of local rum, a pure blackstrap that hits the back of my throat like a struck match. Another man, the color of ginger and cardamom, stands up in his precarious craft and waves us on in.

"Scrumptious," Philip says. "Just leave me here till the next millennium."

I feel relieved to be free of the cocaine, free to think through the next leg of my journey further south, free to consider how to make the next compass heading more inviting than the last. This may seem strange, Skip, but I feel like Hale has given me a second chance to redeem this delivery, and I aim to steer by his spirit voice for as long as I can.

We've traveled to another world as clear and quiet as an alpine lake in Switzerland. In the lee of mangroves, we watch egrets falling through tall scraggly branches like confetti. In one quick tack between shoals, the blue-diamond surge of waves shattering against the hulls is replaced by light green coco palm. We hear the heat oozing beneath leaves, the sun sucking moisture so the rain can fall again, the strum of insects on the prowl for pollen and the flowering rot of things unclaimed.

It's 4:00 A.M. I've been talking for hours and now my watch is over. Oh Skip, please tell me some part of you is here with me now. All I need is one nod. One finger wave from the helm of your hospital bed, your last boat. I promise you this: Before I'm through, I'm going to bring Hale home to you.

CHAPTER VI

I leave Skip's room to make coffee and wait for my mother to emerge from her bedroom. At 10:00 A.M., she cracks her door, peeks out. She cinches her robe and shuffles into the living room while looking over her shoulder as if maybe she left the quiet and safety of her quarters much too soon.

"Tell me about your night," she says, flatly.

I tell her Skip called out for her at 2:00 A.M. and I went in and sat with him and we talked about old times on Lake Erie. That's my first lie. Then, I leave out the important piece. How I'm telling him, in my own sweet and selfish time, where I've been for the last three years.

"The hospice nurses will be here any minute," she says.

"Maybe they can give him a shave," I reply, dragging myself to a chair, exhausted from my night watch with Skip.

"He would like that. And to brush his teeth."

I look at my mother in the quick light of the open refrigerator door, where she searches for a buried lemon. She bobs up with the yellow oval in her hands. As I watch her carefully press a cut lemon over a white cup, I see the weariness of her strength.

"It's better that he die in his own home," she says. "He'd be angry if I stuck him in a home. I couldn't take that, not after all these years together."

"Yeah, I agree. It doesn't get much better than that."

She looks at me with a tinge of spite. "Better?" she asks.

"I mean nursing homes are terrible. This is a good alternative."

"He's been dying practically since you went to the islands. He's a melting candle. One thing after the other. His heart, kidneys, eyes, teeth. He's got bleeding sores all over his body. How come you never wrote or called? I thought you died and now your father's dying and you turn up like some kind of derelict with trash bags. What am I supposed to do with that?"

"I can help. I can stay here. You can rest."

"I don't trust you'll be here for more than a few days," she whispers. "Isn't that your style? When things get rough, you slip out the door. Last I heard, you couldn't wait out the hearing over that marina that went up in flames. You come and go and never say why. What patience are you going to have with a dying man who's in no hurry to go anywhere?"

"That's not fair, Mom." I slouch in the chair, press my fingertips into my forehead, and look out at her through the tent of my fingers.

"Tell me I'm wrong. Tell me everything I just said is made up and I'll take it back." Her mouth is like a pair of rusted scissors that won't open, but they still cut.

I don't say anything. She has every right to regard me as a hungry ghost. I can see in her stoop the weight of my absence and the dread of my return. She switches from madness to miracles in the next sentence.

"I wish I could talk to him about spirit," she says, sipping her lemon juice. "I wish it was something we shared."

"Once a pagan, always a pagan," I reply.

She squints like someone who's looked for buoys too long in the fading sun and she doesn't see me in the pink slash as much as the ghost shadow of her own pain. One thing her pinched eyes reveal: She doesn't know me and I don't know her. We might just as well be standing in the receiving line at Hale's memorial with kind words for strangers and nothing to say to each other.

"Matt, you've got an answer for everything except . . ."

"I've been south. I was doing boat deliveries in the islands."

"I'm not just talking about your latest vanishing act. You can't tell me about the last thirteen years because you've been drunk most of the time. It's all one long blur to you. Isn't it? You were drunk the night Hale died, right?"

"I'm back now. We'll sort this out."

I want to push back with force, but mostly she's right and what she says makes me want to snag another boat, disappear, never finish my story, and never return again to the burdens of

71

the land. I would happily drink whiskey instead of rum, anything to ease the rot gut boil and false safety of living under the same roof with her who wishes I had never returned.

We talk past one another for another half hour until she offers, "The tired part of me wants him to get on with it. The wife in me thinks he'll rally like he has so many times before. He's really a cat with nine lives."

"More like a hundred lives," I say.

My mother snaps back, "The doctor says he's got congestive heart failure. Fluid build-up. His air supply will get caught off. You going to be here for that?"

Watching her nurse her hot lemon drink, I marvel at how she's tolerated Skip's drinking over the decades, his countless boats, his restless spirit itself like some kind of squall skidding over the charts, no one harbor good enough to call home. She adds a pinch of cayenne to her lemon to wake herself up. She sips half-asleep, then she eats half a grapefruit, peeling back the rind to eat the white inner skin.

As I turn to go find the newspaper lying in the driveway as Skip did every morning, my mother startles me. She grabs my arm and says, "I'd like you to write the obit so we have it, ready to go."

"Ready-to-go." It's a Skipper-like phrase, a phrase he's fond of and might use himself if my mother were laid up instead of him.

"Of course," I tell her.

I reach for a pencil and pad of paper as if responding to a command from a new skipper. Now I have a job that gives the day its shape and direction. I can perform a needed task. I can help my mother. I can be of service. I write quickly . . .

Jack Younger was born on June first, 1913 in Sandusky, Ohio. As a boy at neighboring Rye Beach, where his parents owned a summer cottage, he taught himself to build boats. In 1957, Jack built a forty-foot sloop named the Pirate's Penny, *still in commission today. He was a Delta.Tau.Delta at Miami of Ohio where he lettered in football, track, and basketball.*

As a member of the "greatest generation," Jack proudly served in WWII, where he saw action in the Pacific. After 25 years with Metropolitan Life Insurance, Jack took early retirement and sailed his Pirate's Penny *from Vermilion to Florida, where he built houses and owned Jack's Manatee Marina on Merritt Island, still operating today under that name. Jack was a member of the Masonic Lodge, a lifelong sailor, a sports enthusiast, and a master craftsman with an undying sense of adventure.*

Jack (known as Skipper to family and friends) believed the greatest trait was courage, followed by a sense of humor. He passed away in a home he built on Amelia Island, Florida on _____. He is survived by his wife, Emily, whom he loved passionately since 1934 when they met at Miami of Ohio, and by his son Matt.

Even before I finish writing, I feel like I've betrayed Skip, who, as bad as shape as he's in, still wants to crush my hand and kick my ass. I slide the piece of paper over to my mother, who smiles twice while reading, then says slowly, "It says a lot with a little." She takes a sip of lemon juice and adds, "Maybe we'll get a break in the weather today." A sailor's wife with one eye always seeking out the drape of flags or the drift of smoke, my mother's fond of saying, "Weather is always with us," by which she means something like change is always with us, like clouds in the afternoon or crows at dawn. But also she intends another meaning. Weather and change are in our future because she believes one day we'll all be changed, and that will be a good thing maybe, unlike the latest turn in the weather.

"One day," she says, looking again at what I wrote, "when you're old and hurt, you'll wish you had done more. You'll wish you could do some things over. You'll wish your brother were still alive."

There it is, the gleam and velocity of her knife.

I won't let her cut me, not now, not when there's more to tell. After lunch, I pitch and roll and barely sleep inside a change of weather until I find myself talking again to my sailor who lives just outside the thin shadow of his own obituary. Wait for me and I'll wait with you, I tell him more than once.

CHAPTER VII

"Hale, I'm so happy to see you. Where have you been, my son?"
My father's voice scratches low, nearly inaudible, a cross
between a whisper and a moan. I dig my fingers into my ribs as
he reaches up into the night-light darkness, his arms fully outstretched as if straining to touch something several stories high,
believing I'm his other son, the lost one, the god-like son he
wants beside his bed. His words are exactly the words I want to
hear except they're offered to a boy long gone, and still pictured
the way he was, miraculously strong and gifted.

I reach down and clasp his forearms and hold strong.

I want to say Hale's not here, Skip. It's me, Matt, but I don't
correct him. I let him spend a little time with his first son who
never returned from the great salt lanes.

"Where you been? Your mother's sick with worry. She thought
you'd gone down to Davy Jones's locker." My father cocks his head
the way dogs do when they want a biscuit or a back scratch. My
gut churns and I can feel my body wanting to spew ash over the
ashes of my dead brother god who's always present.

When I see my father caged in his bed with rails, it's hard to
see the ghost of myself in him, yet I must be there waiting like
smoke on water. When I close my eyes and find my Skipper in
memory, then I also discover his unruly blue eyes, the round and
sensuous chin, the generous, full-muscled torso and short legs
that he and I share. Though he waits to die and I wait to live,
we are not so unlike. We are just two men looking for a port of
entry, a common truth, a summons, a new heading, out beyond
the hammering we have known.

I talk into the darkness that holds the purple tangle of scars that
is my father . . .

Skip, I don't know if you can remember this, but just days after we arrive in Ft. Lauderdale, Hale snaps some cord to our previous life in Ohio. One day he's flip, morose, relaxed, anxious, loud, silent, his eyes veiled, glassy-gone to an easy place where games are played for high stakes that always seem cheap. He becomes a big shot with time on his hands. You never see this change in Hale because you're too damn busy playing on the *Pirate's Penny*. You've had a bellyful of Metropolitan Life and you figure your boys are almost grown and off to college, so why should you worry about details? Ft. Lauderdale High School has over three thousand students on three shifts with no study halls, so Hale's out of class by noon and he doesn't have swim practice until three. He never eats lunch, so he has hours to weave himself into any trouble that suits him. He boasts to me of gambling on casino boats, smoking dope, fucking college girls from Vassar and Sarah Lawrence. He isn't the go-along-with-trouble type; he's the one who drives the action, cuts the deck, makes the call. He fools nearly everyone because he's the captain of the swim team and a straight-A student recruited by every Ivy League school. The coach of the Olympic Swim Team calls him every week, hoping he'll forego college and devote himself to the glory of the games. All you care about is when the next swim meet is scheduled so you can come watch your famous son take home another ribbon, another trophy, another headline. You don't see the plumes of hell dancing up around your hero.

"You're not so smart," Skip says, corkscrewing his body to face the wall where he sees Hale's photo staring back. "You didn't bring him home."

"You're right. You're always right," I say, slamming my hand into his bed stanchion.

After Hale's death, my parents slip into the stream of constant motion as if they're looking for their favorite son everywhere in the tidal salt. First, they move from Ft. Lauderdale to Islamorada, halfway between Key Largo and Marathon in the Florida Keys, then Stuart, Vero Beach, Merritt Island, Satellite Beach, St. Augustine, and finally Amelia Island—some fifteen moves in all—from nearly the farthest point south in Florida to the farthest point north. Skip builds a house, then sells it in two years. They climb back on board the *Pirate's Penny* and find the next harbor with a water view lot.

I drop out of high school and keep moving by delivering boats up and down the Eastern Seaboard and over to the Bahamas. They become gypsies of no fixed address. Most postcards to them come back undelivered, no such party, no longer there. They don't know where I am, and I don't know where they are. Neither of them talk about Hale even though his pictures are everywhere in their houses, like trophies silted with packing dust. Standing beside a pool, emerald green like a heavenly carpet, Hale always wears the same skinny smile like he's secretly biting down on his teeth.

What do I know for sure about all this jumpy, slingshot passage that we all have in common?

The death of a favorite son can twist a rope around a family's heart so tight it can't be cut, dissolved, or undone. We each keep a whetstone ready to sharpen a knife. We each slice down on the hard wet strands of rope, but no matter how hot the blade's edge, it can't bite through the line and no one can break free.

I've got to keep talking. I want to stop. The glacial pace of my skipper's dying may yet find hummingbird speed. The race is on. I have a lot more to say about the golden son, but first, there's this island I come to. The island wrapped with surf and deceit. The island that Hale helped me reach after skirting the reef.

The Thorny Path swirls behind us, but another's about to kick up in the DR. Moments after Philip drops anchor, he slips on his mask and fins and jumps overboard to inspect the engine shaft and prop. He vanishes and reappears from the murky-green harbor with the frayed anchor line bunched in his fist.

"Son of a bitch was wound so tight around the shaft, even after I'd cut it, I could hardly work it free. We're damn lucky the torque of the line didn't jerk the shaft out of the boat. If we drill out the engine block bolts, realign the engine and shaft, and bolt her back down, we should be back in business."

"Is that a tough job?" I ask, while Philip treads water near the starboard hull, then swims round the boat to continue his inspection.

"It's like the old saw," Philip shouts near the bow, "Nothing's hard if you know what you're doing. I have no idea what sort of mechanics we've got on this island." He swims back to the transom ladder and comes back on board.

"She's not in too bad a shape, considering the last twenty-four hours we were blasted by a fire hose" he says, stripping on deck. "You're one lucky skipper," Philip adds, shaking his head while he drops below to change. Despite my concerns about getting repairs done on *Stardust*, I'm glad to be anchored, even if we're nowhere close to anything we need. In the heat of the day, three men in a skiff come out to greet *Stardust*.

"Bienvenido a mi Luperón," the Customs man says in a musical half-rhyme. "We don't get many *marineros* here. No three sailboats in one, ever. How do you sail it? Too much wind last night. Wrong time of year to sail against the Trades. No? My name's Rafael. These are my assistants, José and Martín."

Rafael already knows *Stardust* has been in distress. Her story is now his story, traveling faster than the waves. Slouched against the combing in his white cotton shirt stained with sweat and tobacco, Rafael wants to hear again about our crossing from the Bahamas. How big are the waves? Does *Stardust* see the reefs? Do the two *marineros* have any firearms, animals, plants, or drugs on board?

I tell him about my revolver.

"Still warm," Rafael says, his hands running over the barrel.

"Sharks," I say. "We fired at them last night."

"We have many sharks," he says.

"So it seems," I reply.

Rafael looks at the other two men and nods his head: "Normally, we check all weapons during your stay, but one revolver, you keep. You have clearance papers from South Caicos?" I consider offering Rafael a bribe, until I remember that the entry card I got when I entered the Abacos in the Bahamas is intended to act as a clearance-out from the Bahamas. I reach for my wallet, retrieve the stained blue card, and hold it up proudly.

"No, no, no, clearance from Caicos," he says, thumping his palm on the cockpit seats.

Philip alertly jumps below as if searching for the form and returns with a tray of drinks. He serves rum and cokes, gin, soft drinks, stale potato chips, cookies, two bruised apples, one mauled orange. The men want to hear more about the crossing and with each new telling, they each fish up a story of their own, eager to revise, interrupt, and finish each other's tales. As a young man, Martín was chased by a creditor ten miles offshore when he ran out of gas and had to paddle back against heavy seas. José once hunted *tortugas verdes* when a *viento terrifico* capsized his boat. He wasn't rescued until the next day by a girl in a home-made sailing canoe who later became his wife. Rafael once left in the middle of the night to track his wife who'd left with another man in a wooden dinghy for the Bahamas. He never found her, but her lover's boat washed ashore a week later. Puckish smiles, feints, and whispers swirl among us. The Customs men take another slug of Captain Morgan rum.

"Which one of you is captain?" Rafael asks, having forgotten about his earlier request for clearance papers from Caicos. I shoot him a puzzled glance.

"Only one of you can go ashore until your boat's repaired," Rafael says.

"*Por qué?*" I ask.

"Since your boat cannot be moved, one of you must stay. Government rule."

"In that case," I pipe up, pointing toward Philip, "that man is the captain."

Philip will go ashore and find engine parts and another mechanic to help him repair the diesel. Philip tells Rafael we need a new engine shaft and an engine realignment.

"He will have to go to Santo Domingo for such a mechanic," Rafael says.

"How about Puerto Plata?" I ask.

"No one there can help you."

I can't tell if we're being conned or not, but I also can't see what other option we have.

"You be happy soon," Rafael smiles. "Your engine fixed. You see."

The other men smile, and Martín asks if Philip and I play *base-boll*.

"We need another Tony Hernandez," Martín says, smacking his fist into his palm.

"Yes, maybe," I say, thinking it prudent to express a willingness to play although I have no intention of doing so. The five of us toast to the inevitable success of repairing *Stardust*. The men leave with Philip in the stern of their tipsy craft. I wave from the cockpit and fall asleep amid a tangle of sheets, wet clothes, bottles, waterlogged books. When I awake, it's dark and the trees are alive with the chatter of insects, the wheeze of accordions, the echo of footsteps. Near the unfinished pier, I see a man and woman swaying beneath a palm-thatched rum bar. A child dances with a piebald goat.

With the batteries dead, I can't read at night. I have only a few cans of tomato soup and salted beef. I'm already tired of replaying the events in Cockburn Harbor and counting up the wages of my lost cocaine. Better to risk a fine than to stay there alone bickering with myself.

Against orders from Rafael, the Customs man, I go ashore.

I strip and put my clothes in a plastic bag and cinch it at the top. The water feels cool and soothing against my wind-chafed skin. I breaststroke along the surface unseen by anyone, a creature of the Thorny Path at home in dark waters. Something feels right, Skip, about swimming naked to the island and reclaiming some part of the original, uncluttered integrity of my intention to make this run south. I climb ashore at a sandbar break in the mangroves. I flick off the excess water and slip back into my clothes. I see a string of Christmas tree lights hanging from leaning poles and walk toward them—my sea legs wanting to roll.

I don't know what time it is. I can't remember the day. I feel like a man who's already passed through shark-bait status, and now I'm ready to live posthumously with less fear, greater strength. I want to sail away from the last few stalled weeks, untouched by the teeth encircling me, and quickly forget about Jimmy Q. and the stolen cocaine. I want to get *Stardust* back in order and get her to St. Thomas. Where a better man might have bent at the knee, Skip, I tell myself the cosmos owes me something sweet for coming through an avalanche of falling water. My ambition is simple: get drunk and wake up with a woman.

I stop at the rum shack strung with colored lights. Large curls of blue-green paint peel off its clapboard. Next to the bar sits a pile of twisted lumber and rusted kerosene cans with caps missing. The dancing couple and the bartender smile as though they've already savored the details of my story in the shape of my torn clothes and dripping hair. The woman's face looks like she has a three-day fever as she clings to her man. The clumps of hair under her arms are slick with sweat. I raise a finger to the dancing couple and walk up a street littered with tires and kitchen trash. The place is uprooted, anonymous, timeless in its enduring farewell to better times. A rat sits on the crown of a fallen mango.

To the west, behind the rum bar, sits a warren of one-storied, pastel-washed frame houses perched on cinder blocks, each one matched with a scraggly orange or lemon tree. What at first seems like a tiny fishing village, with a baseball field facing the ocean, fans out into three main streets—Duarte, Independencia, and Luperón. I pass a carpenter's shop, shoe repair, dentist, welding shop, ice house, bus stop, several smashed-window Fords and Chevys, and a white mannequin lying face down on a concrete slab. I smell the half-sweet, half-rotten smell of cane fields, wood smoke, the stench of chicken shit, the sour tang of rum mash, all of it lingering over the deserted streets like rancid flowers. I follow the beat of music along Independencia to the town square where everyone has come to find music and a bolt of rum.

Pawing couples, chatty mothers with infants, faltering men, and knots of children mingle, shout, and scuttle to the blare of the music pouring from a bar. The men wear white drawstring pants and yellow and green cotton shirts. They have flat stomachs, narrow waists, sharp curves, and ridges of muscle melting into muscle. They notch together on a curb, eyeing the high-haunched, honey-colored women wearing skin-tight stretch jeans and high heels. The men grab women out of the park and dance with them in the street.

The merengue bar jams with women and men who cut a stiff-legged, two-step, confectionery shuffle. Girls flirt with girls as much as with men. From where I stand, it's hard to tell the dancers from the watchers as everyone sways to the rasp and drag of music scored on scratchy records. When the music stops, the park is awash with banter and kisses. I buy a cup of mango sherbet and sit back on a park bench to drink in this carnival—the handsome copper faces, the exaggerated gestures of flirtation and surprise, the eye-winks from the elders, the hips rocking without music.

As I consider lying down on the bench, a woman sits down next to me. I hadn't seen her at the merengue bar. She could be 17 or 27. Her skin is the color of nutmeg cut with cocaine. She could have crawled out of an oil drum or just stepped off a cruise ship. I've never seen a woman so lit with color, balanced between black and white, having already traveled through a slash of black, indigo, mother-of-pearl.

"Want to dance?" she asks.

She talks in a fluttery voice while her supple fingers act out the parts of two dancers. I'm so confused by the zing of her English and the luminosity of her skin, I can't get my tongue to work right. Her black hair is cropped short like a helmet. Her breasts draw a sharp outline under her dress. She takes my hand and guides me across the street to the bar. I'm the only white guy on the street. The sexual jabbing between the men stops while they eye me like some kind of sea creature dragged in from the beach. She leads me through the door of the bar onto a tiny patch of floor skimming with dancers. Her hips rock against mine, teasing, nearly percussive, as she moves only below the waist, while I move only above the waist in clumsy imitation.

As I turn to survey the smiles surrounding me, she draws closer, showing me with her thrusted hips how the dance plies variations on the same two-step pattern. I want to walk off the floor, and I want her to teach me. Inside the speed of the strobe, she slows everything down. "Step forward," she says "Drag to close, step forward, drag to close, 1 & 2, 3 & 4. Simple, no?" It *is* a simple dance, but she moves on every beat with a contrary hip movement to the right, making my heart switchback against my chest. I count the 4/4 time in my head, but my feet can't get it right. When she drags her foot and turns, her dress hitches up on her thighs and the strobe sparkles her skin.

The razor-stuttering momentum of the music continually breaks apart, reassembles, scatters, rejoins. Older couples keep a cool distance from each other. Young couples wrap themselves together like smoke so I can't tell which hip or leg is male or female. Inside this zone of fruit-flooded color, I love watching this woman with melodramatic furrows, stern glances, tempting smiles. Miniature beads of sweat trickle from the turn of her mouth, down her neck to the V of her chest. Her clothes, like mine, are soaked by the end of the first song, and this time I take her hand and lead her back outside to the park.

"I need a few more lessons," I say.

"You're fine," she says. "Now, we get something cool, no?"

I stop beneath the canopy of an ice cream vendor and buy two cups of lime sherbet and a basket of crescent-shaped donuts dipped in chocolate. The sweat on her face, neck and arms is still visible as she dips the plastic spoon into the cup, then balances the spoon in her mouth without her hands. She closes her eyes, moves her feet ever so slightly as the music reaches us with drums, accordions, and one horn with a heart murmur.

She lifts her head after the shine and sweat of the dance floor and offers me this warm, compliant symmetrical smile so unlike my own that's permanently lopsided and dogged-down tight. Her unguarded smile becomes, in my imagination, a cracked doorway, inviting me to enter and unpack my secrets. Impishly, she turns to face me and wets her lips after nibbling the sherbet. Skip, I don't how to say this without it sounding just goat-eyed wishful or delusional, but she leans in, our knees now touching and she undresses me with her eyes, peeling down my layers until I'm sitting there naked enough to startle a hole in the Luperón darkness. She peers into my marrow, tenderly, approvingly, and with her eyes locked onto mine, she offers consolation. "I'll do some wrong for you, if you'll do some wrong for me."

I smell the lime on her breath mixed with the salt stain hugging her collarbone. I wait patiently like a hunter to catch the quick reach of her tongue as it takes another lick and another. Inside the curl of her wetted lips, I feel my own sea knots releasing in my spine and legs. Instead of suspicion, I open my palms in front of her and feel simply grateful to be allowed to linger on the flush of her cheekbones, the soft flame of her throat, the nipples puckering her dress, grateful to invent her heartache and imagine my own history dissolving inside of her. Everything's wrong with the only white sailor in town tagged on a dance floor by a beautiful woman-child, but it all feels right.

"You live here?" I ask, not knowing exactly how to compete with merengue pounding behind us.

"I grew up here. Now, I only visit."

"What brings you back?"

"I came back to dance with you," she says.

Her line is a little too sweet, Skip, and I sense she knows exactly who I am.

The shimmer of her sweat should carry the shine of dread, but already I'm beyond reach. Where a better captain might have returned to his ship, I watch her nibbling lime sherbet while other men circle us with their communal agitation. Whoever she is, I want this light-skinned, blue-eyed Dominican to nudge me away from *Stardust* and her trials and her repairs still ahead. After she finishes the sherbet, I grab her hands and pull her up from the bench.

"Show me your town," I say. "What's your name?"

"Rosario Estrella."

She tells me how Luperón looked better before David and Frederick, two hurricanes that struck in 1979. The storms leveled buildings, killed many people. Her father was knocked down by

83

a piece of roofing and thrown into electrical wires. Electrocuted. She found his body the next day, curled up like a fish, burn marks over most of his body. Holding hands, we walk away from the park, away from the men who shout at her, *"Avión, Avión."*

"What are they saying?" I ask.

"They're excited because tomorrow is the *Pelea de Gallo*, the cockfight. Some will lose everything. Some will win lots of money. They'll be strutting all night because they can smell the spilled blood. It's always like this before the *gallera*."

"Have you ever gone?"

Rosario says her father raised game cocks and sold a magic potion to bolster their courage. One time, she says, her father takes her to the *gallera* after she complains her older sister gets to go. Her father stands as quiet as a priest. He grips her hand when the two cocks face off, beak to beak, across a line scratched in the dirt. His little red cock flies up high, lunges with its blunted steel spurs at the head of a brown-and-white speckled cock, and rips a gash in its breastbone. But her father's red cock is pecked in the right eye, blinding it, making it screech with fury.

Her father massages the cock's legs with his secret oil corked in a purple vial. She stands on a crate, so she's nearly as tall as her father, and looks into the good eye of the red fighter. Before she can tug on her father's sleeve to show him the gleam, the red cock races forward, with its eye swollen shut, and pins the speckled cock by the head, hitting it again and again with spurs. Feathers and blood fly. The men love the fight and can't wait for the little red cock to fight again. She's frightened, not by the killing, but by the faces of the men who want death to help them feel more alive. She says she never understood her father.

"That fight made a big impression on you," I say, thinking instantly it's the most lame thing I've ever said to a woman.

She presses against me as she did on the dance floor and I can feel her naked body beneath her dress. We walk back through the town toward the beach with the merengue bar rasping behind us, the fretful notes giving way to the surf's held breath and release. She enters an alley behind a shoe store. She lingers beneath a tree, reaching up into the branches, her dress hoisted on her thighs. She returns with a handful of strawberry guavas. She places one of the pink fruits in my mouth.

"Take a bite," she says.

She tells me poverty pursues her, always. I wonder what greater poverty is pursuing me and whether the crew of the *Citadel* is tracking me right now. Between poverty and dreams of escape from the DR, she says she drinks too much. "We're like children on this island. All we want to do is dance, sing, and follow the strong man, the one with the secret cock oils. In a poor country, everything's for sale. In a very poor country like the DR, everything has already been sold."

She says no woman has ever held a major political position. There's no party that values women except as mothers. She says if you're not a mother, you're nothing. You're a whore. That's why the men shout, *Avión*. *Avión* means little bird between the sheets. I take a deep breath in hopes of keeping up with the swerve of her hands. "No one listens to you unless you ride the big white horse," she says. "No one listens to the troubles of women."

"How long will you stay in Luperón?" Rosario asks, as I look out toward the harbor and see *Stardust* anchored, her masthead and stern unlit. I hesitate in my answer wondering if she's fishing for clues she can barter, sell, or use against me.

"As long as it takes to get our boat up and running."

"Then, your boat is OK," she asks cautiously. "Nothing else is wrong with it?"

"She took a beating coming across from the Bahamas, but she'll make it," I say.

"Where do you go . . . from here?"

"St. Thomas."

"Never been there," she says, skipping her hands through the air. "I've never left the DR. I'd like to see New York. I have girl-friends there."

She makes it sound painful to live in a beautiful place where the poor don't know how hog-tied miserable they are. She says DR jobs stick to you like dirty underwear. A woman can go to Santo Domingo, make slum wages in a baseball factory. Or she can sell her body and have a view of the sea. Either way, she says, beauty, money, and self-respect never come together. She grabs my hand and we leave the jetty for the beach. We kick off our sandals, walk to the water's edge, and look toward the Bahamas. I can almost feel her eyes working the wind like a boat, measuring the threat of the Thorny Path.

What I see is stolen treasure cascading into water, telling me, Skip, to forget this girl and this night, and to keep *Stardust* easting to Red Hook Bay in St. Thomas. I still believe I can make good with Sam Wells, get the rest of my money from him, and move on to another boat. I turn to leave. I can't afford more trouble, but I also want it. I want her to kiss the salt sting from my eyes, flick her tongue against my teeth, grip me with the flare of her hips.

With her, I whisper to myself, I can be absolved of my memory, my name, my history, absolved of the blood I believe will seep forever from the wound in my hand the night Hale went down in the Gulf Stream. With her, I tell myself, I can forget about the death of our family god and live godless and happy and free of everything I can't fix.

Rosario scoops up a handful of water, touches my face with the spume, and licks the brine from my chin. In one nimble arc, she pulls her dress over her head and tosses it up the beach just out of reach of the waves, then she unhooks my shorts, helps pull the T-shirt over my head. We kneel in the sand on all fours. I look at the stars safe in their distance from the Thorny Path, then at her brown skin in the darkness pulling me out of my heckled brain. The curve of her butt pushes smooth and hard against me, the wetness between us thick and noisy, the easy slide of skin inside of skin like our own tidal surge, a tightening mixed with softness, a bearing down blended with a letting go, our own little cries lost inside the greater beat of the surf that dies and goes beating in my ears after I've come.

Coated in sand on our knees and elbows, we gather our clothes and carry them up the beach to the dunes, where we brush each other off and dress. We walk back past the harbor, toward her house perched on cinder blocks between jagged banana trees. The two small windows in front on either side of the door are cracked, covered with masking tape. The door itself is a peeled green slab soaked in sun and salt air. I can just make out, in the faint moonlight, the sagging, rusted corrugated tin roof. Once inside, she lights a candle and the one large room swells with shadow. I see one dress on the floor, a toppled three-legged crib, a couple of tattered lounge chairs, a table covered with crumbs, a knife, half a loaf of bread, a large red Chase & Sanborn coffee can, and a string of laundry like a spider web laced between two chairs.

"This is where I grew up," she says, without apology.

"It's got all the basics," I say, not knowing how to greet this wreckage.

"It's a dump, but I come here to get away from my work in Puerto Plata."

What looks like a hammock is pinned into another corner and slung over the sagging mattress. She reads my puzzled look.

"Mosquito netting," she says.

She lowers the net down over the mattress, pulls off her dress, and climbs through a slit in the net. I follow.

"Want the candle out?" I ask.

"Let it burn down," she says.

I part the narrow opening in the net and slip down onto the mattress next to Rosario lying on her stomach. I lie down beside her. I stroke her calves and thighs. Without saying a word, she rolls over and takes me into her mouth until I grow hard. Later, we fall asleep beneath the netting with the candle rising and falling like its own sea in league with the swallowing tides. Sometime in the mosquito night, I awake and sense the presence of another person in the room, rustling, kicking off shoes, yanking at a zipper, pulling off clothes.

"Rosario, Rosario, wake up," I say, tripping over my words.

"What?"

"Someone's in the room."

Rosario squints over my shoulder. "That's Catalina, my friend. She's back from the bars. She must have fought with her boyfriend. She needs a place to sleep. It's all right. She's probably drunk."

I smile to myself, having always imagined such a moment, sandwiched between two women. As sea-weary as I am and still rubbery in the legs, I can't sleep. While Rosario curls into herself, my body rocks with the pull of her hips. I fall asleep watching the brown wave of her back, but wake after dreaming of being back on board *Stardust* with Jesse in Nassau who laughs after I lose the Avon raft.

Rosario's rooster drags the dream about Jesse from my head.

I hear its cry before I see that Catalina's gone. I hold my hands to my face and smell Rosario. I look at her nude body, the black helmet of her hair, her legs curled, her chattering hands now crossed at her chest. Her mouth drapes open, lipstick smeared and a thin smudge of blue mascara runs below her right eye. I see in her face she's no teenager. The bottoms of her feet are laced with scars. One toe's hooked and swollen. Her red toe-nail polish splinters along the cuticle.

Already I want the taste and feel and stroke of her.

I want the morning to begin with the night. I get up in search of a glass of water and a toilet and find neither. The main room is more inviting than it looked in the dark. The concrete block is painted a lime green. What I had taken in the night as folding lawn chairs are mahogany chairs with green floral plastic-coated cushions. A radio and record player sit on a packing crate end table. Records lay scattered beneath. A rusted knife glints from a window ledge. Sandals of every color mingle on the floor with costume jewelry.

I open the back door and step out into morning light and see a clutch of women standing on a plank in the mud. They swivel their heads like tropical owls. One woman with her hair bundled up in a blue kerchief nails me with her eyes. She holds a baby hitched on her hip, its fat legs poking out of a cloth diaper. The smell of oil and lard creeps out of her clothes. I smile weakly, offer a wave. I walk a second plank through the mud, past a scraggly calabash tree and a rusted slop pen with a speckled sow, my each step scrutinized by the women as I hurry toward a hut I pray is the outhouse.

Luckily, my hunch proves correct, but the outhouse is a roaring pit of flies. I can't bring myself to sit. I raise myself up on my tiptoes while trying to squat. The chatter of the women increases and I picture them coming to the unlockable door and bursting in just at my moment of greatest concentration.

What do they see in me, Skip?

A white man who fancies a brown-skinned woman and tosses her away?

I stand there behind the door holding the knob, working out in Spanish my exoneration: how I did not pay her to sleep with me. How we met at the merengue bar and she brought me to her home. I craft my sentence, *palabre y palabre*, but when I open the door, Skip, the women are gone and so is Rosario. I know my only real job is getting *Stardust* ready to sail again, but I want to find her.

Skip shakes his head, pinches the top of his nose with his thumb and first finger.

"My daddy always said a man is just a three-peckered goat with no chance to reverse blood flow to his brain. You're living proof he knew what he was talking about."

"You're with me. You're listening. You're here."

"What the hell else am I going to do?"

"I thought you were sleeping. I didn't know where you were."

Skip palms his eyes.

"Here's one thing I can tell you," he says through the thin cage of his fingers, "Even when I'm gone, I'm here, so talk away. You seem to have some destination in mind." Now, his hands bury themselves under his blanket. His eyes flutter shut. He returns to that windless trench between this world and the next where he gathers all his tales of wonder for his next junket.

Skip, I know what you're thinking in there: lust and curiosity is a dangerous combination for any sailor, and you're right, but still, I want another night with Rosario to spill over into the next day. She wants *off island*. I want *inside the island* of her body. Nothing about this rhythm feels safe, yet it's another temptation I can't turn down—no matter what she knows or who she works for.

"Maybe death is something else," Skip says, his words thin and low as if blown into his throat from a jagged shore.

Let's just call my detour into the DR a death visitation.

I've now stolen drugs from Jimmy Q and a boat from Sam Wells and then lost the drugs and *Stardust* needs serious repair. So yes, looking back into the swells, this detour was all of that— a wish to die, but in that dying, I wanted to seize another life which bears no resemblance to the life I've known before.

This hunger for another life is something your other son knew a lot about.

He never revealed this hunger to you, but I saw it gobbling cul-de-sacs, glistening skin, needles, quarts of gin. I helped keep his secrets hidden from you and the greater world that lusted after a piece of his growing fame and wanted to eat of it and be changed by it. I feared for where his appetite for more lives might lead, and finally I was drawn into his hunger and consumed by it as were you and mother. All of us were consumed, broken, and cast away from each other by an eighteen-year-old family god who needed to keep an appointment with a breakneck fever.

CHAPTER VIII

When I look in on Skip at 11:00 A.M., his body spoons like a shrimp tumbling in a tidal curl. At noon, he flickers one eye, then the other. He stirs again two hours later thinking it must be time for something, but what that is, he can't sort out. "Where's everyone anyway?" he asks. "Funny how people keep giving me the slip. Where in the hell do they go? Can you tell me that? You can't tell me anything because you just got here. If you want to visit me, you can't," he continues as I crank up his bed. "I'm long gone. Flown the coop, tweety-tweet, fast asleep. If you want to remember me, get onboard and throw up the rags."

His mouth flares at the corners as if he's auditioning for the circus.

"Ain't nothing a man can't do with a good woman. Just don't stick me in a fucking hole in the ground. I'm not lost, I'm found. I've never been round the Horn of Africa, have you? Hard a-lee. Where's my Emily?"

The next hour passes while he sings a new rhyme:
Don't sigh.
Don't ask why.
Don't cry.
Don't say goodbye.
Sing no sad songs for me.

"Easy now," he says with his eyes clamped. "You're not hauling a sack of potatoes here. Easy, big fellow. This here is precious cargo. Have I ever told you about Cuba? I was in Cuba one time when all hell broke loose. The joint was jumping. You've never seen so many beautiful women, dancing in the street, on tables. Musicians camped on every street corner. Bottles of rum for two bits. Monkeys passing the hat for naked dancing girls. Cuba was the seventh wonder of the world back then until that bearded hothead fucked it up."

Skip convinces three fraternity brothers in 1935 to sail a boat to Cuba during spring break. The ninety-mile crossing from Miami is remarkably uneventful despite the fact that Skip has never done a lick of ocean sailing, but once in Cuba, the boys take to the Havana nightlife too well.

"One lands in jail," he says. "One stumbles into a whorehouse. One loses all his money on dice. I get black-vomit-mosquito sick. Chills and sweats so bad I can't see my own hands. Don't know if I can sail the boat back to Florida, but I do. I tie myself to the tiller. Our sloop arrives safely back in Biscayne Bay and we drive back to Oxford, but I'm in the back seat moaning all the way through Georgia, Tennessee, and Kentucky wanting to die rather than go on living for one more mile. Once you get malaria, you carry the seed of that poison until you die."

I've heard his riff on malaria many times before, and I don't care if it's apocryphal, embellished, or mostly true. I just like it when he says he got black-vomit-mosquito sick because it makes me think he and I are more similar than not. I too feel like I've got some poison ballast water pumped into my bones I'll carry with me until I die, and there's nothing I can do to unload that weight, nothing but keep talking and see where this sickness leads me.

I wheel him to the kitchen for a slice of melon, a cup of tea, a square of toast. He fidgets, twists, pokes, grabs at himself. He's so uncomfortable in his body, I want to help put him out of his misery, if only he will help me end mine. Later, after another day has been pinched so hard all the hours of light disappear in an instant, I sit him on the edge of the bed, holding him in place with one hand while I use my other hand to push the wheelchair out of range where, if he falls, he won't hit it with his head.

I lift his legs over the bed, but they won't bend. They are so stiff and disconnected from his body, they feel like a second person dragging behind him. He wants his sip of water through a straw. He wants more air, more light, then less of both. He says he feels like a lucky man dying in his own house and he strings that thought out into *Lucky me, Lucky you, Don't cry for me, Don't cry for you.* Before he finishes his song, I return to the island and tell him about a long ride.

I spend the next day in Luperón with Rosario and ask her if she wants to sail with me and Philip to St. Thomas. Skip, I know it's a stupid idea because she's never been on a boat and she'll be an illegal without a passport, but I don't care. I figure she's the kind of trouble I need to help me forget the bigger trouble swelling behind me.

I want only to fast forward and picture myself in St. Thomas except for this one wet knot. Why would Rosario pick me out of a merengue bar? I don't know if she works for Jimmy or if she knows Jesse, but this much I do sort out. Rosario seems too curvy and delicious to be true. What's your line about bergs, Skip? Every person's an iceberg. The part you see is the smallest part of who a person really is.

Whoever was dogging my boat out in the Thorny Path won't stop.

They won't let me get away. They will want to reclaim what I took from them. I'm nothing more than a slave to that moment when my knife cut away the cocaine caught in a frond, a slave who must now live skillfully on this island of beautiful secrets, and hope I can get back to the gentle side of the Trades with Rosario on board.

"I want to see New York," Rosario says. "Are you going there?"

"Nowhere close to Manhattan," I say with a mixture of disappointment and relief.

We walk toward the town square where she says we can find horses. Small white egrets peck at donut crumbs. Beneath a mop-headed palm, a trio of old men in palm-woven hats argue about the upcoming cockfight. At an outdoor bar, cooks yammer about supplies, wave at a flat-bed truck, bark orders to boys dumping trash in the road. A black rooster with an oxblood tuft stands leashed by one claw to a drainpipe. Two sows, the size and color of rusted propane tanks, root in dishwater scum while strings of plastic flags whip the air over their heads.

"What are these flags all about?" I ask.

"For the men of the presidente."

"Candidates?"

"Sí. Red ones are for the presidente's man, the fat one who will fix the roads and build schools. Blue and white for the man who will give us more food. Purple for the man who will fight for the middle class. Like all the other elections, this one is a struggle between fear and promise, and it's too close to call."

"Any of the candidates any good?"

"They're all crooks and puppets who don't give a fig for the people, although they all talk sweet."

"Why do the people tolerate the corruption?"

"That's the only question worth asking, but we never ask it, the same way we never think to keep our money in the bank. My father once told me there were little earthquakes on the DR every day, but no one feels them except the chameleons. Which is why they are such great leapers and keep the roosters hungry. He said, we are like the lizards, jumping around, waving our flags, changing color every other day, jumping out of the way of one disaster after another."

"What do the newspapers say about who will win?"

"Gossip, jokes, and letters from America are the only newspapers we trust. No one believes anyone, so we make up our own stories."

"You should run for office," I say, squeezing her shoulders.

"Maybe in the next century," she laughs. "Or the next life."

"Why, is it so impossible?"

"Matt, you don't know how things work here. There are just a few families who own the ballot box. If my last name was Ochoa, Brugal, Bermudez, Barcelo, Cheka, I might ride in a long white car and never talk to you."

"That's the old way," I say.

"The old way is much older than earthquakes and hurricanes," she says, shrugging loose from my grip.

At the edge of the park in the shade of a Banyan tree, a man who must know Rosario waits with the reins of two horses. Only one of the horses wears a saddle.

"Who's riding bareback?" I ask.

"Not you." she says. "You sailors always take your comfort."

I put my left foot in the stirrup, grab the saddle horn, and swing up in the saddle, feeling smug I've remembered the three cues for getting a horse to work with you: *the shifting of weight, the grip of legs, the pull of the reins.* She grabs the mane just above the withers and swings up on the horse. We walk the horses out of town, side by side. A few men stop to look twice at Rosario straddled over her horse, her cinnamon colored thighs gripping the flanks. "*Avión,*" one man calls out. "*Avión,*" he says again and grabs his crotch.

She doesn't acknowledge the men as our two horses climb a narrow dirt road paralleling the ocean. Quickly, we disappear behind canopies of pink and red blooms, coconut palms, ferns, and tall grasses lit with the swollen faces of bumblebees. We pass dirt-streaked men on burros strapped with panniers of charcoal and braids of dirt-tangled roots. We trot by women on foot carrying baskets of mangos, avocados, green finger bananas. Barefoot children trail behind us. She stops one of the children and buys oranges, mangoes, and a couple of avocados big as butternut squash. We ride past shanties with roofs of layered palm fronds, the wobbly structures girded in the center by a brightly painted wooden pole. White wooden crosses lean behind a fence looped with ribbons, strands of hair, and photos. The houses have no electricity. No running water. The faint smell of smoke cuts the air. Darkness pinches the doorways. I see bright fallen lemons waiting to exit from their skins. A pair of boots swing from a branch, the long leather tongues dangling.

Just when I feel lulled by the vagueness of this lush and poor green world, the sound of waves interrupts the hum of perpetual rot and growth. Through tendrils I see patches of surf like handfuls of torn pages thrown into the air, reminding me to push on and finish my boat delivery to St. Thomas. She points to a blur of wings inside a cluster of red trailing hibiscus. "Zumbadorcito," she says. Balanced in air, flickering, an emerald-green hummingbird, no bigger than a thumb, thrusts its needle into a red trumpet, then vanishes, only to reappear at a different flower.

"I'd like to be the Zumbadorcito, the smallest bird in the world with the most powerful wings," Rosario says.

"Why's that?"

"Because then I would carry sugar to every poor girl on the DR."

I say nothing but grab at this sharp twinge in my chest when I let myself imagine that Rosario and Jesse both love to carry sugar to girls. She senses the downward pull of my head and swings around my horse and smacks it on the rump. My heart jumps into my throat as we race beside creeper-hung trees and emerge along an avenue of royal palms lining a scarf of white sand beach. There's no boat or person in sight, just a trio of gray-white pelicans skimming wave tips. We walk the horses to an adjoining cove and tie them off to a fallen pine. She pulls off her shorts and top and jumps into shallow surf. I stand there watching, thinking maybe it would be acceptable to die now when there's no weight to the wind.

After a swim, she kneels in the sand in front of me, soundless, floating, nuzzling, her eyes never leaving my eyes, her long look like a spear in my side. By not looking away, I imagine she sees my whole story threading from West Palm Beach to Cockburn Harbor and across the Thorny Path. The taste of her salt takes me to a feeding depth and I forget that Jimmy is waiting for me somewhere. Maybe I'm wrong and there's no point dabbling in dread over what happened back in Cockburn Harbor. Jimmy has so much money, why would he bother with a wayward sailor like me?

Why not stop here with Rosario? Slip into another life. Erase my name. Never return. I could spend the next year peeling away our clothes, soaking up the cosmos before it disintegrates from its own craving and malice. I'll stay on this island and take as much fire as I can stand until I glide out of my old skin. With her, maybe I can forget the guilt and misery that brought me to this green vault freshly opened for my body to enter.

We ride on and vanish into trees sleeved with moss and flowers and come to a rusted car jacked on cinder blocks. Wet, tropical air has eaten melon-sized holes in the fenders.

The drenching rain, tangled creepers, and insects have broken down the car's original heft and shape. The glassless windows are draped with blue plastic and tar paper. Trunk holes serve as chimney stacks. Thick vines climb over the doors and a sticker on the rear bumper reads, "*The harder they come, the harder they fall.*"

"Rasta man lives here," Rosario says.

"Who's he?"

"Desmond Keane. He came to the DR after his wife was killed in a ganja shoot-out in Kingston."

"Friend of yours?"

"You might say."

She shifts her weight back in the saddle and her horse stops without taking the grip of the bit. She gets down from her horse and shouts, "Hey Desmond, you gonna sleep your sorry-ass life away."

It seems impossible to me, Skip, that any man or woman sleeps inside this sprawling mechanical shack. I hear something uncoiling inside this hulk, and my gut tells me to whip my horse like thunder and get away from this resurrected junk-heap, but then, I look at my reins and realize I've not been looking after our trail and have no idea how to retrace my way. Whatever lives inside this jagged smoke-hole, my crawling skin tells me, sucks the life out of the mouths of the dead. I have no business knocking on the iron door of a creature consumed by so much perpetual desolation.

"Who be telling me the day already here?"

"It's Rosario. I've brought you some fruit."

"Oh sister-sweet. I love you like the wind, but where's my spicy jerked hog?"

"You'll get none of that fatty stuff from me," she says.

I think the conversation might continue with Rosario talking to a junked car with no visible driver; then Desmond pulls up the plastic shade, stares out. His two eyes shine in his sallow face like copper pennies thinning on train tracks. The rusted car door creaks open and Desmond emerges one limb at a time like an octopus from its cave. His dreads fall in a wave and are collected in a fishnet bag looped at his waist. There must be an extra six feet of hair grafted to his body and stored at his side.

Once Desmond extracts himself and wobbles on one leg, I see better into his twice-totaled car. He's removed the car seats to make room for a sagging mattress and a chair with the legs chopped off as well as storage crates. He's cut away the rear panel to access the trunk where he stokes a rusting Dutch oven.

"Where you be escaping to now on that beast of burden?"

"Just out for a ride," she says.

"You always be going somewhere, my darling, but you never get there," Desmond says in a smoke-singed, rolling baritone that makes me sway in the saddle.

"One day," she laughs.

"Who be the white man?" Desmond asks glumly, not looking at me.

"What does a name matter?" she says, glancing in my direction.

"You know, my angel," Desmond says, cracking a smile and revealing red swollen gums, crooked teeth, "you can't be chasing after white man's Babylon."

"Don't get started on that white man jive, Desmond. You ain't running for office," Rosario says, downshifting into a mumble that matches Desmond's drawn-out wheeze. Desmond turns and fixes me with the burnt pennies in his head.

"Only one reason white folks show up here," Desmond says, bending over to pluck a pink orchid off a vine. "This be the only country on God's green where the mulatto is king. Not black, not white, just honey right. Only problem is mulatto comes from mule. So which part of you, my white hustler, is scheming to hitch a mule?"

I don't know what to make of this silver tongue sprung from a junked car. "Why would I want a mule when I've got a horse," I say.

"That's good, that's good," Desmond says, slapping his floppy sack of hair. "I like a Mistah Sailor Man with a snit of humor. But you got that mule-skinner look. Long way back in your eyes."

Desmond talks on about all the white folks who come to the DR for more than rum-and-sun. He says white women come from all over the world looking for mulatto studs. They don't dare try any black bone back home, he says, but where it's hot and far away, danger is just a part of paradise. And white men from all over God's kingdom, he says, come to check out the not-ever-black Dominican women.

"Any way you taste the sugar, you be riding in one of the great sex capitals of the world," he says with a musical hammer.

"I suppose it's only whites who've got the problem," I say.

"You be right, and you be wrong, Mistah Sailor Man."

He says black men also come to the DR looking for the light-skinned woman child. They pump themselves up at a bar, order ice-cold Presidente beers and octopus to make their dicks hard, and then eye the women in the shrink-wrap black dresses. They carry on about the flatness of the nose on this one, the thickness of the lips on that one. How straight the hair. Who has eyes as rare as blue amber. "Black man's pain," Desmond riffs, "is not as old as the white man's barn."

"Can you see it? Can you smell the barn, Mistah Sailor Man?" Desmond says in a fuming trance. "The slave girl be a little worse for the voyage," he stammers, "but her palms not cracked from toil. Her lips not burnt from sun. Her breasts still round to the tongue. White boss man has the power any time white momma too dried up like a barrel of moth-eaten chickweed. Any time he has a craving he can't fill with his own keening midnight stroke. Any time day or night, he can say, now bend over that rail, child, spread those tight cheeks. You know you be dreaming of the whiteness of my seed, blessed by God almighty, oh sweet Jesus, praise be for my desire and for the pain of my desire," Desmond says in a quavering growl.

I look at Rosario, hoping she'll offer some clue as to how I might reply, but she doesn't return my gaze. Her eyes turn glassy. "You're trying to link me with something that happened a long time ago," I say with as much brass as I can muster, "But I'm just delivering a boat to St. Thomas. I came here by accident."

"That what I be telling you, Mistah Sailor Man. There be no accidents. There's only the divine dice throw. You don't know whether you lost or you be boss. But you spinning a web bigger than you need. Your ship's plotted on the human body, not on blue water. The quiver of your smile saying you a sex crime waiting to happen. You come to dark town to lighten up. Meantime, you drinking from a grail with a hole in the bottom. No matter how you work your passage to Heaven, you looking for that sliver of advantage, the lump sum, the payout, the score, the fishing hole where all the big fish feed on the minnows. It's all there in the eyes twisted up with more fear than you can fathom. I don't make this shit up, Mistah Sailor Man."

"I'm just waiting for repairs," I shrug, trying to act bored while I'm equally intrigued by the fatalistic predictions of this twice-totaled, Dutch-oven soothsayer.

"Truth-talking don't come easy to you," Desmond says, retreating a few steps backwards to pull out a bottle of rum from his glove compartment. "Whet your whistle, my friend," he says, holding a label-less bottle by the sweated neck.

"No thanks," I say. "I never drink before happy hour."

Desmond pulls hard on the bottle.

"Never too early to drink down the sorrow of the failed voyage. I've been waiting to get back to Africa all my days. I'm fifty and still be waiting. Your face says you waiting for your ship to come in. I'm waiting for my ship to leave. But this Rasta man can't go back till we drive away the white demons. I'm not saying you be the evil one, but chances are in shanty town you keeping me down."

"Desmond," Rosario says brashly. "I must have woken you from a wild-assed dream."

"Can't wake me from a dream, sister, cause it's all one dream. No start, no finish. Even when I sleep, my spirit thumbing the jungle highway to see when my wife is ready to make her great return."

"What I meant," she says, "You're giving my friend a fine taste of Rasta spirit. And it's not even Sunday."

"He needs some preaching," Desmond says, flashing his spleeve-stained teeth. "When it come time to divide the sheep from the goats, when it come time to pull the water from the rock, you got to know where you stand before the man. What I'm trying to say goes like this, a man got to know what sugar he's chasing even if he says he don't like sugar."

I listen to the horses feeding on a sprawl of pink bougainvillea. The air trembles with rain making the daylight blink. My horse shakes its head. I do the same. I don't need a flea-bitten sermon from this crackpot. What if I am using her? I'm prepared, at some personal risk, to help her leave the DR—even if she's linked with Jesse and Jimmy. Isn't that a fair trade? Desmond's church may be open twenty-four hours a day, but I'm leaving no offering in the basket.

Rosario hands over her bag of mangoes and avocados to Desmond who sits on the hood of his house. "A little more fruit won't bother you any," she says, bending over to give Desmond a peck on the top of his matted ski cap.

"It's just like you, child, to come out from town and not stay awhile. I've got some cards, you know, and dice and we could see what your Mistah Sailor knows about lady luck. I hear tell that with a little luck a dead man's veins will bleed again. Ready to bleed again, Mistah Sailor?"

"We have to get back," she says with a tinge of protest quaking her voice.

"What's so high and mighty back in Luperón?"

"Just things to do," she says.

"My mechanic," I say, "should be returning from Santo Domingo. He went there for engine parts."

"Then, you be leaving our fair island?"

"Soon," I say. "Very soon I hope."

"Then, you take real good care. Real good, Mistah Sailor. The seas don't aim to please. They only aim to take aim."

We ride back to Luperón, mostly in silence, except for a few words about Desmond's saucy tongue.

"I think he's done a little too much ganja," I say, hoping to melt her sudden coldness.

"More like not enough weed," she says. "He's taken to rum and it blurs his vision. You wouldn't know but he has a PhD from Miami in comparative literature. He used to teach."

"You've got to be joking," I say, jolted by the idea that the creaturely man shoehorned into a wrecked car is a gypsy scholar.

"His wife's death broke him. She was a beauty and a soul traveler."

"What's with all the hair in the bag?" I ask.

"He's growing it for his wife for when she returns from the other world."

"Right. You don't believe this stuff?" I ask.

"I know he travels to far-off places. He keeps company with many dead. Desmond's been living out here for years, gathering herbs, experimenting, traveling many worlds most people will never know. I bring him fruit and flowers and he tells me stories about the ghosts of people who can't sleep."

"Like his wife?"

"Yeah."

"You knew her?"

"She was my sister."

"I'm sorry," I say. "You should have said something."

"Would it have made a difference?" she laughs.

"He's still pretty angry," I say.

"Who isn't?" she says, shifting her weight to make her horse switch from a walk to a lope, just short of a gallop. Her animal struggles for air in the noonday heat, jerking its head, spitting tiny carnations of foam as we drop back into the town square where vendors pull their baskets of fish out of the sun and slip them into pockets of shade.

Skip, some part of me thinks I'm just another fish that's been hooked, gaffed, and been iced for later consumption. Some other part of me thinks I'm not a piker, I'm a striker, like Jesse, working the hours before dawn. I can reel this girl in, get back on my boat and leave, and no one will ever see us. I left one island this way. I can do it again.

At 4:00 A.M., I leave Skip's room and return to my father's old room next door. I lay down, no longer able to sleep when it's dark. I hear the whipping of a flag. The rustle of a raccoon in the trash. The frogs throbbing. All of it mixed into an echo from the last reaches of the night world. My brother's voice catches me from the thin whistle of his chest, "Wait, Wait." I call out to him. The rain spits at the cottage. His voice dies in the pour of overflowing gutters. I walk through the cottage cut with lightning. I check the windows and doors, not to batten them, but to see which one he has left by.

"Wait, wait," I whisper to the cottage leaning into the wind. Hale fought my leaving that night out on the Gulf Stream with a whisper, and now I can't afford for him to leave, but he does. Gone again when he was so close I could almost touch the bones in his face.

CHAPTER IX

I sleep through the morning or through my own night watch. The boundaries between day and night have dissolved. I can't get my bearings. Too much light. Too little dark. My lips caked and bleeding. I stagger to the kitchen for coffee, water, juice, any liquid.

My mother walks past me in the hallway between Skip's room and the kitchen, head down, lost in heaven and memory, or so I imagine. She pauses, turns around as if she's forgotten something in my father's room and must retrace her steps. But no, she snaps upright, grabs me by the arm like I'm a bolt of stray lightning.

"You were jealous of him, that was it, wasn't it?"

"What?"

"You wanted to take him down a peg, right? You couldn't stand that Hale always stole the limelight. You got him all turned around. That's what you did."

My father lies within ten feet of us, itching to sort out whether he should live another day or just say 'fuck it' and send his busted frame to the boneyard. But no matter. There's very old business to attend to. It's the thousand-piece family jigsaw puzzle we all want to finish, but never do.

"Yeah, I was jealous of Hale. Who in the fuck wasn't," I say, shaking her arm off my arm. "He had it all—brains, beauty, fame, and no doubt fortune would find him soon enough. All his glory was hard to take, but I was also proud of him. Proud as hell he was my older brother and not someone else's. He was my treasure too. You may not believe it, but I looked after him as best I could."

Shuffle, bang, leap, zigzag, skid.

There's fresh blood in the wind. Fresh blood. Old wounds. My mother scuttles on like the wraith she is, anxious to return to her Psalms 121:8 left open on her nightstand: *"The Lord shall preserve thy going out and thy coming in from this time forth, and even for evermore."*

To dull my mother's knife, I drive to Tiger Point Marina and lust after boats I can't afford to charter, let alone buy. This is where my father kept all his sailboats, and if I had one and I lived on Amelia Island, this is where I would dock and haul out. He and I came here many times to prowl among the deserted craft and dream of how we might restore them to their former splendor.

In every boatyard in the world, there are sleek sailboats with women's names that have been abandoned, left to sweat and mildew beneath heavy tarps and lashed lines, their sails rotting on their booms. Their owners never use these boats. Never visit them. Never attend to them. But they also never let them go. Instead, the owners leave their sailboats locked in cradles which only misshape their water lines. Even after the owners die, sometimes their heirs pay for storage until the boat collapses from its own weight like a beached whale.

Bob Martin, the owner of the Tiger Point Marina, tells me that one boat—*Halcyon Witch* out of Detroit—has been land-locked here for ten years. Why? Because something happened with her or did not happen with her that the owner, even in his last will and testament, will not change and so she sits here, unattended, robbed of youth, dying, never to sail again.

In about half the cases, the owners get behind in their payments or they run up storage and repair bills they can't square up, and the marinas take over the boats, minus the payments because the banks don't want them on their balance sheets. Because marinas make their real money through dockage fees, haul outs, and repairs, and not by keeping a sales office humming, the abandoned boats kept in cradles have no new life ahead of them.

Women we can't let go of: that's what Skip called the many unclaimed or forsaken boats sagging in their cradles. Which brings me to a turquoise Tartan '37 named *Tabula Rasa* built in '76 which Martin has recently launched in hopes of selling her.

She's a lovely Sparkman & Stephens design with hand-laid hull, molded as a single unit. Skip once owned a Tartan '37, but she proved to be too much boat for an aging sailor into his seventies even though I remember him saying fondly, "Her hull tracks like a dream on all points of sail."

Bob Martin tells me the owner of this Tartan disappeared a year ago. The bank that held the paper tried to sell the Tartan for top dollar, but gave up after three months, so he ended up with her. Now, because of a divorce, Martin wants to unload her fast before the bank makes him sell everything he owns so his wife can walk away with half.

"How much you asking?"

"I'm open to any offer over thirty thousand."

"You've got to be joking," I say. "She has to be worth fifty thousand at least."

"Yeah, that may be, but I don't have time to advertise all over the Eastern Seaboard for a buyer. I need cash now. I won't carry back any paper."

"Mind if I go below?"

"You got any money?" he asks.

"Yeah, I've got money. I just can't get my hands on it yet."

Martin snickers, shakes his head. I turn and walk away from the Tartan and toward my father's car.

"I like your old man," he says. "One hell of a sailor. Knows his stuff. Always makes me laugh. How is he, anyway?"

"On the way out."

"Aren't we all," Martin says.

I go below and fall in love with all the Tartan's teak trim. The V-berth is spacious enough for two. The head comes with a shower spigot. The port settee converts to a double. The starboard, main cabin settee, is a roomy sea berth and so is the aft quarter berth. The starboard galley has plenty of elbow room as does the navigation station to port. I take a peek at the Universal 40 engine. *Tabula Rasa* may be eight years old, but she's been well tended. Any way you swab the deck, this boat is a sweetwater steal at thirty grand. I find Bob Martin, eager to learn more about the Tartan without revealing my approval.

"Well, she needs a little TLC, but she's not bad. You got a recent survey on her?"

"Funny you should ask. The bank made me get a survey done just about six months ago. She's very clean. The mainsail has a tear at the luff. The 150 jenny is missing a couple of hanks. The gel coat is nicked in a couple of places near the bow. Small stuff, really."

"Thanks, Bob. for letting me dream a little."

"Any time," he says.

I leave Tiger Point thinking two things clearly: I have to make a play for *Tabula Rasa* and I have to get the combination to Skip's safe. *Tabula Rasa*, I say to myself, I will give you a proper woman's name.

That night I want to tell Skip about the Tartan '37. I talk up her lines, her teak finishes, her roomy V-berth. He talks Cuba.

"Did I ever tell you about Cuba?"

"Yeah, Skip, you've told me about Cuba. How you sailed there during spring break and got malaria."

"I never want to leave, but I have to leave. I'm so sick but I'm in love with everything I see. Giant varnished yachts. Strings of lights over every street. Guitars and dancers. Rum and dresses. Monkeys and strippers. Streets so skinny you've got to turn sideways to get through. I never want to leave and I have to get out. I might die there. I was never more alive. I know all about these islands you tell of."

I lift his head with one hand, fluff his pillow, and give him another sip of water. It's 3:00 A.M. The hour of low rolling thunder. More hot rain soon, like something cooked up in a lobster pot rather than dropped from the sky.

"Can you stand to hear more, Skip?"

"Tell me about Cuba. Tell me a story." He sings an old song we used to sing as a family coming back from Put-in-Bay to Vermilion on Lake Erie.

My gal's a Coker, she's a New Yorker.
I buy her everything to keep her in style.

She's got a pair of hips,
just like two battleships.
Hey, boys, that's where my money goes."

"I can't tell you about Cuba, Skip, but close enough. How about the Dominican Republic?" I go back to this island because I need for my shipwright father to track the path of my undoing, all the way back to the night Hale died and I quit school.

You want to know where I went, Skip? I spent ten years looking at the hole in my hands. The stars became stones. I drifted into any side pocket bar, any marina, any boatyard, any boat delivery, any woman I could snag off the docks. Booze and sex were my night-blooming flowers. B & S, I called it, then just B.S. And that's what those nights were, mostly bullshit I couldn't ever step away from, each night tempting me with false clarity, false summits.

I wanted booze for the night blur. Sex for the morning slide.

It didn't much matter who I was with. As long as she liked to drink, laugh, and not ask too many questions about where I'd been, where I was going, the thrill would prop me up until I could shove off on another delivery. I'm not going to trash these two perfumed flowers completely because, well, some nights they were enough or almost enough. I got hooked on fucking over the emptiness, but after years of this, I'd wake up sick inside and gray on the outside and unable to remember anything about the night before. The woman next to me would look the same way I did, sick and gray. It was as if I were living in the condemned building of my own body. The rent was free. All the utilities were paid. But I knew the building would collapse any day, and I would be lost inside with a woman I didn't know beyond the chaos we both embraced. One morning I said, "Enough."

Which brings me to Rosario.

She reeks with sex, but not the kind that numbs you with its mechanical rituals, its talked-out bargains, its doubts, it midnight recriminations, and slapstick threats. None of that bullshit double-think drags her down. Just full throttle, go-for-broke, eyeball to eyeball tender smashing union and reunion. And she doesn't drink rum, so there's no slur, no bitter speechless mornings, no memory loss, no who-in-the-hell-are-you.

Rosario and I make love every day. Sometimes two or three times. We make love everywhere, inside, outside, standing up, sitting down, until it's not just her body I want to take with me, but also her pain, her beauty, her loneliness, her poverty, her soul. At first, I think what better place to hide than inside the burn of her body. Then, I don't want to hide which means she and I have to keep moving further south.

Seven days after slipping in the waters of Luperón to swim ashore, I've not heard a peep from Philip, nothing until I meet him walking down Independencia Avenue. He's whistling, talking to himself casual sweet like he's just scored a winning lottery ticket. "The men on this island are something else," he says. "My god are they gorgeous and affectionate. Michelangelo should have set up shop here. His David could have been Pedro, Roderigo, Miguel, Fabio. There is, however, the problem of where to find the right marble."

"What about the engine?"

"I took a detour over to Puerto Plata, forgot all about my job, but I'm on it now. I've practically got the problem solved."

"You really don't know how to lie. It's not in your nature. I'll go with you over to Santo Domingo."

"I thought you were supposed to stay with the boat?"

"I got tired of that the first night. I met this woman."

"This woman have a name?"

"Rosario," I reply.

"I like it. Rosario. Rosario. Let me be your Impresario."

"It's been fun I admit."

"Maybe we should stay here and run dive charters out of Luperón."

"Remember Red Hook Bay. We're supposed to be there already. Sam Wells doesn't even know where his boat is, and we're down here playing fast and loose with the locals."

"Momentary memory lapse, forgive me."

Philip and I hail a bus traveling to Santo Domingo over the mountains. The bus driver points us toward *la cocina*, the noisy, stereo-blasting merengue kitchen at the back of the bus. Before the rollicking bus pulls away from the curb, I see a group of barefoot, potbellied children through the open doors. I think they might be there to say goodbye to someone on the bus, but when I catch their flat, bloodshot eyes, I know they're regulars, anchored on the curb for any money or food that might fall from pockets. Their clothes hang in patches from skinny frames. I toss some coins in the air as the bus pulls away. The children rush forward, fluttering over the dirt, yelling gleefully, shouting, shoving, the rags on their bodies flying like feathers as a fight breaks out. Violence comes easily to these island children who skid in and out of shadows like bickering pilgrims.

I want to talk to Philip about this island we've come to, but we both slouch and hide from the one subject that should give us pause: Has someone followed us to the DR? Out of an unspoken retreat from potential trouble, I jump in.

"Think it's over?" I ask.

"I wouldn't cash in any insurance policies just yet."

"You afraid?" I ask, watching a man out the window crawl under a tobacco leaf as big as an elephant's ear.

"Yeah, I'm afraid. But that's why God invented sex."

"We have to get out of here and keep moving south."

Philip nods and says, "In due time."

The bus driver knows only one speed: fast.

He takes great pride in gliding through stop signs, squealing through curves, drifting into lanes of oncoming traffic, relying always on the law of the horn to clear a path. Philip says he thinks the heart is the only insatiable organ, but he's wrong, it's the horn. With a horn, the bus driver taps out messages of greeting, farewell, warning, complaint, and sexual bravado. He dodges ruts by racing his eyes along a fissure of cracked windshield. He doesn't wear a seatbelt.

While the bus careens over potholes, the driver picks up a compulsive radio beat by slapping his pink-palmed hands on the steering wheel, so that it's altogether unclear whether gasoline or music is fueling our movement. When the driver grows the least bit weary of his relentless forward propulsion, he yells for "more rum," and we pass a bottle up from the kitchen, with nearly all the men taking a swig. By the time we reach Imbert, only thirty minutes later, Philip feels woozy. As the driver whips around the town square a half dozen times, shouting for more passengers, Philip hangs his head out the window to gulp air.

The bus guns through leafy tunnels woven so tight the sun is sewn out of the sky. Inside these thick circles of morning shade, I see the silhouettes of donkeys loaded with fruit baskets and sway-backed, mud-splattered horses carrying ceroons of pistaschio-green tobacco leaves. I watch the clash of centuries in an eye-blink, one nearly broken and spent on four ambling legs, the other belching fumes on four racing wheels. I nudge Philip when we come up on rows of tiny white-painted crosses beside the road.

"They could be *calvarios*, the three crosses of Calvary," he says.

As the bus crosses over the northern coastal mountains and into the lush valley of the Yaqui river, the land shifts between low, moist alluvial drainages draped in palms, and soft brown savanna cut with corduroy roads. The latest songs pour from the radio mixed with the chatter of roadside dogs, goats, mules, and the pelt of ten-minute showers. Philip has traveled throughout Europe, Africa, and much of the Caribbean, but he's certain he's never seen such verdant mountain slopes, so many lovely, grassy meadows and fields of black loam as soft and rich as butter—all threaded with streams, breezes, and the smell of fruit-scented rain. You could die in a valley like this, he says, and not regret having left the sea behind.

On the outer ring of Santo Domingo, Philip and I see clay huts and tin shacks, a labyrinth of mud and straw, mountains of stinking truck tires, plumes of smoke, lottery ticket vendors, fruit peddlers, hooks of roasting meat, and knots of men scattered about crumbling plazas. As the bus races past *bohio* shacks, children jump like fleas out of the dust, swerving and yelling to be taken for a ride. Everywhere I see the building up and tearing down of lean-tos, roadside fruit stands, barefoot children playing baseball over rivers of broken bottles. One boy in a black tuxedo and red shoes plays a wheezing accordion like a roadside undertaker.

At the hub, I see spacious courtyards, gargoyle cathedrals, and villas facing the sea, all made from coral stone, as though the sea itself has been harnessed, powdered, and mixed with earth and lime and cut to size. I stumble from the bus, woozy from the rum and exhaust, yet thankful to be alive after dozens of near-misses with pedestrians and cars. Philip and I walk down wide boulevards lined with royal palms, through Romanesque arches, past pink marble benches shaded by banyan trees as wide as trucks. Everywhere, we see filigree gates leading to gardens of white angel's trumpet, star apple, guava. As in every city, the rich of Santo Domingo carve out enough quiet to make their residence a sanctuary amidst the stink and noise.

Just six blocks from where the bus stops, Philip finds the Hostal Nicolás Nader, an old palace in the *zona colonial*. The rooms are spendy, but we plan on staying for only one night, maybe two. In the afternoon, the Dominicans sleep, but he's not tired. He considers looking for a little afternoon recreation, but decides instead to find a marine mechanic with parts and tools who's game to travel with us back to Luperón. The front desk clerk tells Philip there are hardware stores and garages out on San Martín boulevard. We walk up Duarte to catch a *guagua* heading west. We leave the world of the stone fortress and enter the broken glass archipelago of Chinese restaurants, cigar stores, laundry mats, merengue bars, and hookers on the hunt. We get off at Drake's Marine Hardware and find a man elbowed over a service manual looking at raw water pump impellers.

"That's the most vital piece of rubber on the whole engine," Philip says.

"You got that right," the man replies, puzzled by the crowd of rubber flanges to choose from.

"That double-toothed cam is mounted inside the pump body," Philip says. "Then the impeller fits in, then the gasket, followed by the pump cover and the six retaining screws. Looks like #3607 is the number you need," Philip adds, reading upside down.

"*Muchas gracias,*" the man says.

"*De nada.*" Philip smiles.

"What can I do for you?" the man behind the counter asks.

"It's a long story," Philip gestures. "*Cómo te llamas?*"

"Luís."

He tells Luís about *Stardust's* crossing from the Bahamas to Luperón in a blow. How the anchor line is knocked loose from its bow netting, wraps around the shaft, and jerks the engine off its bed. The engine, he tells Luís, has been installed on a pair of fiberglass angle irons which allow vibrations to pass through the hull. Philip then tells Luís he needs someone to help him realign the engine. He describes the drill he needs to reset the bolts, the propeller coupling, the screw-jacks for supporting the engine, the feeler gauges, the rear seal, as well as five quarts of diesel oil.

"I can help you," Luís says. "When do we go?"

"Tomorrow morning," Philip says, never once looking at me.

"Don't know if I can find the parts by then, but I'll try."

"You have a car?"

"*Sí.*"

"*Bueno.* The skipper and I are staying at the Hotel Nader at the corner of Luperón and Duarte."

"I know the one."

The two mechanics shake hands and Luís smiles broadly at the prospect of good paying work.

"*Cuánto?*" Philip asks.

"A hundred dollars for my time, twenty-five more for the car, plus parts."

Philip smiles at the price, which probably inflated by Dominican standards, but he's never any good at haggling so he just nods. For him to spend one day on a job in Ft. Lauderdale costs a client over five hundred clams.

That night, around 11:00 P.M., Philip and I walk out to Santo Domingo's oceanfront Malecon. It's one long open-air

113

disco packed with slink and tease. Philip scans the sweat-gleamed faces for an entry point.

"I'm curious," I ask. "How do you meet men?"

"I meet them everywhere, in libraries, grocery stores, bookstores, even churches. Some of my best nights are with married men. All their lives they fantasize about having sex with men, so they sneak out into the street and invent destinations that don't exist."

"Really, married men? Come on?"

"They drag so much weight into the dark and return home with even a greater weight. The weight of the unlived life," Philip says, his eloquence always a current to contend with.

"The unlived life would not be one of your problems," I say.

"I give them *las noches para recordar*," Philip winks.

Outside the Jaragua hotel, Philip meets Tomasito.

The Cuban tells us he has escaped from Castro's clutches by swimming to the naval base at Guantanamo across a shark-infested bay. He kills two silvery beasts with a kitchen knife before he makes it to safety. That's his first story. I drift away as Philip and Tomasito blend into strobe-pulsing Club Babylon, each in perfect step with the other's hips.

I see two men slouched at the bar watching Philip and his partner.

One has bleached white hair that hangs in a clump. The other is mostly bald, bleary-eyed with lightning veins shooting across the bridge of his nose. They look familiar, the way a half-eaten sandwich looks familiar.

I try to catch Philip's eye, but he and Tomasito turn away and head toward the exit. I have to get to Philip before these two men do, but there are so many sweaty, tipsy bodies in my way. I see Philip and Tomasito kiss and go separate ways. Philip slips into a crowd. I lose sight of him and of the two men, but I figure they are as close to him as I am. Philip must be walking back to our hotel, but which way will he go? I climb up on an embankment and see his strawberry-blonde head turning up Calle de Marzo. I start running, pushing people aside. I lose my bearings. I run ahead toward El Convento de Los Dominicanos near our hotel. One block away, I see Philip and a car pulling up behind him. The two men I saw back at the club get out. They now wear masks and carry baseball bats.

Philip starts running, but one of the men is just as fast. He throws one leg forward and trips Philip from behind. Philip grabs his left leg. He tries to stand and run again, but before he can, both men swing their bats. Philip crumples to his knees. Philip grabs his own leg. He tries to stand, run again, but before he can, both men swoop down and swing again. Philip twists on the pavement like something has snapped in his spine.

I run hard, but another string of cars blocks my path. The second man swings again, high and low. Philip rises to his feet and rushes into the belly of one man and slams him against the car. Before the tackled man catches his breath, Philip switches behind him like a wrestler, crosses his hands in a headlock. The second man in a mask rushes at him swinging. Just before Philip takes a baseball bat to his kidneys, he drops the other man's head forward, leans his body weight over him, bears down like a vise, snaps hard. The man sinks from his arms.

The second man roundhouses the bat, but this time clips only air. He pulls off the mask and, for a moment, the two men circle each other in slow motion, sucking air. Philip spits blood sheeting down from his nose and eyes. The cars clear away, and I run full bore into the back of the man and knock him down. Philip gets up before I do and lunges on the fallen man, grips him by the throat with his left hand. I grab the baseball bat and clip the top of the man's skull. The man slumps sideways. I hit him again across the bridge of the nose. The man's head bounces against pavement. I hit him again at the back of his skull. The man doesn't move. I drop the bat and can't straighten my fingers. Philip tries to stand and falls over. He tries again to stand. This time he crawls away from his attacker whose neck droops on his chest.

I drag Philip off the avenue and beg him to walk with me. He staggers forward for half a block. I wave some money at another man and he and I carry Philip around the back of the hotel, up the stairs, and put him to bed. He wakes at noon coughing blood. Philip's face is like a welt of cast-off truck tire. His eyes are swollen nearly shut. Philip tries to talk, but he can't shape the words with his tongue.

"The two guys are dead," I say. He nods.

"We've got some shit now on our hands," I add, holding his weight on my shoulders.

"Make-up," Philip squawks. "Get me make-up."

"What?"

"I need a wig, shoes, bra, make-up, crutches."

I leave him curled up in a ball and return in an hour with a plastic bag full of the things Philip wants, everything but the crutches. Philip tries to lift himself up in the bed, but his crimped back forces him back down.

"Put it on," he says.

I take the powder, rouge, and lipstick from the bag and work on Philip's face. Last night, Philip had a temporary lover on his arm who dreamt of spending the night with him. That same man would not recognize him today.

"More powder," Philip says, as forcefully as he can.

An hour later, I finish with the make-up, the lipstick, the wig. Philip's breathing is shallow and raspy. His eyes, two gray flames, sputtering. His mouth swollen with a jagged stump of bottom teeth.

"Help me up," Philip whispers.

"This is madness, my friend," I say.

"If they find me," Philip squawks, "I'll never get out of the DR alive."

I slip the bra around Philip's chest, help him step into a white cotton dress. I call the mechanic at the marine diesel on San Martín to pick us up and get us out of Santo Domingo.

Luís, the mechanic, and I escort a puffy-faced woman through the door and down the steps of the Hostal Nicolás Nader and into a car. Luís drives while I hold Philip's head from leaning against the window. Four hours later, after pounding out the miles behind trucks spewing diesel fumes, Luís pulls into Luperón, and we guide Philip into a five-bed clinic where a doctor takes X-rays, and tells Philip he has a broken jaw, three shattered teeth, five cracked ribs, a ruptured disc, a concussion, bruised kidneys, possible internal bleeding. It might take weeks for him to heal, maybe longer, maybe never.

His fears are well-placed. Maybe he never will get off this island.

I wonder if I can leave him in the DR and keep pressing further south. I plan my future moves, because the past is now boiling around me like molasses in a vat. I get a rum and cool down. I need to talk to Philip about what happened in Santo Domingo, but he's in no shape to do anything but sleep.

I need to keep *Stardust* moving, but after Philip's beating, all I can think about is Rosario. Yes, the sex is wildly delicious, but something else about her creeps inside my rum haze. I want to cut away her mosquito netting, help her enter a future worth securing, rouse her belief and mine that another life is possible. Inside the clutch of her body, I imagine something beyond the fierce pull of memory and nights I can't remember. Sadly, Skip, I'll have to fall much farther into the pull of her mulatto skin, before I want to take again the sailing air.

CHAPTER X

After two weeks of breakfast glare, my mother and I invent an armed camaraderie. We have no training in the common rituals of cleaning a man's body. We have little skill, but we get better. It seems like cleaning my father takes twenty minutes, but really it's only five before Skip is cinched up in a new diaper, new pajamas. We lean together and roll him upright. We wheel him out to the porch or in front of the TV. Hours rush by inside his languid, nodding world beyond all borders where everything is seen, but nothing is acknowledged. We wheel him back and put him in bed. "We'll fluff him," my mother says, and "give him a drink." She offers this instruction more to herself than to me.

"If he fusses in the night, talk to him like a Dutch uncle and tell him to shape up. You tell him he was in the Navy and he did things in WWII that make this look like a picnic." My mother wavers between tough talk and silent, unseen corners. I'm humbled by her willingness to make of this chaos as much harmony as she can muster.

After we finish cleaning him up, she kisses him on the forehead and heads off for her bedroom on the other side of the house. I too leave his room and pick up a medical book she has checked out of the library and left in the kitchen. I read about congestive heart failure. As his heart weakens, the blood will back up in his veins and lungs. A tidal wave is coming and when it arrives, his body will suffocate. I listen to the breathing of the house, and instead I hear his breath churning. Skip cries out with a fierce start. I jump from bed as if a ship's bell has struck. He's sleeping with his eyes slit open.

"Chop her down," he bellows. "Chop her down."

He looks at me like I'm a fool for not retrieving his bolt cutters from the garage, when he says again, "Chop her down before she takes us down." Those words, *chop her down*, are all I need to picture again the night he and his crew sail the *Señorita* back to Vermilion after a race at the Toledo Yacht Club. Long before I become one of his crew on board the *Pirate's Penny*, Skip owned a NY 30 named *Señorita* that still sails today out of Newport. Designed by Nathanial Herreshoff, the '43 *Señorita* is one of only eighteen NY 30s ever built, in 1905. One of the world's most coveted racing sailboats, the *Señorita* is sleek and wicked-fast with an enormous gaff-rigged main. As a six-year-old, I remember watching her big sail billow above me, thinking, *my father is dragging the clouds. What will happen to us now?*

The race is part of an annual October snow flurry series. After placing third overall, *Señorita* leaves the Toledo Yacht Club in the late afternoon with the main flying wing and wing. By 7:00 P.M., the wind gusts at thirty-five knots out of the northeast. Skip comes up into the wind and lowers the main. No matter. Under jib alone, the *Señorita* surfs down snarled waves. By nine, the wind gusts to fifty knots. The standing rigging, the blocks, the turnbuckles—all emit a high-pitched hum. Skip loves the fury of this homeward sail, a fury he calls, "the bite of the hot saw." His *Señorita* is less than ten miles away from her dock in Vermilion when he leans down and listens to her wood hull groaning under the funnel of this wind. He hears something he doesn't like and before he can douse the remaining jib, the mast snaps over the bow and the *Señorita* stalls in her race homeward.

In those next confused moments, the crew panics while waves pour in over her stern and the *Señorita* staggers sideways, her jib scooping water and acting like a weighted sea drogue, her halyards spilled over the decks, her bow thrashing in the waves.

My father yells, "Chop her down before she takes us down," but no one knows what to do. His experienced crew is accustomed to heavy weather, but they're stunned by the raw consequences of a dismasting. This is the one moment of terror none of them has trained for. They do nothing but stare at the tangle of sails, mast, spars, and rigging while the *Señorita* flails like some wounded animal on a death skid. Skip tears open the stern lazarette looking for the bolt cutters. Either he forgot to stow them or someone has moved them to another location.

He jumps below into the port quarter berth and returns with an axe. His crew cinches their lifejackets, knowing that without the mast, the *Señorita* can't return home, but with the mast still attached and all her rigging pulling her under, she's easy prey to this Lake Erie straight-line blow.

I see him standing on the cabin top leveling the axe against the spruce mast. He's spitting back at the truth of the moment damned to overturn his *Señorita*. He's feeling the bite of the red hot axe screaming in his arms and he's smiling like a king at the splintered destruction. "Chop her down before she takes us down," he shouts because he doesn't know what else to say inside the teeth of this beautiful misery he has come to. The crew leaves him there alone, until he breaks through the remaining layers of wood, then calls out for them to help lever the fifty-foot mast and pitch it into the lake. The crew leans away from the rat's nest of halyards, sheets, sails, and spars, afraid the snarl will drag him and them overboard, so they put no muscle into the task until he drives them with commands that come easily. This is where he always wants to be, eyeball to eyeball, with the great wave of nothingness that will snap, splinter, and break us all and sweep us out into the snaggle-tooth gale of no return.

How does my shipwright father waltz his beloved *Señorita* home that night? He jury-rigs a mast and sail from the sprawled wreckage and sometime around three in the morning, he sails his damaged beauty into Vermilion—all hands on deck.

"How are you, Skip?" I say, never following up on his request for the bolt cutters which are hanging somewhere in his work-shop along with assorted running tackle and axe dating back fifty years.

"Couldn't be better," he says. "You know what they say. There's nothing sexier than a dying man."

"I hadn't heard that," I say, leaning over him to wipe his brow, thinking he looks like he's been bushwhacked by a school of hammerheads.

"Men I've known for thirty years can't stand to pay me a visit," Skip says with a frown, "thinking they might catch what I've got. But some nice-looking gals I've never met can't get close enough. It's a strange world I've come to. Just wait your turn, you'll see what I'm talking about." I don't have to wait, because I already know that sex and death tease and track one another like sun and shadow.

"Have you seen your brother lately? Where do you suppose he's got to? You know he was accepted by the Naval Academy in Annapolis. His bags were packed, but then he left them behind."

I pull up a chair, soothe again his brow with a damp towel. He seems neither pleased nor displeased, then he smiles.

"Just like old times," he says. "The two of us heading out for god knows where. What do you say, you and me go find Hale and bring him home."

My father's gray-green, bloodshot eyes remind me of Philip's as he lay in a clinic, immersed in panic and sweat. While Philip hollows out the contour of a moan, I suspend my fear and replace it with a fool's belief that I'll escape any threat with more long hours of rum and naked abundance.

I work with Luís, the mechanic Philip found in Santo Domingo, and we manage, with lots of miscues through language and flailing gestures, to drill out the sheared bolt, re-mount the engine, and realign it.

Between looking in on Philip and working with the mechanic, I spend less time with Rosario. I talk with her at night about joining us to St. Thomas and she says, "Not now. Enough talk," then our usual sexual fury hits like a Lake Erie squall and I know I can't leave this island without her. A week after Philip returns from Santo Domingo, I meet her on the loading dock and she says she's returning to Puerto Plata.

"Where can I find you?"

"I'll find you, Matt Younger. There are only a few streets. It's a little gingerbread town inside a paperweight."

"We're leaving our next meeting to chance?"

"I wouldn't call it that," she says. "More like necessity."

She wears a fetching poppy-colored dress that reveals an ample stretch of thigh and clings smartly to her breasts. I see a few idle workers on rafts beside the docks, catching themselves in mid-sentence to glance up her dress. All the men watch her turn and walk off the dock, her white sandals clicking on the wooden slats. On the same morning, against the doctor's wishes, Philip checks himself out of the hospital and finds a boy to row him out to *Stardust*.

"Permission to come aboard, skipper?" Philip asks.

"To hell with that," I shout. "How'd you get permission to check out of the clinic?"

"Your friend, Rosario, paid me a visit. Said I should stay on the boat. That I would be safer with you."

Philip struggles to maneuver up the transom ladder. "Wait a minute," I say. "Let's not lose you in the drink after all this." Luís and I each grab one of Philip's arms and drag him up the ladder.

"Think you're ready for sea duty? You can't carry a teacup."

"Don't worry. I'll be fine," Philip says. "Couple more days and I'll be walking."

I pay Luís and shove him off.

"I've got to get out of here," Philip squawks as soon as Luís is out of earshot. "Somebody in Santo Domingo is likely to find me if I stay here. I need to keep moving. And the last thing I want is to stand trial in the DR, especially when it comes out I'm as a queer as a three-legged horse."

"Those two assholes jumped you. It was self-defense."

"Yeah, right, but I'm alive and they're dead."

"I killed one of them too, remember?"

"I know, but they were looking for me, not you."

"Who were they, Philip? I'd seen them before somewhere."

"I don't know," he says, but he turns away from me in mid-sentence.

"What do you want to do?" I say, scared that Philip will be discovered onboard and *Stardust* will be impounded.

"I want you to hide me until I'm well enough to get on a plane. Since we've already gone through Customs, nobody should board us in Puerto Plata."

"That means I'm stuck here without crew," I say, selfishly, feeling both confused and angry by having to scramble, repair, and shove off quickly.

"What about Rosario as crew?"

"I'm working on that."

"Look, I'm sorry," Philip says, trying to get settled on a boat rocking beneath him.

"Sorry about what? I got us into this mess and I'll get us out. We'll wait until morning to leave so it'll be easy to shoot the twenty miles up the island without having to tack every five minutes."

"I'd like to go now," Philip urges. "It's just twenty-two miles to Puerto Plata. This bunny hop would be a good test for the engine." Philip holds his ribs and winces when he talks.

"Why not?" I say. "There's no point sitting here pounding rum when we could be burning diesel."

"Fire it up," Philip replies, "and let's see how good you did without my wizardry."

As the engine sputters and spits smoke and water, I prop Philip behind the wheel and go forward to weigh anchor, nervous that our departure will be observed and recorded by someone I can't see. I tell myself it's got to be easier to finish repairs in Puerto Plata and find a good coastal chart for the rest of the island. After complaining about the Trades to a couple of locals, they told me the fishermen's trick of ducking behind the capes during the day and easting at night through the big bays when the Trades peter out. I don't like the idea of navigating a rugged coast at night, but tacking against the Trades is no longer an option.

After we round the northeast set of breakers at the harbor's mouth and swing due east, I put *Stardust* on autopilot and help Philip down the ladder and into a bunk. Philip looks like one spreading purple bruise, but something else worries me more. His strength and lightness have been replaced by a raspy cough. He falls asleep as soon as he hits the bunk.

In an hour, I skim the headland of Punta Patilla, turn southeast for Cabras Point, take one flop to the northeast, hoist the main, then motor-sail the next twelve miles to Owen Rock, unmistakable for the hulk of a cargo ship cracked open on a shoal. Off to port, I see smoke billowing from the Puerto Plata power station. The San Felipe Fort looms on the point. Behind the fort lies the yacht basin and docks. To starboard, I make out the commercial pier and due south, high up in the air, half-hidden in mist, I see the statue of Christ the Redeemer perched on top of Isabel de Torres.

Like you, Skip, I've never been a believer, but I tip my hat to the Christ, thinking, what the hell, it can't hurt to show a little respect. As we enter the channel, I see what a godforsaken backwater we've come to. Boats of all shapes and sizes knot up like hurricane salvage in the dirty, congested harbor. The boats at the concrete pier use a Med-mooring style with lines crisscrossed at the stern to keep them a half boat length from the dock as well as an anchor off the bow to hold them steady. For Philip's sake, I decide to avoid the dock, anchor out in the cramped harbor, and hope *Stardust* doesn't get her anchor lines fouled with another boat's. To add to the dreary slosh, Puerto Plata has a commercial pier for cruise ships and seagoing tugs, which means they throw off prop wash strong enough to tear loose an anchor and cast a boat against the concrete pier. It's not exactly the sort of quiet, protected harbor I envisioned for making further repairs. After I get the anchors set, I grab the ship's papers for a visit to the comandante.

"What are you going to tell him?" Philip asks from his bunk where he sprawls like a wounded spider.

"I'll tell him there are two of us on board. We're bound for St. Thomas just as soon as we make repairs. The other passenger, meaning you, is recovering from food poisoning."

"What if he wants to come aboard for an inspection?"

"That's fine. We've got nothing to hide. But I don't see why he'll need to since we already cleared in Luperón."

"The less I show my mug the better," Philip says.

"Yeah. I know," I say, thinking his face is practically its own verdict. I've seen better peaches caught in the bottom of a crate. I tell him to stay below until the swelling subsides. I hail a dock boy who rows me in. I find the *comandancia* located across from the commercial pier and the fishing fleet. Three men sit around a desk gawking at a magazine. The comandante waves me over for a look. A chesty blonde wraps her oily legs around a candy-striped pole while a black man reaches from behind, pinching her nipples.

"*Me gusta la teta muy grande,*" one man exclaims.

"*Sí, sí.*"

"What do you think, señor?" the man sitting at the desk asks me.

"*Me gusta,*" I say.

"We have an aspiring Latino among us," the comandante says while standing up. The other men laugh and return to thumbing their girlie magazine.

"My friends are very happy," he adds. "We now possess a lifetime supply of such amusement."

"Don't tell me someone's now running porn?" I ask.

"We fished a dead guy out of the drink two nights ago," the comandante says. "He came in on a sailboat. We found ten grams of cocaine, a couple pounds of reefer, and all these beautiful women," he says pointing to several boxes near his desk. "You must pardon our amusements. What can I do for you?" the comandante asks in a polished, rhapsodic English. The comandante carries his late middle years with an elegant, barrel-chested sturdiness. He wears his generous black hair slicked back and shining. A pair of gold teeth set far back in his jaw glitter when he talks. He looks smart in a neatly-pressed brown khaki uniform, but what I linger on is the pearl-handled Colt .45 revolver strapped to his right thigh. It looks like a museum piece pinched from Buffalo Bill's Wild West Show.

"I'm on *Stardust,*" I say.

"Is that a new American drug?" the comandante laughs.

The comandante's joke sticks me like a barbed hook.

"Your name, sailor?"

"Matt Younger."

"What's your business in Puerto Plata?"

"I'm here to make repairs, then sail to St. Thomas. We cleared over a week ago in Luperón," I say, handing over my ship's papers.

"Puerto Plata is drug-free, my friend," the comandante says, glancing at my doctored papers. "Violence is rare. We like it that way," he adds, keeping a somber unblinking gaze anchored on my eyes while he reveals a straight set of glistening teeth and moist red lips that look freshly painted.

"How long do you expect to be here?" the comandante asks.

"Don't know exactly. I need to repair a forward hatch and pick up a crew member."

"You lose someone overboard?" the comandante says smugly.

"My mechanic," I say, "is very sick. He's going back to Miami."

"What's wrong with him that our sunshine and rum won't cure?"

"Bad case of food poisoning, or maybe it's seasickness," I say, reaching for something serious enough to warrant Philip's departure, but not so serious as to arouse suspicion or a visit from a doctor.

"A sailor who gets seasick is bad luck. No?" the comandante says.

"*Exactamente*," I offer, gathering my stamped papers off the comandante's desk and turning for the door.

"By the way, did you hear that a couple of norteamericanos were killed in a street fight in Santo Domingo? Know anything about this?"

"Can't say that I do," I say. "Never been there," I add, sucking back on my bottom teeth. "This is one big island you've got here. You could spend a lifetime here and not see it all."

"Yes, it's big," the comandante says. "Some decide there's so much to see, they never leave their cruise ships. Others stay in resort compounds and never risk our streets and countryside. Still others are led around by tourist guides and never see anything interesting. They come here from some place far away, but they never have an adventure. I hope that will not be your story. Enjoy your stay and our nightlife. And take a few bottles of Brugal with you when you leave. Best damn rum in the islands for the price."

"Never touch the stuff," I say, wanting, at that moment, to nurse an entire bottle of his lauded Brugal to calm my frayed nerves, but also suspecting one bottle would not be enough to dull the shine of the comandante's pearl-handled Colt .45.

CHAPTER XI

Like you, Skip, Philip mostly sleeps. Isn't that what the dying do best?

It's as if you're in dress rehearsal for the long flight while you cruise back through the rooms of sensual delight, re-examining the jewels, your head lit from the inside like a movie theater, the images flickering into the rich and abundant dark. Philip curls toward sleep, but the chug and rasp of his breathing keeps me topsides where I sleep in the lee of the wraparound cockpit dodger.

"Where's your gun?" Philip groans from the companionway.

"What?" I ask.

"I'd like to keep your gun handy," Philip says.

"You don't even know how to fire a gun. Do you?"

"I just want to have some protection," Philip says, his hands trembling as he hands me a cold Presidente beer.

"The comandante's the wrong guy to fuck with," I say. "He chucks people in the drink and forgets to fish them out. If someone wants to question you, you better go along."

"I'm going to get out of here before that happens," Philip says, too weak to keep standing, his upper lip beaded with sweat. "The gun?" he asks again.

"It's in the starboard hanging locker under the flares."

I climb down below and retrieve it for him. Philip returns to his bunk where I show him how to load and unload the .38 double-action Smith & Wesson.

"I hope you don't ever use this," I say, sensing from the cut and bruise of Philip's face that the violence begun in Santo Domingo may yet return for a second blood payment.

"Easy for you to say. I've probably got more goons looking for me."

"Not likely," I say, trying to disperse my own dread of what I've started and don't know how to stop. "The comandante doesn't want to rattle the tourists. This thing will blow over. Nobody wants more trouble. You forget this island is a favorite vacation destination for Germans and Canadians."

Philip's routine affection for people banks into a sharp curve of paranoia, his playfulness stolen by the clench of pain. His milky right eye twitches. His jaw looks like a sack of tiny red potatoes. His front teeth are wobbly and blood-stained. His obsession with sex is replaced with a preoccupation for safety. I spend hours each day reassuring him he'll get back to Ft. Lauderdale, and not in a black box.

One day, I go ashore to buy food and rum, but forget my money clip. I return to *Stardust* and find Philip, not in his bunk, but in the damaged starboard hull, the one with the hatch blown off during our crossing of the Thorny Path. He doesn't hear me come aboard. I don't find him below, but I hear him. I return topsides and step gingerly forward. I peer into the hull and see him undoing the latch on one of our large ammo boxes. In the glare, I can see down into the hold where he squats in shadow, but he can't see me. He opens one box and takes out a bag of duct-taped cocaine, then another, all perfectly dry, all perfectly safe, all dangerous as hell now that we're anchored within a few hundred yards of the comandate's gaze.

I lay down on the deck and stick my head in the hole of the hull where the hatch had been.

"What the fuck do you have in your hands?"

Philip jerks up, hits his head against the side of the hull.

Dazed, he says, "Jesus Christ, Matt, you could have given me some warning."

"Warning, that's a good word," I say into the cavity of the hull. "You told me all the cocaine had washed overboard or the bags had broken open and the cocaine had washed out. I forget now your exact words, but you said the shit was gone."

"There's an upside to this, Matt."

"You sorry son of a bitch. I want you off my boat now."

"Let me explain."

"Why?"

"Because your life depends on it. You have no idea what you're up against."

"Jesse?"

"Maybe Jimmy Q is the king of cocaine, but she's the queen."

"I'm listening."

I help him out of the starboard hull and watch him limp back to the cockpit. There, as we descend the companionway ladder, he looks at me like a hurt and searching child, both wanting to talk and afraid he'll be punished for saying what he knows.

"There's a lot I never told you."

"Starting with why you were rooting around in the ammo boxes now?"

"I thought the cocaine might help kill the pain."

"Isn't there a song like that?" Then, his song begins with a few broken notes like he's chewing a piece of gristle, his cracked lips seeking spit, his tongue tripping over the stub of his busted, lower teeth.

Seven years ago, Philip tells me, Jesse leaves her daddy's shrimp boat, flies to Nassau, and meets up with a couple from Michigan bound for the West Indies. They don't know a turnbuckle from a turnip so she quickly becomes their maritime maven. Only problem is, she makes a play for the man's wife, teasing her at first with quick shoulder caresses, undressing in front of her, and squirming into tight T-shirts. When she buries a wet kiss at the base of her neck, the older woman wiggles out of her suit. The husband gets jealous and drops Jesse off on the docks in Providenciales while his wife chokes back sobs. The bump turns out favorable for Jesse, disastrous for the Michigan couple. She hears later their boat pitch poles after hitting a reef. A rescue boat finds their half-eaten bodies in the shark-laden waters off San Juan.

A month later, Jesse meets Jimmy in a cabana in Provo. After serving her a half dozen rum punches, he offers to fly her around the Caicos in his plane. He throws down a steady cash chatter that floats her a notch above the stink of shrimp still clinging to her jeans. She pegs him as a rummy until they rise out of Provo, not in a rust-bucket Cessna, but in a Lear jet. Once airborne, he hands her a 16-ounce paper cup with no straw. She lifts the lid and sees the cup brimming with white powder. Three days later she wakes up on board *Citadel*, his sixty-foot cruiser. She only remembers snorting coke straight out of that cup until it's gone. She can't find her clothes, but she doesn't care. After living for better than five years in diesel-splashed quarters on board her daddy's *Miss Edgefield*, Jesse has no trouble imagining herself as a kept woman on board a floating penthouse.

But she's no kept woman. Jimmy makes her earn her keep.

"Why does she tell you all this?"

"Because she has a plan. She's always got a plan and another one in case the first one doesn't take and another one after that."

His mind revs faster than his mouth. He trips over words. I have no way of knowing if what he tells me is true, but here's how Jesse undresses her story for Philip:

For each uncharted leg of drug-running, Jimmy designates green-light players. Jesse delivers any freight by water and collects the tariff, but Jimmy never pays her in cash, not a dime. He doles out just enough cocaine to keep her looped. When she returns from a junket, she drifts inside the *Citadel*, fluttering between a giddy dreaminess about her freedom at sea and an eerie premonition she'll die coked up and naked as a molting shrimp. Some nights she even longs for the long nights on board *Miss Edgefield*, her father at the wheel, dragging for shrimp gold off Cumberland Island, Georgia, just north of Jacksonville.

Jesse makes so many runs, Philip says, since that first night with Jimmy, it's hard for her to know if there's any boundaries left. She steals sailboats from moorings and marinas. She finds new gunk holes where cigarette boats can hide. She loads and unloads cargo in the middle of the night. She makes a name for herself in the Bahamian drug trade.

When she returns to Cockburn Harbor, she lets Jimmy burn himself down with the thrill of her body, but nothing in his body is worth a damn. The wires from his cock to his brain sizzled out long ago. It sickens her to think of his sullen paralysis while she taunts him with come-hither looks. He bleats and sputters while his body turns turtle. She hates his porn-talk impotence. She hates herself for her enchantment with his money that she never sees, and she hates her own body for wanting his powder that dulls her decision to break away and live another life. Which is when she thinks of Dwight Stone, a new Customs official at Provo airport who bristles at Jimmy's control of Cockburn Harbor. Stone begs Jesse for one hour alone. She agrees. In exchange, he gets on the horn at airport control and tells Jimmy he's got his jet pegged on radar and will bring the heat in when the plane lands. Jimmy dumps the cocaine out the cargo door and it lands on the western tip of Provo. After that, all Jesse needs is to convince Jimmy to bait a delivery boat skipper to go after the cocaine.

"That would be me," I say with a long, tired face that reaches back to the bar in Cockburn Harbor where I didn't have the common sense of a horsefly to walk away from Jimmy Q.

"Here's the clincher," Philip says, the sweat pouring off his face. "She needs to steal the cocaine from you without Jimmy knowing she has the boat and the cocaine, so she can get away clean."

Philip pauses with his story about Jesse and squints through the companionway as if trying to see a different vision of himself in the green hills canted above the harbor.

"She set me up in Nassau," I say, "with the missing Avon. I knew it then. I just couldn't prove it and I didn't think such a mishap would force me to stop in Cockburn Harbor, but she bent my ear good."

Philip nods, head down, exhausted, frightened.

"Let me guess," I say, "she convinced Jimmy to tell me about the drop in Provo, betting I would go after it. Jimmy went along with her plan because he wanted his cocaine back, and Jesse padded the deal with some new sexual fantasy."

He nods again.

"You're only missing one piece of the puzzle," Philip says. "Jesse never wanted *Stardust* to make the crossing across the Thorny Path. She knew if the boat landed in the DR with cocaine on board, it would be hard, maybe impossible, to get it out. She wanted me to throw you in the drink during the crossing so then she could commandeer the boat. She was the captain of the *Citadel* that followed us out there."

"Jesse, our winsome bikini cook, wanted to test my long distance swimming skills?" I say, feeling the queasy chase of the

Thorny Path all over again. Skip, in case I had any doubts before, I now know I've embarked on some kind of demonic detour leading through the Pit of Corruption across the Five Rivers of Hell to the Gates of Death itself. My little adventure in Provo proves the old saw, "*Heaven sends us good meat, but the Devil sends cooks.*"

"The way Jesse puts it, all I have to do is bump you through the lifeline. You know, man overboard. An accident of sorts. Then she comes on board and sails *Stardust* to Belize with the Trades in her favor. She vanishes with the boat and the cocaine. She counts on me coming through, but I'm sure she didn't bank on the storm and your heading for the Silver reef."

I press my fist into my chin to make sure I don't throw it at Philip. He cooked up a deal with Jesse that almost worked in her favor.

Philip sips a glass of water. "I didn't trust her," Philip says, pulling himself up the companionway into the cockpit. "I had no intention of throwing you in the drink."

"That's why you got jumped . . ."

"The two guys in Santo Domingo worked for Jesse. I recognized them from the Sunset Lounge in West Palm at the same moment maybe you did."

"How was she going to ease your conscience?"

"With $150,000."

"Thanks for taking a pass on the nest egg," I say, relaxing my fists.

"Why go to all the trouble?" I ask, searching the cuts and bruises of his swollen face.

"I thought if you saw the coke was gone, you'd leave the boat for long periods of time once we got to Red Hook Bay. I'd still get my money from Jesse if I made it easy for her to get her hands on the coke. Now, I don't care about the money. I sure as hell don't want to meet up with Jesse or any more of her thugs. I just want out of here. I want to get back to Miami to see Derek, my old lover."

"Let me play this back. You didn't want to kill me, but you still wanted the money?"

"Pitiful, isn't it? I thought Derek and I could move to Brittany. Use the money to start up a diesel repair shop. After you left to find the coke in Provo, Jesse got in touch and made me the offer. She'd been on board the *Citadel* all the time we thought she was in Miami getting us a life raft. That's when I made up my mind to take another tack. It was all so stupid."

"You might have told me then."

"Greed got in the way."

"That's quite a tale," I say, wondering if any of it is true.

"As soon as I get more steam, I'm going to make a break for the airport. I'm pissing and coughing blood. I can't stay here much longer."

Given Philip's side bet with Jesse, maybe I should have been nervous about him staying on board, but he had hardly the strength to walk, let alone haul away the bags of cocaine. Now, I just want to be rid of this two-timing Frenchman before I have another body to explain. Skip, I can't be sure of anyone, not with Jesse at the helm of this detour. Any damn fool can smell the foul breath of the hellhounds circling, but instead of making ready for the next battle, I start drinking rum. All I want to do is keep Philip talking because I can't stand my own pickled brain and the thought that Jesse hovers over the DR planning my demise.

"Derek?" I ask, crawling into my bunk. "Tell me about him."

In a halting rhythm, Philip tells me he's been with Derek on and off for ten years. They met in Miami in a parking lot outside a gay bar. Neither comments on the weather, on the music, or where the other lives. They just tell the story of their lives and much later down the beach, near dawn, they find their way to a hotel room. Then, in the last year or so, their bare-assed romance cools. The man Philip used to talk with all night becomes moody and withdrawn. A man with a ravishing appetite for all things sensual, Derek stops wanting sex.

Philip says, ever since his boyhood in Brittany, he's been better at leaving than returning, always eager for the pulse of harbors and piers. "Safety's oversold," he says, but now he wants to win back some of that safety and make a new life with Derek.

"I want to meet him," Philip says, closing his cut and swollen eyes, "on the other side of this dream called the body."

CHAPTER XII

I clean out the starboard hull, rearrange its contents, look again at how Philip pried loose the panel after the starboard hatch was blown off. I unbuckle one of the heavy ammo boxes and look again at the duct-taped bags of cocaine inside. I look at the bags, Skip, thinking two things: they represent all the money I'll ever need and I must dump them overboard during the night.

I tell Philip he has just one job before he jumps ship: "Hide the cocaine."

"Where exactly?" he asks.

"Someplace where even God can't find it."

He crawls inside the engine room and builds a false panel and smears it with grease and oil after packing in the bags of cocaine. I make a replacement hatch out of clear Spanish cedar which I fiberglass and fit into place. I fill up the water tanks and refuel. I replace filters, clean injectors, check the impeller and exhaust system. At the end of one tedious week, I've had about as much tranquility and convalescence as I can stand.

The cinders from the nearby power plant rain a fine black dust that catches in my throat. The harbor surge makes me feel like a chunk of diminishing laundry soap. More than once, a poorly anchored boat tears loose from the mud and drifts down on us in the night. I want to move to the dock to finish repairs, but Philip insists on keeping a distance. He mends slowly. His facial cuts scab over. The swelling along his ribs goes down. Still, he needs medical and dental care.

I forget about Philip's troubles and his deceit once I decide to go ashore.

I tell myself if the cocaine has gone undetected this long, it might remain a secret for one more Saturday night. From my thwart in the water taxi skiff, I hear the clank and cough of bicycles, motorbikes, cars, amid the clip-clop of horses and the ever-present blare of car horns. So many people neither work nor play in Puerto Plata, but linger on the threshold of another life that only exists in the trembling depths of late-night songs. Their eyes, counseled in ecstasy and despair, say *the road ahead is uncertain, the road behind is closed.* Low scudding clouds throw down shadows on the mountain slopes below the Christ, but regardless of their speed, they too seem trapped by the heat and rain. Everywhere I look I see the old sweltering decay and the silvery evanescence of a faded Victorian madam. I can almost taste the salt and grease sliding off the sea grape leaves. The stink of hurricane mud is cut with a sweetness rising off the fruit stalls swollen with mountain sour sop, tamarinds and mamey apples.

At the town's main square, couples mill around a two-tiered wedding-cake bandstand as though waiting for a priest to hitch them. Inside the bars, the priest is ill-equipped for the medley of delivery boat captains, shipwreck divers, amber traders, hookers, drunk Germans, quiet Canadians, card-trick artists, cruise-ship workers, and fast-talking boys who carry their steepled shoeshine houses in their hands.

I stop at the Hotel Castilla for a drink and to keep an eye out for Rosario.

The hotel swarms with interracial couples strung together like rosary beads. Just as Desmond says, white women, pale as chalk, lean into black men like they've found the Rosetta stone. White men pull at strings of mulatto women like taffy. The air floods with pouts and teases, unfastened with the rolled r's of rapid conversation while the breathless beat of merengue pipes in from car and bus radios, and from the hotel itself. It's a scene laced with so many untrackable plot threads, so much sexual intrigue, I have to order another rum just to applaud the apparent triumph of innocence and comedy over sin.

While I wait for Rosario to tell me something I don't know about our sexual dance, I talk with an American woman who looks rich enough not to care about the morning after. She has fitful, raccoon eyes, the start of a double chin, and skin the color

135

of double-fallen yeast bread. I don't want to talk, but she's had more than a few rum punches and her night is not going to end without at least one detour.

"My husband died a year ago," she says.

I consider saying nothing, but figure with just the right word or two, I can cut her off and force her to look elsewhere for conversation.

"Too bad," I say. "Everybody's gotta go sometime." I take a slug of rum, thinking that should crimp her voice box so I can drink and think in peace.

"We didn't have sex for twenty-five years," she says, leaning into me.

"Fuck," I say, in disbelief that this conversation is just getting cranked up.

"Fucking is a lot more important than couples give it credit." she says firmly, as if making a business announcement.

"Shit," I say. "Get me out of here."

She grabs my arm. She orders us another drink and tells me the whole unraveling tale, right down to the zippers and button-holes. There's the brilliant, controlling father who becomes the brilliant, controlling husband who's forever out of touch with his feelings and his body. I'm quickly reduced to clichés.

"History repeats itself," I say.

"Not anymore," she replies. "The one thing I want before I die is to have a hot passionate lover, not necessarily a soul mate, but someone who can fuck like an angel horse with no desire to return to the barn."

"I like that," I say. "Angel horse. Sounds like a novel for eight-year-old girls." That's when, thankfully, she pushes off. She turns her back to see this handsome Dominican man at the bar. She lays a hand on his arm and opens her purse. So it goes, I think. Money can't buy you love, but it can buy you an angel horse. While I take off my sunglasses to rub my burnt eyes, I hear the one voice I need to power through the wake of this last encounter.

"Hey sailor, want to buy a girl a drink?" Rosario asks, pulling up a chair and waving to the waiter. She wears a strapless, satin green dress fished out of a carnival trunk that makes her body shimmer like some agile triumph over the ugliness breaking the bones of an ordinary day in the DR.

"Took you long enough to find me," I say quietly, not wanting her to see how relieved I feel that our submersion can begin again.

"I've been making plans."

"What kind of plans?"

"I'm thinking about taking a trip, maybe to South America or New York."

"How 'bout St. Thomas first, then hell, I'll go to South America if you want to."

"I've already got one dream cooking," she says, knotting and unknotting her hands.

"Let me cook up another one for you," I say. Before she objects, I describe surfing down a ten-foot curl with the moon riding over our shoulder.

"If you point at the moon nine times," she replies, "you won't go to heaven."

I look at her face aglow with the light of the bar and imagine her kneeling in a church praying for a way out of her poverty, believing with her catholic knees that if this life fails to deliver some modest reward, she'll gain it all and more when the lights go out on this cruise-ship, merengue town.

"The worst is behind us," I reassure her and myself. "From now on, we sail to the east at night when the Trades are not against us. *Stardust* is not the greatest boat for going to windward, but she's tougher than she looks," I say.

"So you think it's a good boat?" she asks, cautiously.

"It's a great boat for sailing the islands," I say. "Not such a great boat for long off-shore distances. She'll make a good dive charter boat. Please say you're ready to come with me?"

"Tell me more," she says, forgetting what I've already told when she came to visit Philip and me on board *Stardust*.

I tell her, Skip, about the difference between monohulls and multihulls, between sloops, yawls, and ketches, why *Stardust* is an unbeatable witch downwind. I tell her about the basic points of sail and how the only secret to sailing is knowing where your boat is in relation to the wind.

"After we get to St. Thomas, what then?" she asks.

"We find another boat and deliver it further south."

"That's it? One boat after another? And you don't know where you're going next, except south?"

"It's a not a bad way to go."

"I'd like more than that," Rosario says. "I want a home somewhere."

"You want the United States?"

"Why not?"

"It's no picnic in America," I say. "The cities are rotten with crime and drugs. Good jobs are hard to find. Harder to keep."

"I wouldn't mind more money. More opportunity for women. Regular hot showers. Less Spam and eggs," she argues as if rattling off a list of political demands.

"You still think New York's the land of milk and honey?"

"I don't know what it is," she says. "All I know is, there are tens of thousands of Dominicans living there, keeping this island afloat with their cash envelopes that fly in here every week. Without those cash envelopes, this island dies. We become another Haiti. That's a fact you'll never read in the newspapers, but it's true."

"New York's a graveyard," I say, aiming to shore up my case.

"Then, how come it's got so much money?"

"It's not about money," I say. "There's no beauty there. Just the rich and the poor walking past each other. At least here you can ride up into the mountains, look out and see the ocean. You can breathe in the beauty. It's better than a paycheck."

"It's hard to marry an ocean."

"Is that what we're talking about? Marriage?" I say, wondering now if Rosario won't leave the island with me unless I marry her in one of those five-minute Dominican services used by foreigners on the run.

"Don't make marriage sound like a jail sentence," she says. A young boy about ten flutters near our table holding a camera. More confusion grabs me by the wrists. I've been afraid Rosario is linked to Jesse and yet now Rosario defends marriage and seems to want me as her groom.

"A Polaroid of the señorita?"

I wave the boy off, but Rosario cries, "Sí, sí, sí." She swings her chair around and throws her arms around my neck.

"*Ahora*," she says. The boy clicks his dented box camera. While he waits for the film to develop, Rosario grabs ten dollars off the table and stuffs it in the boy's shirt pocket.

"Hey, wait a minute," I object. "I can buy a camera for that."

Rosario presses her fingers to my lips, hushing me. As soon as the film rolls out, the boy peels it off, tosses the picture on the table. I pick up the photo and glance at the slightly drunk couple. I see a man with scraggly blond hair, his burnt eyes drawn down. He drapes an arm around a honey-colored, woman-child lit with wonder and mischief. I look away from the photo and back again and this time, I find a sailor holding his breath in a windy place and I wonder if he's any man I know. I turn the photograph and write your Florida address on the back.

"What's this," she says, "43 Spanish Moss, Fernandina Beach, Florida."

"In case we ever get separated," I say, "you'll know how to find me."

Rosario laughs, slips the photograph into her purse, takes twenty dollars off the table, and nudges it over to the bartender. We walk upstairs to a room. Not much more than a sagging bed without pillows and jalousie windows with wrought-iron railing beneath. She pushes open the bottom of the window and a pink bar of light nicks the floor. Inside the pink, I see a chartreuse chameleon, the size of my thumb. He sprints the railing and freezes, his tongue nailing the air, his long glossy tail brushing the iron railing. In his paces, is he watching us undress each other or does our dance hold no appeal? His body holds fast and quivers as if he's a hummingbird in disguise waiting for the perfect moment to raid a flower. He seems so at home in a stripe of shadow, it's hard to imagine he prefers the danger of the hard, oven light. She smiles at the lizard and sticks out her tongue the way he does. She lifts her toes under her fallen panties and flicks them at the creature. He dodges and disappears only to return to the ledge, the narrow band of his chest ballooning in a huff. Straddled on the railing, watching us, the chameleon owns the room with his speed and silence and regards us for what we are, temporary inhabitants, a bit of amusement he can easily wait out. After I drink in the chameleon's gaze, I take Rosario as she bends over the bed.

In the grip of our frenzy, I lose track of this green animal engine at the window although I sense in his bravado and retreat my own desire to disappear inside her cinnamon-gold skin and lay claim to a color that does not belong to me. Not belonging, I want the color all the more—all her history, her knowledge, the startling blue abyss of her eyes, her island scent dredged from the sea slime and mixed with the sprawl of bougainvillea.

At first when she and I met in Luperón, I only heard the growl of that engine between her legs and pictured the splotches of her behind where my hands gripped her cheeks. Now, I want to be possessed by her soul looking out on the light that rakes the Thorny Path. When we've finished in the half light and dressed without speaking, I go to the window. A ragged, gray seagull stands one-legged on the railing, and I wonder if our voyeuristic dragon with the swollen chest has been devoured like us, or if he has escaped the plunge of the beak so he might rule again on some other evening from an uncertain perch.

"Ready to dance again?" she asks, springing down the stairs. She grabs my hand and we leave the Hotel Castilla and its brightly-lit ornamental park. We run through narrow streets. Rosario turns sharply through an alley, across a bougainvillea-draped courtyard, past a tall wrought-iron gate, past sleek black cats with green marble eyes, past stray children with mangy dogs, and walls of dense flowering vines. We emerge on a barricaded road across from a nightclub called La Lechuza.

Once through the door, I let her go, order a bottle of rum, and tell myself I want to set aside my worry beads and enjoy the show. With a rum undertow, I can easily escape the grip of any full-length mirror. I can glide down through the layers of sweet, burnt molasses until my name is just another word without a history. I drink a glass in one gulp, then another. I roll a cold glass across my forehead, look out through the translucent curve, and see Rosario dancing with a blonde in a short black dress. Not dancing so much as lifting, bending, one skin swallowing the other, the way the night inhales a flare launched from a sinking ship.

I turn back to the bar to order more rum, forgetting I already have a half-full bottle. I look again to the dance floor. The blonde is gone. Rosario gyrates up close to a Dominican woman as another song skitters through its horns, then jams through a series of crescendos. I veer onto the dance floor, my shirt sticking to my back, my eyes tearing from the last slug of Brugal. This is the point in the voyage, Skip, where the ocean runs dry and the fish flop on the sand. I start shouting from the shallow burden of my disorganized, drunken life.

"Who's the blonde?"

"I don't see any blondes here," Rosario says.

"Don't play games."

"You're drunk," she says.

"I may be drunk, but blondes in black dresses jump out in a place filled with . . ."

"Filled with what? Mulatto whores?" she scoffs.

"Can we talk somewhere?"

"What's wrong with here?"

"Who was that woman?" I shout over the music.

"Never seen her before tonight."

"Where's she staying?" I demand.

"What's so important about this blonde?"

"She reminds me of my cook from Cockburn Harbor," I say. "Did you catch her name?"

"She didn't say," Rosario says.

"You're lying."

"If you know everything," Rosario scowls, "why are you asking me?"

Rosario clings to another woman, raising her arms so their bodies press together. I grab her by the wrist, drag her off the dance floor. I pick her up, not caring where her fists fly. No one in the bar throws more than a glance at us as we tumble into the alley.

"That's really good," she says. "The tough sailor proves he's got balls. What's this about? You're afraid of my dancing with a blonde American?"

"I didn't say she was from America. So, you do know her?"

"No, I don't," she stammers.

"What did she want?"

"To go to her hotel," she says.

"For what?"

"She didn't want to sit around and read from the Bible," Rosario says, pulling away from me to stand against a wall. I take a step back, astonished I've not seen all along that Rosario's a hooker. Still, if she's a hooker, why has she never asked me for a dime? Does it mean she's retired from the trade or she's just running up my tab?

"Come on," she says. "Don't look at me like you've seen a ghost. What do you think poor girls do here for spending money."

"I don't care what you've done for money," I say. "I don't even care if you know this woman. I just want you to come with me to St. Thomas. *Stardust* is ready and I've got some money," I say.

"What kind of money?" she asks, inching closer.

"Some."

"Let's see it."

"Don't have it yet."

"What do you have? A treasure map like the ones they sell on the Malecon for all the shipwrecks on the Silver Reef?"

"I have a kilo of cocaine on board," I boast.

Skip, as soon as I say this I laugh, remembering one of your stock lines, *you can't put the milk back into the cow.* I try to shake off the rum haze. I make a damn foolish mistake telling her this, but I've made so many mistakes by now, told so many lies, dodged so many questions, I almost don't care anymore who discovers the milk that won't ever go back into the cow.

"You know what the comandante does to drug runners?"

142

"I can imagine," I say, slowing down my speech so my tongue won't trip.

Stupidly again, I tell Rosario a half-truth. How Jimmy Q gave me a kilo that's worth about sixty thousand. About how I want us to sell it and use the money to cruise the islands.

"Who else knows about it?" she asks.

"Just Philip, but he's leaving," I say. "Back to Miami. He's had enough tropical adventure for one lifetime."

Rosario presses me for details. I say nothing about the total amount of cocaine that's on board, nothing about its true value, nothing about how I stole it from Jimmy Q, nothing about the threat forever looming over *Stardust,* no matter if she stays or goes.

I slap my face trying to wake up to the fact that I've just split myself open to more trouble. I grab her by the wrists and press hard. I want answers. I want to know who she is now that I've told her about the cocaine. I figure she owes me, but she pulls free and retreats into silence laced with strategy. As we walk along the Malecon, I look past the break wall toward the Turks & Caicos, now locked behind the Trades. There's nothing but blackness to unfurl. Nothing to lighten the way back.

Whatever else she tells herself about working in the lobbies of dilapidated Victorian hotels, she too fishes for pesos in a poison surf. She suffers through each night to dive again and again with other Germans, French, Americans. Good money, not enough, never enough to scour the oils, never enough to scrape off the skeins of hair and forget the occasional beating. Never enough to escape Paradise for good.

We see thin brown boys perched above a ledge in the moonlight just east of the harbor reefs. They make their bodies an arc as they dive for coins near the curl of sludge and shit that Puerto Plata every day dumps into the waters off the Malecon. As if cleaning off one of their found coins to find the embossed face beneath, she tells me about turning tricks in Puerto Plata. She hates it, but she doesn't know what else to do. She looks at the backs of the skinny boys. Her shame and repulsion is not with the swimmers, but with the shudder that she's one of them, diving every night into spools of human hair like that first night, eons ago, when she sat backwards astride a paunched German, older than her father, and invented a straddled merengue, a dance hinged from her hips, pressing her groin into him, rocking, sliding, until she felt him wiggle. She leapt from his lap and led him off to a hotel for a ten-minute collision. When the German went soft and pulled out, he grabbed her by the head and thrust her face down into his crotch, pressing his thumbs into her scalp. She gagged and the German threw her against a wall, spat on her and left.

As we approach the Customs office, I see the comandante leaning against a piling, smoking a cigar. "*Buena noche*," the comandante says, nodding to us as we stroll arm-in-arm like a genteel married couple. Rosario returns his smile. I realize they know each other. Of course, she knows the comandante. If Rosario has worked the bars, cruise ships, and harbor, she knows everybody. The comandante draws near Rosario and puts his arms around her. "*Èsta es mi bonita chica*." He kisses her tenderly on the forehead as if lightly kissing a doll. "This is my favorite girl," the comandante announces. "So smart, so clever, so ready to get ahead with her life," he now says with a hard click of his jaw.

"He talks that way to all the girls," she says.

"You didn't tell me you had a woman staying on board?" the comandante says.

"A woman?"

"Not more than an hour ago, I saw a woman leave your boat with a large handbag. She didn't look so good. Lots of makeup. I thought your first mate was a man?"

I want to tell the comandante he must be mistaken, but I don't want to correct his memory, stir his anger, drive him to caress the pearl handle of his gun.

"I don't know how else to tell you this, but Philip, my mechanic, sometimes likes to dress like a woman. He's an artist. Always on the lookout for material. Likes to play with mascara," I say.

"What does he have to hide?" he asks, blowing a smoke cloud above his head.

"It's a hobby, his dressing up like that."

"You know we've been looking for an American who's linked to the deaths of two other Americans. Do you think your friend, dressed as woman, is someone I should meet?"

For one brief moment I consider telling the comandante that Philip killed both men in Santo Domingo in the hope of buying myself some good will for when I leave Puerto Plata with Rosario. After all, had Philip told me that he and Jesse were working a side bet, I might never have gone after the cocaine.

"Don't think he's your type." I reply.

The comandante offers a toothy smile that would score glass.

"That's funny. I like a man with humor. It serves him well when life kicks him in the teeth," the comandante says, flicking the ash of his cigar and stepping into his office, no doubt, to make a call, alerting the airport police to detain a man in drag bound for Miami.

Rosario reads the lines of panic shadowing my face. "I'll go inside," she says as I slump against a light pole, "and see if I can help the comandante forget about this woman from your boat."

"No, don't," I say weakly. "The man's evil. Philip will just have to fend for himself. You don't have to do this. Please don't go in there."

"It's OK," she says. "The comandante doesn't scare me. Even a strong man likes to have his pants unbuckled."

I flinch when she says this about the comandante, picturing her quick fix.

"Go back to the boat and wait for me," she orders, strolling through the high arch of the Customs office where I imagine the comandante reaching for the phone to call the airport guards. I turn slowly away from the Customs office, glancing over my shoulder. I sit up in the cockpit for hours drinking rum, waiting for Rosario, but she never turns up and neither does the comandante. I figure she must have succeeded in distracting him. I hate thinking of her being subjected to his freakish endearments almost as much as I hate myself for letting her go. As the lights at the Customs office blink off, I go below and see Philip's note peeking out of the broken spine of Rimbaud's *Drunken Boat.*

Time for me to leave this drunken boat and return to Lauderdale. Still a long way from being on the mend. Sorry I couldn't join you for the next hop. If I were you, I'd leave on the next tide. Forget about Rosario.. Dump the sweet stuff. Take Stardust *and go. You can do it alone. Yours, Philip.*

I read the note again, wanting it to reveal more. I strike a match, burn the note and look around for what Philip has left and what he's taken. True to form, *Stardust* is shipshape, clean enough to eat off the floorboards. Philip stowed loose charts, tools, food, sails. How did he do it when he could hardly move? There are only two things he's forgotten to pack, a large lavender, wide-toothed comb and a T-shirt. And there's only one thing missing: my gun. While I stir the ashes of his note in a small bowl, I glance at the book of poems, busted from its binding by wind, salt, and humidity. My eyes fall to an underlined passage, *I know the night and dawn arisen like a colony of doves, And sometimes I have seen what men have thought they saw.*

CHAPTER XIII

I answer the door expecting to meet one of Skip's many care-givers or hospice nurses who have become more frequent, but care today comes in another package. A short, elderly man with horn-rim glasses, starched white shirt, bow tie, and black wing-tips stands primly on the doorstep. I figure he must be an under-taker, a preacher, or an insurance salesmen looking for a quick grab. I aim to turn him away fast so he can park himself on somebody's doorstep who is dead or dying. His bow tie alone is as out of place in Skip's house as a long-finned Cadillac.

"Hello, I have an appointment with Emily Younger," he says with a slight Georgia drawl.

"Sure you do," I say. "Who are you, an insurance peddler?"

"I'm Emily's jeweler. I've known Miss Emily for, what, close to ten years."

"A jeweler who makes house calls, right?"

"She asked me to stop by and have a look at her wedding ring."

Shit, did I ever read this moment wrong.

My mother must be real worried about money to be consid-ering hawking her wedding ring. She wants to have it appraised so she'll know how much cash she can raise if Skip's dying drags out or if after he dies she'll have nothing left to live on.

"She called and said the diamond was loose in its setting. She wanted to have me reset it and polish the gold band, of course."

Wrong again. "Come in, Mister . . ."

"Sunman," he says, wiping his feet and adjusting his bow tie.

I find my mother in her bedroom reading her Bible, her fin-gers tracing chapter and verse, her mouth working over the words, silently, patiently. She doesn't see me or want to see me or the cur-rent passage makes a much greater claim on her than my entry.

"Mom, there's a Mr. Sunman here to see you about your ring."

She looks at me with a sideways glance, and for first time I don't see a glare sweeping out from her bloodshot eyes. Just exhaustion.

"Have him come back, please."

I bring Mr. Sunman back to my mother's room. She pries her wedding ring off her finger and places it gently in his extended palm.

"We've been married for fifty years," she says. "I don't want to lose that diamond now."

"I understand, Emily."

He takes out his eye-piece and holds it against his right eye with his right hand. In his left, he holds her ring. He brings the ring toward this eye-piece and holds the diamond there for examination, turning the ring in the changing light.

"It's a pretty stone, Emily. Age has not altered its beauty, but it is loose as you say. Let me see what I can do to make sure your diamond stays secure."

She smiles. She likes this man. Trusts him.

She has no problem giving him the ring even though she immediately touches the place where the ring rests firmly on her left hand.

"How long will you need to have it?"

"Less than a week," he says. "I'll take good care of it."

"I know you will, Mr. Sunman."

My mother returns to her Bible. I show Mr. Sunman the door. We pause there. He wonders what I want. I'm not sure myself.

"Mr. Sunman?"

"Yes?" he replies coldly.

"I've got a stone I want you to look at. Actually, it's a pearl. A conch pearl. I've got no idea what it's worth, but I'd like to know."

He scrunches his nose, lifts his eyebrows, stammers.

"OK," he says, "Let's have a look." I leave him at the door, no doubt miffed he's been mousetrapped into a two-fer. He came to look at a diamond. Now he's being asked to examine a pearl.

I return and find him tapping on the door frame. I remove the pearl from its soft velvet pouch and hold it in my hand and lift it close to his face. John Sunman rubs his eyes, licks his lips once, and takes out his eye-piece. His breath quickens. "Excuse me," he says nervously, "I've never seen a conch pearl quite like this one."

"It's a beauty, isn't it?" I say.

"I didn't catch your name."

"I'm sorry. I'm Matt. Matt Younger."

"I didn't know. I thought Emily and Jack's son died a long time ago in an accident."

"That would be my brother. I'm the other son."

"Well, other son," he says, now smiling warmly, "This is your lucky day. My firm specializes in diamonds, rubies, emeralds, and other traditional stones, but I was trained in Key West at the Emerald Lion. The specialty there is conch pearls and I've examined dozens of them. You might call them a hobby of mine. I read every auction catalogue in which conch pearls are featured."

"What's the big deal about these pearls? There are conch shells all over the Caribbean. Dime a dozen, right?"

"There are millions of conches, but only one out of ten thousand produces a pearl. They resist all attempts to cultivate them. They are wild, no two are alike. A pearl like this, well, the odds might be one in a million you'd find something like this. May I?" he asks, picking up the pearl from my hand.

He examines the pearl with his lens.

"See these lights caught inside the pearl, that's called a flame structure. Even apart from its magnificent size, the flame of this pearl makes it something any museum or private collector would pay dearly for." Reluctantly, he places the pearl back in my hand.

"What's it worth?"

"A great sum of money."

"How much?"

Mr. Sunman swings his head from side to side as if calculating the odds of determining a fair value for a pearl that's taken his breath away and left a sweat at his wrists.

"The low end would be $150,000."

"My God," I say. "And the high end?"

"Over a million."

"Are you sure?" I ask, the sweat now beading my upper lip.

"I know one private collector in Key West who would sell his home, his boat, and half of his other pearls to own such a rare beauty as this."

"What would you require to sell this pearl for me?"

"10% commission is standard."

"Fair enough," I say.

"You've got something here, Matt Younger. I don't know how you came by such a pearl but it's most definitely a rare find, what they call, in my business, a rarity within a rarity. You need to protect it with more than that little pouch."

"Do you have a card?"

He takes out a card from his wallet. "Let me know when I can be of assistance. It would be a pleasure to play a role in the destiny of such a pearl."

John Sunman turns to leave, still shaken by what he's seen.

"Tell your mother again, not to worry about her ring."

"I'll do that," I say. "And I'll be calling you soon about the pearl."

"Please do," he says, wanting to turn back and look again at the pearl a second time, but instead he walks away from our cottage with bold steps as if he were now, not a man bent by years of lens magnification, but a man who'd been cartwheeled by lightning.

I stand there with the pearl, Philip's found treasure from Cockburn Harbor, with rivers of fire light running through it, and I laugh when I think how stupid I was on stealing Jimmy Q's cocaine, how I fully believed I could turn his powder into a freedom that would let me outdistance my own grief, how because of the cocaine, I lost so much I can never recover, when I might have gazed into the flame structure of this found gem and allowed its fire to pour light on all my dark places.

That's a lot to ask of a pearl, I tell myself, but this is no ordinary pearl. It's a plump, wild-grown, hot raspberry gem that lets you look deep into it as if it were a globe holding not just rivers of light, but rivers of dark, rivers you can't see, rivers that take you home.

CHAPTER XIV

What are the qualifications for being a dying man's night nurse?

I suppose they're not much different than the ones mastered by a mother listening for the tremor of the crib. You must let your body accept that sleeping and not sleeping are one—the way the ocean and its shore are fate-assigned to hear only the other. This I know how to do because Skip trained Hale and me to jump in and out of four-hour race watches on board ship.

Even when I sleep, I sleep with one ear pinned to his room the way I used to listen to the snap of sheets or a sudden wind shift on a long night crossing. Several times in the night, I hear his thin cries that sound more like the yelping of a pup looking for reassurance from a mother no longer there. Why do I rush to his weak animal sounds? I think maybe Skip's come to the rare moment of the deep six, but when I enter his room he's quietly composed with his stiff legs making a tent of the sheets.

After a week, I stop rushing to his door.

Instead, I listen to his cry of "Em, Em" as he calls out for my mother. The journey of each sound makes my mother's abbreviated name linger in the bones of the house, and I can't help but hear the honey of her short name as his pagan version of Om—the sound that allegedly contains everything that was, is, or is yet to be. His "Em" both startles and soothes, and makes me not want to rush to his side, but to have him quiet me with the immeasurable power of Em—the most basic sound containing all the other sounds of our family story. What does his unstoppable will to live tell me? *I will break away, but I will not be broken as long as I can make the sound of Em.*

Jack and Emily Younger have slept in different rooms for thirty years.

They have gone to their separate beds with the AC off, the overhead fans running, the windows cracked. The tree frogs, crickets, cockroaches, chiggers, palmetto bugs, and raccoons keep the Florida night awash in a creaturely flurry, but that dull roar only comforts my parents. I do better with water slapping the hull. Now, I no longer sleep, but rather cat nap beside my father's bed, his last boat. This keelboat he's building is a humbling thing, but I need for him to take his time because I have more to tell before he lights out for the ocean river he dreams of.

I hold his legs up while my mother scrapes and wipes, and Skip mewls like a gull with a busted wing.

"We're turning shit into gold," I tell her. My mother cocks her head toward me, permitting herself a half-chuckle.

"This is as good as it gets," I say. "You and me cleaning up Skip, working like this, side by side. We make a good team. Maybe we should go into business together."

"You're pressing your luck," she says, with a fleeting smile. This is the only warm look she offers during all our hard work. The machinery of our individual pain surfaces less often or, as she believes, the cards themselves are keen on concealment. After dishes, she retreats to her Bible and I return to my confession. If I were a religious sailor of any endurance, I might say she seeks out the light of the New Testament while I feel condemned to wander only through the Old one.

"When are you leaving?" she asks, after we've fluffed him.

"No immediate plans."

"I don't believe that for a minute."

"I hadn't given it much thought."

"Just give me a couple of days after he dies before you clear out."

"I'll hang in there, Mom."

"No, you won't. It doesn't come naturally to you to hang in there for anyone but yourself."

One step forward. Three miles back. I could get down on bended knee and weep another ocean and it wouldn't buy me any grace or mercy with her. Still, I'm humbled by the enduring side chapel of her pain, how it flickers, but never stops, never ceases to turn me back into shadow.

Her pain lashes as much as Hale lingers in this house.

I can sense him everywhere looking for entry in the gloaming and this searching of his makes me think something transfers back to life from death. The crossover the body makes must be a two-way hatch. What leaves, returns to fill in the blanks of push and pull. I feel Hale staring at me from a long way off, the loneliness of disappointment and chance imprisoned in his gaze. I aim to bring him closer so we can struggle for breath and talk our way out of our tangle. I move fast. He moves faster, not yet ready to make full contact.

When my mother sleeps, I rise again and go sit with my father.

Skip, I can imagine what you're thinking about now: how could I get this far into a jam with the wind against me? How could I get mixed up with so many shady characters in such a sunny place? The captain part of me, with a *Stardust* I still aim to deliver for Sam Wells, tells me to go hire any able-bodied man in a bar and call him crew, but I want the one thing no boat needs, fire. Fire is more fierce than love, money or food and that's what Rosario's all about. She offers no reassurance, no trust, no confidence, no safety, but she does throw off an unstoppable blaze, and I think with her on board, I might singe, sear, or otherwise burn any man, creature, or storm blocking my path further south.

Yet nothing's simple and easy in the DR.

If I stay shipwrecked here for a hundred years, how much will I ever know about this island brimming with smashed mangoes and scarlet-kerchiefed Haitians slashing at cane? The whites savor the Dominicans like butterscotch. The Dominicans treat the Haitians like lackeys. The government makes good money off all the hidden sexual rules. So many dance moves and tax collections are linked to the limp of the ball and chain. I want the careless beauty of this island, but I can't pick up the tempo—its soft tongue clicks and percussive shoe leather, its warring grunts and sugary winks.

With each rushed unbuttoning, I see only more of her mask.

A dock boy brings out a note from Rosario. It reads: "I want us to go to Samana before we leave the DR." Skip, it sounds promising, right? She says, before *we* leave the DR. Against my decision to get off the island as fast as I can, I agree to take a bus trip to Samana Bay because she wants to see a certain waterfall before *we* leave the island. In over my head, I board a bus with her and head east in the direction I want *Stardust* to go.

Once in Samana, we grab a second bus, a smaller *público*, and travel west of town. We stop at a *colmado* on the highway and buy icy Presidente beers. We leave a dirt road and climb a path inside thick woven green leaves. A light rain splashes our faces while the sun burns holes through clouds. We have the trail to ourselves. The coconut palms shoot out sideways from steep slopes, their trunks wrenched upwards with mathematically impossible curves to catch the sun. The air stings sweet with rotting fruit. At the waterfall summit, the water hangs back, not wanting to plunge, not wanting to shoot out into air and fall into a gorge and down a hundred-foot cliff. I drape my arms around her and taste the sweat on her neck, thinking this is all we know to do. Like island lava blast from underground pools, we just keep burning down and cooling off in a performance neither of us understands.

"Wait," she says. ""There are some pools below. You can have me down there." She says those words, "you can have me" with such casual splendor I want to set aside any doubts about who is using whom. It seems so impossibly right that sex with her is this clear and undefended. So right that she and I should take and take and not feel guilty for our greed. We loop around the top of the waterfall and follow a path back down. At the pools, we strip, plunge into water, then climb up on rocks.

How do I give her nakedness its due?

How do I honor the broad sail of her torso and the tightly curving orb of her backside? Inside the leafy green of this wet place, she glides again with ease into the lowest of three terraced pools. The cinnamon-amber of her shoulders is lit with layers of successive resin flows. If only I could paint the rare brown beauty she is and capture the pendulous cloud of her breasts cut with pink-orange sky. If only there were enough time to invent a way to stop time, so I might allow these fugitive Samana colors to seep under my skin, so they might find me again when I'm a dying sailor.

In some less wild place, Rosario might be secretive about her body, or quick to keep her clothes within easy reach, but she's oblivious to everything but the pleasure of the current rushing between her legs. She throws handfuls of water into the air and waves for me to come into the eddy, but I don't want to stop watching her framed by a colonnade of royal palms, pink orchids, breadfruit trees. This is not a performance I'm watching, but a perfection.

Great fear and hesitation wait for each of us down the road, but here in Samana, there's nothing but the lovely pull of skin to propel us into the slow end of the waterfall. Only later, after we nibble oranges and drink Presidente beers, do we spread out a blanket. First she says, "Do whatever you want to me, but I want to feel you come inside." Still later, in the tangle of switching positions from front to back, she says, *"Chíngame como una puta."* Whatever gentle affection once flourished between us now turns into a fierce shredding of skin, her face crimped with something like shame and contempt toward herself, toward me.

We board a bus back to Puerto Plata around noon with a group of Dominican children tugging our sleeves, clamoring for coin, seeking comfort. I'm annoyed by this invasion. The roar of the waterfall is replaced with the cries of children who want more of everything they think we carry in our pockets. I look at her thinking she too, after our sexual immersion, must be impatient with this pestering chatter, but her eyes throw off a wild shine. She laughs hard enough to cry.

"I've got an idea," I say to Rosario, who plays patty-cake with one of the girls. "After St. Thomas, how about if we come back here? We could even keep a boat in the bay."

"No one lives in Par-a-dise," Rosario says impishly, her voice drawing out a trill as high as the voices of the children. "You only come here to visit." For the next two hours, she jumps around the bus orchestrating word games and songs I can't follow. She uses her hands like a baton and laughs easily at the frisky pranks of boys and girls, enchanted with the speed of their inventions. She holds one sullen boy on her lap until he starts to clap and tap. Later, in the burnt light of late afternoon, she sits becalmed, listless, somnambulant. She looks at me from some other silent, interior quarter, neither happy nor unhappy, but rather suspended. Whatever joy I take from her, she always takes back and buries somewhere else I can't find.

"Thanks for helping Philip," I say, breaking into the cage of where she has retreated.

"He might be in jail," she says, not looking at me.

"The comandante would have paid me a visit."

"Maybe you're right. What now?" she asks flatly, looking out the window at a girl kicking a path through a mound of coconut trash, tin cans and tire welts.

"I want you to come with me," I say, reaching out to grip her waist.

"So you don't get lonely out there?"

"Maybe," I say. "But if anyone's been hungry, it's been you."

My head throbs as the bus hits a mile-long stretch of potholes.

"I'm leaving tomorrow morning," I say. "Tell me you'll be there on the dock."

"Still thinking about it," she says, with a long look that follows the girl walking through trash at the side of the road. "You want me to be something I'm not. You've created a story in your head about who I am, what I can do for you, but it's not a story I can read." She takes my hands as if soothing the hands of a child.

"I don't care who you are," I lie, wanting her very much to be the source of my forgetting and my finding.

"You want us to run in the same direction, but you must know there's danger all around us that can't be changed."

"I don't know what you're talking about," I lie again, weighing the risks that Rosario *might* be Jesse's accomplice and shipmate. I storm the distance between *might* and *is* and find nothing to stop the surge of faith that she'll come with me. The half of her that's mine I still intend to make whole. "I need to know now whether you're coming with me."

"I'll let you know tomorrow morning early. I'll meet you at *Cristo* at 6:00 A.M."

"Where?"

"At the Christ statue, up on the mountain."

"Why up there?"

"For good luck. We'll ask Him to bless our voyage," she says, uncurling her hand and revealing a piece of golden amber, the size and thickness of my thumb.

"What's this?" I ask, intrigued by the clarity of the gold in my hands.

"The only stone that floats," she says. "It's your proof you'll see me on the mountain. It's the most valuable thing I own. A gift from me." I pinch the thumb-shaped piece of resin between my thumb and forefinger, hold it up against the window, and see two mosquitoes coupled inside, their wings and legs wrapped around each other in a sexual death grip.

"Is this who we are, two mosquitoes fucking each other before they die?"

"They're survivors of the fire," she says. "Keep it, for luck."

"I want you," I say, needing something like love to carry me out of the backwater of everything I can't release on my own.

"I know," she says with a broad, open smile not unlike the one I saw when we first met on the dance floor in Luperón. She returns to playing with the children. I want to get back to Puerto Plata. I want this bus ride never to end. I want my whiteness to vanish inside the sexual blur of her mulatto skin and I want to get off this island now.

There's nothing to do, Skip, but wait for the first light of another day. *Stardust* is ready. I've repaired her jenny. I've realigned her engine. I've made her hatches watertight. I will leave tomorrow and Rosario will come with me. This much I know.

CHAPTER XV

I turn away from the children and Rosario and fall asleep on the bus ride back to Puerto Plata. When I awake, she's gone, Skip. I head toward the Malecon, thinking maybe I've only dreamt our sojourn in Samana. Maybe the waterfall never fell. Maybe the love we spoke of was just another beautiful lie in a beautiful place. While mapping out the truth or falsehood of Samana, I see something that also feels like part of my unending dream puzzle: the name *Jimmy's* is painted in black letters on white concrete.

Inside, Jesse nestles in a wicker chair, as quiet as a bowl of passion fruit. For a half turn on a winch, I think, *walk on by*, but my curiosity, fear, and anger slow me down and steer me toward her. She wears a pink silk blouse, canary-yellow skirt cinched with a white rope belt, and a straw hat tilted down for shade. Her plump green parrot rocks on her shoulder. I walk past the waiter, pull up a chair.

"I'm told Jimmy serves a mean grouper with mango-lime chutney," I say, inventing a menu entrée.

"Wouldn't know," Jesse says. "I only come here to drink and think."

"Come on. What are you doing here?"

"I've got friends in town. And you?"

"Boat repairs."

"Thorny Path too much to handle?"

"It kicks pretty good, especially when you're on the dodge from another boat."

"Wouldn't know about that," she says, sipping her rum punch.

"What would you know about?"

158

"The beaches are pleasant," she says. "The rum's cheap, not too dark. My parrot Rosie likes the merengue bars," she says, feeding a spoonful of rice and peas to her swiveling green parrot who snips at me with its black wooden tongue.

"You've got Rosie upset," Jesse says, as the bird ambles from one shoulder to another.

"Breaks my heart," I say through clenched teeth.

"*Whack his pee-pee. Whack his pee-pee*," Rosie shrieks.

"If you're looking for Jimmy's coke," I half-whisper, "it's gone, washed overboard, kaput."

"Oh please," she groans, throwing her arms up while the parrot jumps in unison. "You think I give a fuck about the coke you stole from Jimmy. That's chump change," she smiles with a spark of frosted diffidence.

"So you're working with Jimmy?"

"Our paths do cross now and then."

"Where's my Avon life raft? Where's my thousand bucks?" I shout, happy to have multiple grievances to lay at her feet, but also reluctant and unprepared to duel with the woman who engineered Philip's rendezvous with two baseball-bat thugs.

"Look, I'm here to get some R&R before I go back to work."

"And what work is that?"

"I deliver boats like you," she says, her eyes flashing around the open-air restaurant as though looking for reinforcements. "It's not much of a career," she adds dryly. "There's no retirement plan. No health insurance. But it beats working on a shrimper."

I draw my chair up closer and lean into her face where I smell lemon-peel clinging to the rum swizzle-stick she holds in her teeth. Over her parrot's head, the Malecon quivers and strains forward into its usual hunger for merengue, fish stalls, coffee, rum, and sexual distraction. It's like watching oil snake across water, the rainbow swirl of it sheltering the pretty girl hawking painted, hollow-log masks, guiding the blind boy balanced on his father's shoulders, pushing the gray beard with his wheelbarrow of straw hats and Christ statues. The street itself slides behind Jesse's shoulders like a series of waves and counter-waves stumbling over reefs of the poor and the cruise-ship rich.

"I don't know what you're all about, but I want you to stay clear of *Stardust*. If I ever see you near my boat, I'll throw you overboard along with your fucking parrot."

"Tough words for somebody who's been chasing a whore up and down every back alley in Puerto Plata."

"What do you know about Rosario?"

"She's a favorite twenty-dollar girl in this town."

"Not anymore," I pounce. "She's my new crew member."

"What did you say?" Jesse snaps back, her voice quavering, her shoulders raised, her fingers bending a cigarette. "Rosario's not going anywhere."

"So you do know her by more than reputation?"

Jesse says nothing while she feeds her parrot a lime wedge.

"Were you dancing with her the other night?" I demand, pinning her against the back of her chair. Before Jesse can reply, the parrot skims over her shoulder and bites my cheek, drawing a thin ribbon of blood.

"Even my parrot's got a better grip on this place than you do," she says. "You don't know shit about what's going on. This is a very dangerous place. If I were you, I'd leave your boat here and catch the next plane for Miami."

"How did you know I was in Puerto Plata?" I fire.

"I didn't. I told you, I vacation here. After the Bahamas, this island is a refreshing change of pace. By the way, whatever happened to Philip? I've been looking for him," she asks.

"He left the island."

"Why so soon?"

"He got beat up. Don't suppose you know about this?"

"The comandante's the only one who keeps score around here. Or maybe you haven't figured that out yet," she says, stroking the ruffled crown of her parrot. "I know you may find this hard to swallow, but you and me, we're not that far apart. We've got a lot more in common than you think. The only difference is, I get what I want and you keep dreaming about it. You're probably stupid enough to think you're still going to deliver *Stardust* to St. Thomas. This island is your last stop. The comandante will see to that. You'll never get out of here."

"The comandante and I are on good terms," I say, testing her bravado with a souped-up lie.

"No one's on good terms with him. Not even himself," she says.

"Just tell me what you want, Jesse."

"I want everything you want," she says. "And a lot more."

"But you have Jimmy Q," I say, knowing by now I don't want to duel with this pro. "You have boats, planes, hotels. You don't need to mess with me. I just want to get *Stardust* to St. Thomas in one piece and get on with my life."

"Too much has already happened," she says with a look of wild sorrow that makes me think, for a moment, she'll help me swim out of this octopus ink. Then, with something like regret cracking her voice, she says, "Deals have been made. Lives have been lost. Nothing can be undone."

"Why not?" I say, placing my hands on hers. "We can make another deal. Let me try."

"There's no going back from here, you know that as well as I do." She turns away from the verandah, the parrot riding shotgun on her shoulder, the two of them vanishing into a crowd of Dominicans.

I suck on an orange slice and reel in the last few minutes, trying to sort out what Jesse left in, what she left out. I want to despise or pity her, but I can't summon anything more than a cramped desire to put as much water between myself and her as possible. When the waiter comes, I realize the barracuda has struck again. She slinks away without paying her bill. I drop a twenty on the table and grab a box of matches with *Jimmy's* printed on the top along with the picture of a whale, only its flukes showing.

I walk into the harbor *comida* and buy as many cans of Dinty Moore stew and hard English biscuits as I can carry. There's no time to get Jesse right. No time to figure out how she might complicate the next twenty-four hours. I walk back to the dock, weighted down with two sacks of groceries. While I argue with myself about the meaning of Jesse's return, the comandante stands at the Customs office fixed like an unblinking sentinel.

Here is a man, unlike me, who appears to live happily among burning coals without ever needing to grip the fire-tongs.

"I'd like to have a little chat," he says. "Come inside." Inside a belt of sunlight where I stand, the rain bursts like rum from a broken bottle. Rain clings to my shirt and face. My wet clothes stand in stark contrast to his dress khaki uniform.

"Shipping out?" he asks, sitting behind a mahogany table red as the skin of a rotten mango.

"Tomorrow," I say bluntly, not wanting to stay in his company any longer than necessary.

"When are you planning to pay up your harbor fees?"

"How much is it?" I say, spitting the words.

"The harbormaster tells me you owe $452."

"What? There must be some mistake."

"I don't think so."

"*Chinga madre*," I mumble.

"What did you say?" The comandante takes out his Colt and spins it on the table. "Let's play a little game," he says. "I'll spin the gun and if the butt points toward me, you pay nothing. If the shaft points toward you, I'll shoot you now. Then, it will be easy for you to forget you owe me any money."

"I'm not playing your stupid game. You jacked up my bill."

"We're cheating you, Matt Younger?"

"Yeah, you're cheating me," I say, standing up and turning toward the door. "You can't get away with this."

The comandante smiles, but no teeth show. He says, "We're here till midnight, as always, if you want to pay up tonight."

"How convenient," I reply.

Minus the $200 I'd paid to the mechanic from Santo Domingo and the twenty I just forked over for Jesse's unpaid bill, I have about $700 left of the four thousand that Sam Wells, the owner of *Stardust*, gave me in West Palm Beach. After the comandante pockets his share, I'll have a little over $200 bucks to get to St. Thomas. As I stow my cans of salt stew, crank up the engine to top off a charge on both batteries, I realize the son of a bitch has me twisting on a gaff. Maybe Jesse's right, and the comandante has no intention of letting me leave Puerto Plata.

The afternoon breaks down into more risk and reward than any God should allow. Someone has scribbled on the blackboard in my head in large white chalky letters, but I can't decipher the script. Does Jesse know the cocaine's still on board? Why is the comandante pissing in the oil pan by wanting more money than he's due? Why are there two guys rowing out to see me? I scurry below. "Goddamn it, Philip, why did you steal my gun?" I mutter. I peel off my shirt, kick off my sandals, run topsides, and prepare to dive off the transom.

"Jimmy would like to see you," the one slightly bald Dominican man says while the boat is still twenty feet away from *Stardust*.

"Jimmy?"

"Your friend from the Bahamas. He'd like to buy you a rum."

"Where?"

"At Jimmy's."

"Of course," I say, thinking that now my goose is fully cooked and just waiting to be carved up and served. I climb down into a rowboat and go back to the dock with the two men. The three of us walk past the *comandancia*, then turn onto the Malecon. Jimmy slouches at a table inside a spool of cigarette smoke. He wears a wrinkled white cotton sport coat, a Pittsburgh Pirates baseball cap, and a T-shirt with an image of a big wave breaking that reads, "*When it swells, ride it.*"

"Glad you could join me," Jimmy says, his Adam's apple glinting like the head of a railroad spike.

"My pleasure," I say, wishing for all the world I still had my gun.

"Isn't this a great little town? A heaven to die for. You know it used to be the port of choice for pirates back in the sixteenth century?"

Jimmy pours a glass of rum over crackling ice and slides it to my side of the table.

"Yeah, I've seen the fort," I say, taking a hard swig, thinking it could be my last. "I figured it wasn't built by Disney."

"It didn't do any good. Pirates owned this island for a hundred fucking years. And now I own it or will soon enough."

"I assume you didn't drag me here to talk history," I say, feeling like a patsy for getting myself shrink-wrapped again by a cocaine pirate preacher.

"Why not? It's all the same story. Pieces of eight, back then. White powder now. What's the difference? What's in short supply, always jacks up the sticker price. Tell me I'm not right as rain. You took the bait. And you did good. You've got a gift. You found the drop, stole it, got it on board your boat, gave the *Citadel* the slip, and disappeared."

"Almost disappeared," I correct him. "And we lost the coke overboard."

"Pity about that. At first, I thought you'd stashed it under the floorboards, but the comandante told me his men looked around. If he says it ain't there, it's history."

"He's on the payroll too."

"Him and me are old friends," Jimmy says. "Good man. A piece of Gibraltar. Look, I think you might like my business. Boats, guns, women, and the occasional hit to remind you that life is a bad joke where nobody gets out alive. The upside is, steady work. There's always the next candy boat. The next adventure. The next girl. We've got plans for casinos, swanky retreats, whorehouses, you name it. Hell, it's better than the Navy. Here, try my hat on," Jimmy says, tipping his cap like a slugger.

"No thanks." I say.

Jimmy smiles weakly, "I've got another offer, my last offer."

"I can't wait," I say, knowing there ain't no way I'm going to be able to stiff this guy twice.

"I want you to go to French Harbor, Roatan, in Honduras. It's a sleepy island with no electricity, no police, no trouble. There's a sixty-foot Hatteras moored there. I want her delivered off the coast of Brownsville in one piece."

"Texas?"

"Right."

"Hell of a trip."

"It's worth $250K with $100K up front."

164

"What about *Stardust?*"

"Fuck that piece of junk. Besides, it's going to be impounded once I tell the comandante to link your fag friend with the death of the two Americans in Santo Domingo."

"How do you know about that?"

"Little birds talk to me."

"What's Jesse doing here?" I ask, thinking I really have slipped off the chart by talking with a man who takes pride in betrayal, corruption, the occasional murder. I hear my soul blasting a hole through my spine, telling me to run fast in any direction, but my rum brain tells me I can live another day, even if my soul departs and never returns. That's right, Skip, you should know this about your only living son: I've come to that part of the story called *insanity*.

"She's been working for me since she was a teenager," Jimmy says. "I taught her everything. She covers the sea. I do air. Ain't she a pretty shrimper for a wasted old crop-duster?"

"That's rich," I say. "You two are the perfect couple."

"She can suck the sparkle out of a silver dollar and spit back change. That's why I married that Florida cracker."

"You two are married?" I ask, feeling like there's no way out of this funhouse I've built except through more fear and astonishment.

"Cozy as Ozzie and Harriet," Jimmy says. "We're even talking babies. Imagine that? Me sitting around telling stories from the coke wars to a little snot, saying how I bought this customs man and had that one knocked off, how we landed planes on little scratch-hole runways no longer than a cunt hair. How we owned islands and governments. How we recruited sweet kids in Florida and turned them into ace criminals. You up for a second round on Jimmy's merry-go-round?"

"What if I take a pass?"

"Carry or die."

"Clear enough," I say.

"Look, I believe in second chances. You've got real talent for this work. I like that in a sailor—controlled recklessness, spunk, an asshole with a set of balls. That business of sailing your boat

165

through the Silver Reef. That was a good trick. You do a couple of deals with me and you can live high on the mighty pirate hog. That's a promise and a Jimmy Q guarantee. And don't worry about Jesse. You'll get used to her after a while."

"When do you want me on the plane?" I ask, wanting only to get free of this conversation any way I can.

"Tonight."

"How about tomorrow morning?" I say.

"I'll book you a seat on the 8:00 A.M. flight."

"My money?"

"Waiting at the airport," Jimmy says, pleased with himself. "A man in a black-and-white fisherman's jersey will have your down payment in a briefcase."

"I'm a little short till then."

"*Quanto*?"

"$500 would do," I say, digging a hole for myself that seems plenty deep already.

Jimmy reaches into his pocket and peels off five one-hundred-dollar bills from a gold money clip. "Here," he says, throwing the cash across the table.

"Go ahead. Find yourself a girl who'll take you for a pony ride. Live it up," Jimmy says. "You're a lucky man with a future. Think about it. Make a half million and never wear a suit and tie. Retire before you're thirty. Take on a second career as a public servant. All that or die tomorrow if you trick me one more time. Carry or die, it's a simple choice, no?"

CHAPTER XVI

I return to the Malecon, looking north toward the Turks & Caicos, wishing I were still there, pinned down, wondering what the hell to do next with the Trades blowing down on me. Skip, as bad as that place was, it feels easy compared to the human boil of Puerto Plata. I tell myself all I need is to stay alive long enough to meet Rosario at the Christ. I need much more than this, Skip, but I reduce all my requirements for happiness to one meeting on a mountain. I have about eighteen hours to kill before we meet, and nowhere to go in the meantime that's safe.

The sky runs ragged with scarlet and orange streaks as if drenched by a flame-tossed ocean. I stop in the shade of a wrought-iron balcony to watch the sky bleed off the page. I squat in the road and feel blood seeping from the side of my face where Jesse's parrot took a bite. "First the mountain," I tell myself. "Then, I'll sail away from these shifting sands for good. And fuck Jimmy."

"Looks like the cat got the best of the dog," a man says, squatting next to me. I look over and see Rosario's brother-in-law, Desmond. His bright copper face drives away the sunset. His dreads hang by his thigh in a netted bag. His eyes swivel in his head like he's just been tossed from the car wreck he calls home. I hadn't seen them before but his fingernails must be six inches long and painted the blue-green of the Thorny Path.

"Didn't think you had anything to do with wicked cities," I say.

"Had a night sweat vision about Rosario. Thought I'd look her up and tell her what I saw."

"You'll have to go to the mountain to find her," I say.

"You do right by her, Mistah Sailor Man, when you make contact."

"Hope to."

"Not so sure you know how."

"I'll try not to let that compliment go to my head."

"You never know what you don't know, and you don't know much." Desmond says, rocking on his haunches.

"Care to translate?"

"The heart is a cockeyed compass, its needle as likely to be set by true north as it is by the southern harbors where the fickle girls swim. If you want her, tell her that. Putting the desire out might be as good as having it. But maybe you can't 'cause you still got dollar signs for eyes. And that means Jimmy. That bad spirit will kill you. And you won't know you're walking dead till you start smelling up the beach."

"You know Jimmy?"

"You live in the DR long enough and that typhoid Mary finds you coming up short. He's like a second Columbus."

"How so?" I ask, knowing full well I won't get a word in once Desmond gets on a downwind roll.

"My sleepwalkers say he be the juicy worm in the apple. Hires little girls to do his skulking. Keeps them high as Pluto. Makes 'em steal keys to all the important doors."

"Don't tell me," I say.

"Rosario's worked for Jimmy for an eternity times two. Wants to get out. Don't know how. If you try to escape, Jimmy throws you to the hogs running through the cane."

"Why are you bringing me up to speed?" I ask, knowing now that everyone on this sailing trip knows more than the captain about what's going on.

"Maybe is another big ocean, but maybe you can help. Don't like white men. Don't trust them. Don't trust you 'cause you could be holding out a dog biscuit or looking to have me torn apart by dogs. Maybe if you were dead, I could trust you. The sorry fact is, I need you alive. I saw what Columbus and his boys done. Nothing pretty about white folks. But Rosario's blood kin. She's headed crooked in the arms of Eve."

"What did you say?"

"You heard me."

"What's this woman's name?"

"It rhymes with love," he says with a pasted smile.

I drop my head into my hands.

"Jesse's married to Jimmy," I say, not looking up.

"Only in the funny papers," Desmond scoffs. "You get married and divorced to someone in the DR while standing up in an octopus bar. Jesse don't know her own heart 'cause Jimmy sliced it up. She hates him but she loves what she hates. Everything's upside down. A snake eating its tail. She's a jailer who sells freedom. He's the warden who keeps all his jailers locked up."

"Rosario's coming with me," I say defensively.

"How many times you heard her talk about men?" Desmond says, slapping his thigh.

"Then how do you explain our. . . ?" I protest. "We've probably had sex every day for a month."

"It's right there looking at you like a spark in a piece of buried charcoal," Desmond says. "She's thinks your thing could be just the thing she needs."

"What pill do I take now, doc?" I ask, wondering how to decipher the meaning of charcoal spark.

"You got three problems picking your bones," Desmond says pensively as if arguing a case before a judge. "No matter what they say, Jimmy and Jesse want you dead 'cause you are just too much bother. Rosario wants you alive. And I want you to keep Rosario out of the evil wind blowing down between you all. Ain't no way I'm gonna let her die in a druggie shootout like her sister, my soul wife vision guide. You only one both smart and dumb enough to give Jimmy the slip."

"Should I try to get Rosario on a flight out of here?" I ask, at a loss for how to slip past Jesse and Jimmy in one piece.

"Tend to your boat, my man," Desmond says.

"I'm not sure the comandante will let me leave without another inspection."

"Don't worry about the comandante. If you've got Rosario on board, you'll be handy dandy."

"How can you be sure?"

"Trust me, all will be revealed in due time."

Desmond duck walks around a corner and leaves me squatting in a pink marbled swirl of shadows. I listen to the sound of the Trades clicking in a nearby palm. Somewhere, far down an alley, I hear the scrape of a merengue soul comb against a washtub, and for the first time, I realize that telling the truth in the DR is an alien concept. There are only grains of truth and all of them tumble and dissolve in the brisk currents that lead here.

It's two in the morning. The rain pings inside thunder. The wind scratches the screen. There's so much, Skip, I've never told you, so much I need to tell you so you can know the real Matt Younger, such as I am.

Let me start with a poolside memory before we plunge beneath the waves . . .

You and I and Mother are at the Florida state finals swim meet. I'm watching the glow in your eyes as you watch Hale, the captain of the team. He's always the anchor man in any relay. Maybe it's because you hate swimming yourself that you find him so god-like as the smooth length of his body knifes the lane so there's virtually no splash, no wake, just this thin line of smoke rising out of a razor cut. You who love to be on the water, but never in it, are mesmerized by his seamless kick, charge, and flawless somersault off the wall. "How in the hell does he do that?" you say to me, but you might have said, "Only in heaven are sons this perfect," for how enchanted you are with his performance. I yell and clap just as loud as you, the tears welling my eyes because the whole auditorium, even Florida's senator who writes Hale's letter of recommendation to the Naval Academy in Annapolis, can see that Hale's the master of the game and will not be beaten, not now, not ever. No one ever comes close. He doesn't even have to seek the spotlight because his times are so good. No one in the country has better clock times in so many different events. The Olympic trainers shower him with letters every week. They lust for a chance to mold him into their champion. To me, in our shared bedroom, he scoffs at their adulation, and you never ask him why he doesn't want to be crowned an even greater hero than he already is. The fact is he doesn't give a fuck for glory. He's repelled by it. For everyone who wants him to become a Wheaties box, he seeks out some other point of danger that'll insure that never happens.

When he reaches out with his stroke, he's not looking to scoop water but to grab the dark matter of the universe that can't absorb light. The knife stroke you admire is his invisible signature. He never wants anyone to see him or catch him. You never know how he cringes from the spotlight. You never catch him sneaking from the house with this funhouse glare twitching in his eyes. Never hear him rant against the safe and the familiar. Never meet his skanky, painted women and his string of night friends sprung from the underworld. You never see in him the restless prince broken loose from the castle.

I tell myself I can't be the one to end the world's love affair with my brother. I can't blow the whistle, lower the boom, launch the ambush. I can't tell anyone the truth about the mighty Hale Younger because no one will believe me. They will only pity my jealousy, reject my conclusions. No one knows what dark matter is, where it comes from, and why there's so much of it, and you and Mom never knew who Hale was and neither did I.

Now, for the bucket with a hole in it, the one we all use to bail with . . .

Hale is scary quick in math and science, almost too smart and easily bored with the pitiful college requirements of Ft. Lauderdale High School. Where I barely squeak through Algebra II, Hale breezes through calculus, trig, physics. Due to overcrowding, the high school runs three shifts, the first one starting at 6:30. By noon, Hale is on the beach picking up coeds on vacation. He's just turned eighteen but looks twenty-three. Blonde, handsome, and Jimmy Stewart wholesome, he stands tall with broad, square shoulders and a strong back built from miles of butterfly kick. As much fish as man, Hale has his own plans for becoming a Navy Seal after Annapolis. So what goes wrong in his life and in mine? Why does Hale one day turn an ear to a man with an offer? Boredom? A one-time act of teenage rebellion as he grooms himself to join the best and the brightest? Can Lust, Gluttony, Avarice, Sloth, Wrath, Envy, Pride lay any claim to his descent?

Hale asks me if I could stand to make $40,000 bucks in one night.

My older brother, the good, the brilliant, the gifted, the one you stake all your silver on, the one who will redeem any shortcomings in our family, that one asks me if I want to make forty thousand in one night. He might have asked me if I want to drive the getaway car after he robs a bank, but I go along with him because it's Hale Younger talking. He's the wise one, the strong one. He and I shall go out upon the deep waters where he can do no wrong.

All I have to do is go with him out in the Gulf Stream on a cigarette boat and meet a freighter. Why in the hell didn't I say no? One night we drive to a beach between Old Rhodes Key and Key Largo. Dirt roads. Scrub palm. No light poles. No signs. A rare deserted spot within the scrim of South Miami. We meet a boat there at a fishing dock. A Cuban named Reinaldo slouches at the wheel. He wears a gun. We step on board. As the twin Mercedes fires up, I say to Hale, what are we doing here? Hale says it's easy money. So easy, you won't believe it, he says, like he's done this before. Tied stern to the dock, the boat turns the blub blub of its idle into a growl and shoots into the salt darkness like a comet. The razor-thin bow never cuts through waves; it rises above them, shearing off curls. In less than an hour, we meet a freighter ten miles off shore in the Gulf Stream. What do we have to do, I ask him, with an arm around his shoulder. Work fast, say nothing, Hale says. But what are we getting? It's simple, he says. We pick up a couple dozen crates of cocaine and get our cash.

The *Argentine* rocks in the waves like some lonely panting sea beast. Its silhouetted hulk is streaked with rust and chain marks. No visible captain. No running lights. No life. The chug of her enormous engines holds her bow into the edge of the hot-pouring Gulf Stream. The backwash seethes white around her transom and throws off eddies thick as cream. Our cigarette boat rides the shear of the freighter's hull.

One man throws open a cargo door and hands us banana crates. We work with the rise and fall of the waves. I try to meet the man's eyes on board the freighter. Reinaldo sees another boat approaching at high speed. He lunges for the throttle. The cigarette boat lurches backward and bangs against the freighter. Hale has his arms extended, reaching for a crate. He catapults overboard. The waves pinch him between the two boats and suck him down.

My left hand flings behind me and catches against the cargo door as it slams shut. I jerk my hand back from the dark hull. I fall to the cockpit floor as the boat leaps forward. I black out. I awake smeared with blood and a scream trailing from my mouth like a skipped stone back to the freighter and the slap of water against the hulls, and the sight of Hale using the water-lift of the boat to time his grab of the last crate. The cigarette boat bolts back to the dock.

Reinaldo throws a thick pile of bills at my feet. Get out of here, he says. My brother, my brother, I cry like something split in two with an axe. Why did you leave without him, you son of a bitch. He could have made it. He could have got back on board. You don't understand. He was a fish for Christ's sake. Let me have this boat. I want to go back out there. Find him. He could still be alive. I don't know what you're talking about, the man says. What other guy, I never saw another guy. Get the fuck out of here, he says, waving a gun. I scoop up the wad of bills and run. I drive with my claw-like hand thrust under my armpit. The blood and tears grind into my eyes until I can't see the white lines of the road. I pull off, blank out. I drive to an emergency ward in Coral Gables. When they ask me about insurance, to cover the cost of suturing the wound, I pay cash. I throw down big bills just as they were thrown at me.

I drive back into Ft. Lauderdale with first light.

I take a back road thick with okra and strawberry fields, thinking no one will see me, but I'm wrong. I count twelve turkey buzzards standing severed from the sky like a row of slouched and baldheaded undertakers flush with cash and aproned in blood. I lay on the horn and each in turn gives a diffident, spraddle-legged hop out of the path of my wheels. They feed on a roadside dog. I watch them in the rearview until I can no longer see their long pink faces flashing beneath black coats, but I know they know I carry the same smell of death under my wheel rims.

In the next few months, my hand takes on the feral twist of a hunted creature digging for pockets. I tell you and Mom a highway breakdown story, how a jack collapses as I'm changing a tire on my VW bug, and it smashes my hand. I don't recognize myself in the mirror. When you ask me, Skip, if I know anything about Hale's disappearance, I say hell no. You punish me with silence. I punish you with lies.

Somehow, you know I'm guilty.

Maybe that's why you never express any sympathy for my empty socket. Mother avoids looking at me as if she too knows the origin of my missing finger. I want to buy a 6-string guitar but I don't because I'm convinced the fret board of any guitar will resist the shape and feel of my damaged left hand, for it too, like you, will sense the truth behind my lies and turn silent and unforgiving.

The night I decide to quit school and run away to sea, I can't shake loose from another memory and another story I've never told you about.

I'm riding my Schwinn home from a game when a Studebaker wagon skids past me, dips off the shoulder into a slight ravine and flips over. I'm the first person to get to the car and see a man's face as he hangs upside down in his seatbelt, the wheels spinning and the engine still running. I try to open the car door, but it's dented shut. The driver can't free himself and there's no way I can force the door open, so he and I just look at one another on an innocent street in a well-lit neighborhood in Vermilion, Ohio. With the engine sputtering and the window bound tight by the bent frame, I can't hear his words, but his look is clear enough. *This shouldn't be happening. This is my street. This is my neighborhood.* His face is wet with sweat. His eyes, swelling and anonymous. I tell him not to panic because that's what you always tell me, Skip. I know he thinks the car might catch fire because the engine's still alive. The longer we look at each other, the more I think the car might burst into flame. And then I do step back because I'm ten and I don't know what else to do and I don't want to burn. The man's Studebaker has flipped at a bend in the river road where there are no houses. I call out, but no one hears me. I call again. I will have to leave the man in order to get help. Maybe, somewhere inside his own scalding tears, he knows I'm just a boy who will have to leave and find someone, but another part of his face says, *stay here, stay with me.* I jump back on my Schwinn and I pedal so hard I fall off my bike and skin both knees. Then, I hear the explosion and I know the fire has found him before I can find help. You are out sailing with friends. I sit on the porch and listen to the sirens from a long way off racing to the river.

The look of shock and disappointment on the man's face, the enduring puzzlement, the bewildering shame of having nodded off at the wheel while driving home, that look I saw again for only a second on Hale's face as my hand smashes inside the slide of the cargo door and he catapults backwards into the drink.

This shouldn't be happening. This is my street. This is my neighborhood.

All that confusion I saw in my brother's face followed by *stay here, stay with me.*

Ever since the failure of those two nights, I feel certain trouble will eventually trip me up and I'll land face down in the drink. Most nights I just sit up and wait for the inevitable. My missing pinkie always reminds me how a nudge or shove on land might have changed Hale's decision to go out to the Gulf. As children making our first innocent deals we would reach for one another's pinkies and wrap them tight, look each other in the eye, and say "pinkie promise," and we kept those promises as if the world and its pleasures depended on our finger shake.

What should have been my promise to my brother?

God damn this sorry world to hell . . . I should have been able to keep him from vanishing into the slouch of his own Mr. Hyde. With each new swimming accolade, each new magazine article, and each new academic achievement, I could see him slipping into a greater hunger for something he couldn't win. Late at night, he would leave by our bedroom door with this glare fixed in his eyes that made me want to call out to you, Skip, but I never did. I should have been able to get him help before a drug freighter took him to task. Instead, I insure he'll finally be challenged in the water and will, at last, be broken by an ocean river so big it can swallow oil tankers on a sunny day. As far south as I go into the islands, his blood cries to me from the Gulf, so I'm always back there with him, hating him for not loving himself enough to avoid such a dark and fugitive place without reprieve.

CHAPTER XVII

Like my failing skipper, I sleep through much of the next day.

I too have become a creature of sea memory, more comfortable in the night when the thunder and rain lay down the law and I can picture a swell rising beneath me. But there are some differences between us. For him, memory is a long wave making itself new each day. What's cast up with the last tide withdraws by nightfall. What cracks open and is carried off by gulls returns for examination another day. For a sailor confined to a bed, all he sees, imagines, and hears is blue-rolling movement, a heartbeat older than stars. I want simply for my memory to be erased by an ancient mountain of water so high I can't see the top of the curl.

The day is over before I get up.

Before I start my night watch, Emily comes to tuck in her sailor home from the sea. I watch her from the doorway, thinking what a life, these two. Forty-five years in lust, in love, in marriage. So many logbooks from so many boat trips, most of them now lost or left behind. What cost, this adventure? I wonder what price you pay for molding to a sailor's caprice, for packing and unpacking his grief after his hero son drowns at sea?

On their first sail, the bending of love nearly breaks.

They will leave Sandusky, Ohio on a day sail. That's what he tells her it will be, a light, easy reach, nothing more than a day sail. Instead, he catches some freshening air and decides to sail the *Vivian,* a twenty-four-foot sloop he'd built the summer after he finished high school and named after his mother, to Put-In-Bay, the lovely harbor on South Bass Island with good protection except from the north. This is no easy reach. It's a twenty-mile sail across open water. Experienced sailors only need apply for this outing. It's also August on Lake Erie, meaning anything can happen before you can turn around and get back to land. One hour out, the sticky air smacks open. A series of line squalls tracks the *Vivian* like a magnetic needle. The waves break hard and fast over the bow. Skip thinks they may sink because his bailers can't keep up with the drenching attack. When they arrive in a wet dark shiver, they're startled by the fierceness of what they've shared. There's not a dry inch on the boat, not even below decks. A raw silence stings after he drops the hook. She hasn't thought to bring a change of clothes, a hairbrush. There's not a blanket in sight. No food. This was supposed to be a day sail, not a night sail. She can't remember seeing the sun. She feels queasy and panics, realizing she's bone-cold from the inside out. Even her bra and panties are soaked. She bites her lips until they bleed.

How does Skip salvage this maiden voyage with the Emily he'll marry, but has not yet proposed to?

He hails a water taxi that takes them to Lonz winery located on another smaller island in the harbor where they find a party in full swing. An accordion player sashays from table to table with a monkey in a red suit. A woman in silver bangles circles the monkey with the shimmer of her hips. A deck of cards flashes across a round table. In ten minutes, everyone at the winery calls out to one another on a first-name basis. Another woman staying at the winery loans my mother some dry clothes. Emily quickly forgets the crossing that nearly broke her with its falling walls of dark green Lake Erie water.

Bend but not break—this is the unspoken by-law of their marriage-voyage.

But after Hale dies and I quit school and vanish the first time into South America, their unraveling starts through Skip's serious drinking and his restless urge to keep moving. You always hear it said that no one life counts for very much, but one death? That's a different story. After a perfectly beautiful day of sailing, my mother will turn to Skip and say, "No parent should outlive a child. Only God can make this right."

Emily re-jiggers his pajamas so they aren't bunched at the knees and makes certain his rubber bed pad is dry. She smoothes out his sheets and snugs the cotton blankets to his chin the way he likes, and finally, fluffs his pillow. She leans in close and he whispers through the gravel of increasing lung congestion, "I did a lot of things wrong, Em, but I did one thing right. I met you. You're the one. I got lucky. Don't worry about me. What did you do to your hair? I love it like this. I'm just ducky. I got lucky. I saw this boat today down at Tiger Point. She's a beauty. You should see her lines. She's old, but I can bring her back. Pack up the old Chevy and let's go there just for a peek. We could take her out, just you and me. It's all good water ahead. All good water, Em. I got lucky when I met my Em."

She wants his tender rambles to reunite their bodies on some bunk, and she doesn't. She wants to stay and she wants to hide in her own room on the other side of the house. She wants the beginning and she wants the end. She wants to return to the blue Atlantic light of their wild middle years. She wants death to come. This time she sits for just a minute stroking their joined fingers. When she leaves, I enter. I sit next to my only skipper and start talking again.

I'm so taken, Skip, with Rosario's easy laying down of her body, I can't see death blooming around her. All I can do is watch and wait, knowing that with each hesitation, I may never get out of the DR, just as Hale never got out from under the churn of the Gulf Stream. I should be busy reviewing the charts and harbors, checking all of my boat's vital signs. I should be scrambling to redeem my failed contract to deliver *Stardust*. Instead, from the stern, I see Jesse approach the comandante at the government dock. He strikes a bright looming figure at night, well-groomed and hidden behind uniform, glasses, and pearl-handled gun. He and Jesse seem friendly, chatty, then like business partners at odds with the deal points. She leans her tits into him. He squares up, all jaw and holster. The comandante draws her away from his men and they walk together inside the Customs office. The two of them together make me hold my breath.

179

This much I know: Jesse is on Jimmy's payroll and she has her eye on Rosario. I need to find Rosario and get her off this island. I hail a boat and come ashore. I walk toward the *comandancia* and park myself in the lee of a bait-and-tackle stand next to it. Two hours pass beside the stink of day-old bait which gives me all the time I need to imagine the variety of traps that lay before me.

Jesse and the comandante leave Customs and vanish into the alley. I follow. They split up in a few blocks. I want to follow Jesse, but I stay with him. She might lead me to Rosario, but he's the boss with the gun, the one who'll decide if Rosario and I leave the DR in the morning. He circles back to the Malecon to Jimmy's place. The bar's empty of patrons. Jimmy's two bodyguards are asleep. The comandante walks past them. I follow him and press myself behind an opened door that looks into an office where Jimmy sits behind a desk. With a desk lamp and a stack of papers spread out before him, Jimmy could be a mid-level corporate manager staying late to catch up on his buy and sell orders. I plaster myself against a wall, every muscle taut, my throat pulsing, my tongue pressed against the roof of my mouth. Jimmy never hears the comandante enter his office.

"I've got something, Jimmy, to help with your insomnia," the comandante says.

Without looking up, Jimmy says, "How good of you to drop by. What did you bring me?"

"Some high-priced candy, my friend. 100% pure heroin."

As Jimmy raises his head, the comandante draws his pearl-handled .45 revolver and thrusts it in Jimmy's face. He stands with his legs apart, braced for balance and spring, his face a flame of concentration.

"What's this, comandante? Don't be stupid. You don't want to shoot Jimmy Q. He's your ticket to Paradise, your patron saint, your island brother."

Skip, I'm standing close enough to both men to see the sweat on their faces. I can see the room angles they reach for with their eyes, and I can hear their every word fill the room like a hammer on tin.

180

"No, I don't want to kill you. I want you to shoot yourself with this," the comandante says, holding the syringe with his left hand while, with his right, he squares the mouth of the gun against Jimmy's head.

"This is so unworthy of you. We're just beginning to make good deals since you came over from Santo Domingo. How much money do you want?"

"It's not about money. It's about Rosario," the comandante says. A shiver runs from my head to my feet when I hear her name.

"Rosario? Who's she?" Jimmy says.

"She's one of your drugged-out hookers. A girl that two of your men beat up, raped, and left on the beach for dead."

"Sometimes things get messy," Jimmy says, looking distracted by the comandante's allegation. "Surely you're only fantasizing about this girl. Look, if it's another one you want, no problema."

"Rosario's leaving the DR tomorrow," the comandante says, "and you're not going to stop her." I want to believe he's talking about Rosario and me leaving tomorrow, but how would he know this? Why would she tell him of all people?

"Jesse's the one you want," Jimmy says cagily. "She's the one spreading lies about me, about my men. I'm on your side. You can trust me. We're partners. Jesse I can replace, but not you."

"Jesse's no princess, but I trust her more than you," the comandante says without hesitation.

"Fuck her," Jimmy shouts.

"Your fucking days are over. It's time for Jimmy Q to take the long flight, but with no airplane." The comandante holds out the syringe. "You're going to inject this into that blue vein in your neck or I'm going to pull the trigger. Which shall it be?"

"This is no way to treat a friend," Jimmy whispers while I strain to hear through the cracked door. "We can deal this out," Jimmy says. "How 'bout let's start with a home in Barbados. Hell, I'll even throw in a Lear jet. A couple of blondes from Miami? You're much smarter than this. That tin badge you're wearing is nothing compared to what I've got in store for you. How would you like to be the head banana of this whole fucking republic. You could be the next presidente. We could do it, you and me. This little coke business is just the beginning. There's still casinos to build on the north coast. Then, the heroin trade. How many millions do you want? What's your favorite currency?"

I can see sweat beads pouring down Jimmy's forehead, his eyes flickering, his chest heaving, the machinery of his fear now running out of fuel. I look over at the bodyguards. They're still asleep. I squeeze tighter behind the door. As the comandante takes another step closer, Jimmy jams his hand under the desk. He also must feel the comandante's hand plunging a needle into his neck. Jimmy pulls a gun free, but before he takes aim, his head swoons, the color leaches from his face, and he falls backwards off his chair. He never launches a scream, but the thud of his head smacking the floor wakes his bodyguards.

Without seeing me, the two men burst through the office door with their guns drawn. The comandante drops to one knee and squeezes off six shots from his pearl-handled Colt .45. Each of the bodyguards jerks into the air from the force of the bullets before they too crumple to the floor. The comandante looks down at Jimmy, who glares out at the world with ballooned eyes as if he's a bottom fish drawn from the depths too fast. The comandante nudges each of the dead men with his boot.

I inch away from behind the door. It creaks. I leap down the hall as a bullet smashes the door, throwing splinters behind my back. I run hard, picturing again the plunge of the needle, the flash of his Colt, Jimmy falling backwards. The comandante follows, but I outrun him. I now know the streets around the Malecon well enough to zigzag back to the band shell in the center of town where the mishmash of hookers, treasure hunters, cruise-ship tourists, and shoeshine boys all flirt with the shiny edge of things just out of reach.

At the Hotel Castilla, I order a bottle of Brugal and consider my crumbs of frying bread jumping in the grease. The comandante has just killed Jimmy because he's angry about Rosario having been raped by Jimmy's men, but I don't buy this allegation any more than Jimmy did. If the comandante would kill a man who could make him rich, he sure as hell would be willing to kill me for what I just saw him do. And who is behind Jimmy's death by syringe? My former cook, Jesse Dove, the wandering peacock of cocaine menace. She put the comandante up to this rendezvous, but what does Jesse promise that makes him stick the golden goose with a heroin needle?

With each glass of rum, Skip, I drop a little farther into the bilge of this island until I'm hurled back to the chasm of the Gulf Stream where Hale tumbles over the gunwale, and the back flush of the freighter sucks him under, and even though he's part fish, he can't hold his breath long enough to resist the eddy of the prop wash. With each jolt of rum, I pull back the belt of Sargasso weed and snag him, and he looks at me with this radiant smile saying it's OK bro', I'm better now, there's no death where I live, I made it safely home. But I don't believe he can be so clear and wise after drowning under tons of black water so I move on, north for another boat, then further south until I wash up here and get drunk again with bullets flying after me.

Just like the old blues song says, "*I'm guilty and I'll be guilty for the rest of my life,*" but when I meet Rosario, I say "Fuck guilt." For being so brilliant and bound for the U.S. Naval Academy, Hale's just my dumb-fuck brother banking on easy money, and I'm shit-stupid blind for shipping out into the Gulf with him. With Rosario, I can blast new blood into my brain and change my life. With her, the rum tells me, I can untangle myself from the waves that drew Hale down.

The devil in a dress finds me. Jesse hurries into the hotel lobby, panicked, jumpy, distressed. She sees me at the bar, comes over, takes a gulp of my drink.

"Matt, I'm sorry about what I said earlier."

"You're never sorry, are you?"

"I'm in a jam with the comandante. I'm leaving tonight."

"How are you leaving?"

"I'm catching a plane."

"Rosario, where is she?"

"I haven't seen her."

"I don't believe you."

"The comandante has it in his head I'm running the coke traffic in and out of the DR and he wants to take it over."

"Are you running it?"

"No."

"He just killed Jimmy," I say, the rum talking more than common horse sense.

"Oh, my God. I'm next," she says, taking another gulp of my drink. There's some truth to her fear because Jimmy, before he died, pointed to her as the true source of the comandante's woes.

"I hope you didn't come looking for help," I say.

"No, I just want you to know I'm sorry for everything and I hope we both get off this island alive."

"That's my plan," I say. "Leaving tomorrow for St. Thomas."

"Good luck," she says.

I say nothing, not knowing what to make of Jesse Dove, not now, not ever. I nod and she bends over as if to kiss me on the cheek and I resist. This time, I turn away before she does.

CHAPTER XVIII

After hours of looking for Rosario in the bars and hotel lobbies of Puerto Plata, I walk away from the ocean up Avenida Colon toward the *teleférico* that carries tourists up the side of a mountain to the Christ statue. Before I turn left to walk up the hill, I glance into the bulb light of a *mercado*. A swart pig's head swings from a gambrel while another pig, a white one, splays on the table, its sockets a snarl of flies. I see a man under the eaves wearing a bloodstained apron and a thin-ribbed dog licking the stringy glop oozing from the pig's snout. As garish as this scene is, so is the moment that follows, when a young woman wearing a scooped-neck white top dances merengue with a mop handle, the dull wet stick alive in her hands as she lathers the pavement, soaking up the gummy mucus of the man's butchery, her hips sliding back and forth along an invisible line as if married to the pull of the stick.

I turn around and bump into an old woman with a basket of hog snapper, their orange tails a semaphore in the last spill of sun. She wears a stained straw hat over a red bandana. She rests the basket on one knee, wanting me to look wisely upon her fish and buy. Like other women I've met on the docks, she needs to sell her fish, so she'll get one fish to take home. I catch the smell of rum on her mouth. She's tired and she's strong and despite the furrows of her brow, she carries more than a hint of her former shine. She walks barefoot and her feet are toughened from walking. She probably lives in the hills above Puerto Plata and walks to the sea before first light. The sadness I read into her face is the sadness of a woman who no longer dances on a island where merengue is the only heavenly transport anyone cares to ride.

I reach into my pocket without picking out a fish.

She waves me off, saying, "No fish, no money." I bend down and touch her feet. She smiles, shakes her head as if I'm a foolish tourist unworthy of the evening, and she leaves before I can give her something or say goodbye. I wonder who is the greater Beauty—the young woman dancing with the slick mop or the old fish vendor eager to take home her one fish. I turn away from the last streets holding Puerto Plata together and climb through a valley of squat houses with rusted tin roofs that look like so many playing cards on edge. Lanterns, candles, and bulb light from inside the houses reveal holes in the worm-scored siding. Nothing here stands ready for the next hurricane. When I arrive near midnight, the cable car's closed and sits as empty as an egg drained of its yolk.

The summit of Isabel de Torres stands over eight hundred meters, but on this night it's reefed by clouds. All around me in the half-lit darkness, the clatter of insects, the flurry of bats. Every few minutes, I hear the occasional shriek as though something with broad wings plummets from a branch to take a prize by the neck. I pass vacant huts flanked by banana leaves and hear piglets scrabbling the cassava. The terrain wants to become machete-cut farmland, but it can't win against wild shoots. The higher I climb, the muddier the ground and the harder it becomes to hop from stone to stone. The interlocking curves of the trail make me feel as if I'm looping in circles, slightly dizzy, yet still climbing. I stop for more air and my ankles find sinkholes. I wonder about Philip and picture him waddling off the dock in his dress and wig, packing a gun in a handbag like a circus villain. How many other sailors travel as far as he into the salt lanes on one stray melody?

I sit down on the trunk of a fallen tree and figure the summit must be near.

I long for a hit of Brugal, no ice required. I look up, hoping that the raspy breathing I hear is the sound of good clear water rustling underground. Instead, I see a miniature burro with floppy ears, big as conch shells, a stubby pinched tail, a straw-saddle loosely swaddled around its distended belly, its hide galled where milk cans have rubbed. The burro nudges against the cactus fence and nibbles on tubular white flowers, its eyes as narrow as thrown streaks of moonlight. I climb up on its sway-back and pinch the rope bit between my fingers. The animal doesn't move when I kick its patchy flanks. Giddy up, I whisper, giddy up. The burro won't budge. I make a kissing sound and say *arriba la montaña, arriba.* He finally steps away from the cactus fence and we climb out of that antediluvian world of looped branches and hissing night flowers.

After a time, I see small clouds of dust leaping in moonlight where a man reins his horse and steps away. I lead the burro off the road and lash it to a sapling. I walk through scrub palm to the park entrance of the Isabel de Torres Nature Preserve. The horse rider is a night guard. He dismounts and slumps into a chair with a bottle of Brugal in his hands. He wears a holster and revolver.

The man is not a threat to me, and I mean him no harm, but I want his gun. If death waits for me in the morning, Skip, I want to wait for it with a loaded gun. I lay on my belly behind the folds of a squat bush and give the man another hour nipping his bottle.

When I see his head roll to one side, I creep out into the clearing, holding a heavy stick. The man looks dead. As I close within twenty feet, the horse smells me coming and whinnies. The guard spins off his chair, half-sprawling, digging for his gun, shouting, "*Alto, alto.*" I rush forward, tackling him. Before the man gets his bearings, I unsnap his holster and pull the gun loose.

"*Soga?*" I ask. "*Donde está soga?* Rope?"

The man shakes his head.

I poke him with the stick and say, "*Soga del caballo.*"

The man looks puzzled until I point to the reins. I wave the gun in his face. The guard inches forward to slip the bit and halter from the horse and holds it out to me like an offering. I reach for the leather reins and the man swings the steel bit, catches me in the face, drawing blood. The guard swings the halter again, this time over his head like a lasso.

I point the gun at the guard's chest and say, "No, No, Stop, *Lo siento*. I only need to borrow your gun. I'm not going to shoot."

The guard drops the halter and I lash his hands and feet with it. I rip a large swatch from the man's shirt, stick it in his mouth. I take out my marlin spike and cut a thin piece of the reins and use it to secure the gag. With his feet bound, I drag the guard out of the clearing onto a bed of pine needles not far from the entrance gate. I retrieve the gun and holster, then look for the man's horse but it's gone. My watch says 4:30 and I tell myself I'll soon see a few faint streaks of pink. I throw the holster in a gully, stick the snub-nose revolver in my pants, and walk toward the torso of the Christ.

I look down at my blood-stained hands and hope to gulp a blast of ocean air once I stand at the summit. Isabel de Torres is still wrapped by clouds. I crane my neck to see the expression on the Christ, but all I see are outstretched arms vanishing inside swirling white sheets. I lie down on a bench, close my eyes, and ask for deliverance. Because I have no one else, I ask of the Christ to be forgiven for what I might have to do in order to get Rosario off this island. I drift into sleep.

I see *Stardust* sailing from Puerto Plata, her mainsail pulling while the jib swells and the big boat pushes through the first swells of the harbor entrance. The diesel chugs like new. She looks ready for sailing eastward to St. Thomas. The morning is bright and crisp. Someone besides myself stands at the wheel. The person's hair is long like mine, blonde, and pulled back into a ponytail beneath a cap. Jesse and Rosario stand together at the wheel. They smile up at me on the mountain.

I remember, just before I left Cockburn Harbor, how Philip told me *Stardust* was missing a set of spare engine keys. I hear the name of Jesse's parrot, Rosie. I see two women slow dancing in a hip-grinding merengue bar like two ribbons of silk blending the light and the dark. Why have I not tracked the flight of this blended ribbon more clearly? Did I find it impossible that two beautiful women would make a match on a dance floor?

As I raise my head from the bench, I see clouds peeling back the face of the Christo. To the west, I see the mountains of Haiti, buckled green behind rain. I see the coastal mountains encircling Luperón and the vast undulations of cane sweeping like an army of green arrows toward the airport—all of it owned by the Brugal family and worked by Haitians for less than a dollar a day. The cables of the *teleférico* rattle and hum. My watch says 6:30. I rush to the cable car ticket booth. No one's there. A sign says cars leave every ten minutes. I wait twenty minutes. At 7:00 A.M., a young woman arrives to sell tickets. She's surprised to see anyone at such an early hour wanting to go down the mountain.

"*Habla inglés?*" I ask.

"*Lo siento,*" she says, shaking her head.

"*Quiero boleto. Boleto!*" I demand.

The woman says, "*Un dólar.*"

I throw money through a window slot. The sleepy-eyed woman takes her time tearing off a ticket from a thick roll.

"*Tengo prisa,*" I say. "*Prisa.*"

A cable car stops at a platform, hesitates, then swings before me like a pendulum. I enter the empty cable car, and as the car jerks and lifts into the air, I glance back at *Cristo*. I'm not prepared for his robust smile, his unmistakable euphoria. Where are the nails cloven through the feet, the green patina of tears, the wailing doubt? I turn to face Puerto Plata rising up below me and Skip, what I saw in my dream, I see again.

In the middle of the harbor, I see *Stardust,* the only trimaran in Puerto Plata, heading out on a brisk fifteen-knot breeze. She clears the thumb of land where the Fort stands, and slips past the line of breakers on either side of the channel. High up in the *teleférico* I shout, "Jesse's stealing my boat. Stop that boat. Stop her. That's my boat."

Suspended between earth and sky, I can't tell where my dream stops and the morning begins, but when *Stardust* turns northwest with the wind behind her, I can feel my sea legs wanting to fold and roll. When *Stardust* cuts behind Punta

Cafemba, I slump inside the cable car. I've got what I came for. My doom is complete. I've lost Philip. I've lost my delivery boat. I've lost the cocaine I once believed would redeem my past and pay future dividends. With a stolen gun in my pocket, I wonder if I might have to use it when the cable car stops rocking on its greased wire and deposits me below.

As sure as the Trades are blowing southeast until September, Rosario is with Jesse in the cockpit. Nothing's left of my boat delivery, Skip. Nothing's left of my beautiful plan. Nothing but a crumpled cable car ticket from Jesus the Redeemer who lives, with an irrepressible joy, up on the mountain above an old city of pirates.

After I step off the cable car and touch ground, I run for a cab, the gun bulging from my right front pocket. The driver peels from the parking lot and I decide to swing by the harbor to make sure my eyes have not deceived me. As the cab bolts down Avenida Colón and hugs the corner at Duarte, I glance to my right and see police cars. The driver says, *"Narcótico es muerte,"* the driver says.

"Jimmy?"

"Sí, sí, sí, Jimmy Q."

"Who killed him?" I ask, knowing the answer, but wanting to hear what he says.

"No lo sé."

"Ahora, aeropuerto," I say, thumping the top of the front seat. *"Pago cincuenta dólares."*

"No hay mal que por bien no venga," the driver says.

Skip, the driver says there's no bad from which good doesn't come, but I don't believe him. Not now. Not ever. I scarcely see the rolling golf courses of the Playa Dorado Hotel or the miscellany of tin shacks just outside the hotel fence, leaning like so many rows of busted teeth, the flocks of skinny, barefoot children waving madly as my cab enters a curve at high speed. What does any of this random beauty and despair mean to me now? All I have left is a stolen gun and a story about a Dominican woman who gave me a piece of amber with two mosquitoes entombed.

As the cab swings into the airport grounds, I take the gun from inside my right pocket and wrap it inside a newspaper left on the back seat. I pay the driver before the cab stops and jump out. I drop the gun in a trash bin. I walk toward the airport doors to buy a ticket, and I see Jimmy's man dressed in a fisherman's jersey. He leans against a large wooden box overflowing with orange and pink flowers. At his feet, I see a briefcase. I think the man must know by now that Jimmy Q is dead, or maybe he's from Santo Domingo and hasn't yet heard the news or maybe Jimmy's legacy is designed to keep business moving whether he's dead or tending to his bar.

Now that Jimmy's gone, I can take the money and no one will know.

One hundred thousand is enough money to buy another sailboat, a very nice one. It would be so easy to smile, bend down, and pick up the case. My fingernails dig a little tunnel through my hands. My feet slide in the man's direction. I come within ten feet of the flowers, stop, look at the man with the briefcase, then turn toward the glass doors of the airport. I walk faster. I want to be on a jet, even a Dominican one, the most accident-prone jets in the world, more than I want the next boat. I elbow a path to the ticket counter. The plane is due to start boarding in twenty minutes.

I smell someone approaching behind me through a reef of cigar smoke.

"I don't think it's time for you to leave our island," the comandante says quietly.

"I have a plane to catch."

"Not today," he says, his eyes hidden behind shades.

"What right do you have to detain me?"

"Oh, the list is so long, Mr. Younger. I can't begin to tell you about all the things you've done. But let's start with the gun we pulled out of the trash can. We'd like to know if it belongs to Aldo Perez, the night guard at Isabel de Torres Park. He has three cracked ribs and a gash on his head. He's going to press charges. And we would like to find out what you know about the death of a drug dealer named Jimmy Q and the deaths of two Americans in Santo Domingo. It seems wherever you go, there's so much trouble. We think you can help us grasp the significance of all these events."

"You have a warrant for my arrest?"

"There's no such thing as a warrant in the DR, my friend." the comandante says. "But you need not worry too much. For God knows what reason, Rosario likes you, and because of her, I will see to it you won't die in the DR today. Maybe tomorrow, but not today."

CHAPTER XIX

Inside a cramped room on the barbwire grounds of La Vega prison, I can scarcely tell I'm living near the north coast of an island air-conditioned by the Trades. My private locked room stands next to the latrines, and though the sea is just over one mountain, I can't smell the salt air through the stench of piss, shit, and lime. My job's a simple one: to swab down the latrine floors and slop the hogs with the rotten fruit and moldy bread tossed out by the prisoners. My life seems not merely stalled in a trance of shame and anger but stillborn, gone, vanished beyond repair. I don't know whether to smile like the village idiot or weep.

The comandante has no intention of linking me to the deaths of two Americans in Santo Domingo, but he wants someone to hold in connection with Jimmy's death until a "complete" investigation is made. The night guard from the Isabel de Torres Park brings assault charges against me. The guard spends three months recovering from a concussion and demands I pay all medical expenses, plus lost wages, plus a fine of $5,000 U.S. dollars. I have exactly $450 dollars in my wallet, the princely remainder of Jimmy's gratuity. But since I have no way to get more money, and I'm too ashamed to ask you to bail me out, I agree to accept, in lieu of going to trial and risking a stiffer sentence, a three-year prison term. The comandante uses his influence again and I have to spend only three months working in the prison, a period of time equivalent to the guard's convalescence. I have to clean the latrines but not live in a cellblock among the prisoners. "A blessing," the comandante assures me. "White men, especially blondes like you, are so desirable here."

The trick that keeps me alive is inventing stories for Rosario.

If I could imagine a life for her, I tell myself, I have a chance of offering a new life to myself. At first, all I can do is replay our movie, but slowly I replace the burn of sex with the tug of words. We talk for hours. We get to know one another. I rebuild the story from the beginning when I first walk through the pig-trash streets of Luperón to meet her at the merengue bar.

"What does Rosario seek from Jesse?" I ask myself.

This is my best guess, Skip.

Jesse's one of God's sea-tamers who knows how to bend the waves to match her desires and get Rosario away from the DR. Maybe she promises to take Rosario to New York, where all dreams take hold for good. Tame the sea and you can tame the land. This is the promise Jesse offers to her. Follow me and I'll draw all pain out of your body and blow life back into it.

And what does Jesse dredge from this deal?

With each caress of Rosario's skin, maybe Jesse tells herself she'll outdistance her nightly sex charade with Jimmy and her phony-baloney marriage. Maybe Jesse convinces Jimmy to offer me another pile of drug money—so the comandante will grab me with a sack of cash. All I can do is light the flare of my speculations and watch them fizzle out. What do Jesse and Rosario say to each other on those first days on *Stardust* flying west from Puerto Plata toward Central America? In my little room, next to the foul-smelling, windowless prison, I act out the parts with my hands, like puppets.

Skip, this may sound presumptuous, cheap even, but as I count the bars of La Vega prison, I'm more like you than not. I hover between sleep and waking, not knowing if I want to twist on a cot or die quick. No one I know can find me. The past is unsalvageable. The future, remote.

My skipper stirs, turns toward me, listening. His bony frame has lost nearly all its muscle tone yet he still retains the uncanny power of a crushing handshake. How can this be? How can the memory of muscle find its expression after the shape of it is gone? Touching his arm under the blue cotton sheet, I trace the origin of his arm strength back through the years of pressing against a weather helm. He can't last this night. He must.

At the end of three months to the day, the comandante returns to La Vega prison with a letter in his hand, stating the terms of my next incarceration. For the remainder of my three-year sentence, I'll work in the Puerto Plata Customs Office. As I walk past the barbwire compound, I see fists, toothy grins, a flash of metal, an arc of spit, and I hear a medley of catcalls. Watching me watch the prisoners, the comandante breaks into a hint of a smile.

"What if I try to get away?" I ask the comandante as I trade my gray-striped uniform for my shorts, T-shirt and flip flops.

"I'll shoot you on sight," he says, flatly.

"What do I have to do?"

"Handle all the delivery boat skippers. Who better than you to examine boats, check for contraband, see if a ship's papers are in order?"

"My wallet?" I say, digging through my clothes, "Where's my wallet?"

"It does appear to be missing," the comandante replies, "but you won't need a wallet where you're going."

"What about my drivers's license, my credit card, my six-pack Captain's License? They're all gone."

"Six-pack Captain's License? What's this? A license to drink?"

"It's a Charter boat Captain's License that allows me to carry 6 passengers."

"You should be relieved. Now, you'll be responsible for only one passenger."

"What do I use for money?"

"You won't be needing any. You'll have a roof over your head and two meals a day. We don't eat breakfast. Just coffee. Very black."

"How will I ever leave this place without a picture ID?"

"You'll just have to invent a new identity," the comandante says. "You seem to be good at that."

"That's perfect. No money. No identity. No Captain's License."

"Trust me, Mr. Younger, what you'll find here in Puerto Plata with me is a three-year picnic compared to just one night in the Huey prison where I'll send you if you give me any trouble."

"Trouble?" I say. "I've never known any trouble."

"It's the most violent, rat-infested sardine can on earth," the comandante says, massaging his knuckles. "Gang fights, mattress fires, and riots are as common as hurricanes. After being sentenced, some men slit their own wrists rather than step through the Huey prison gates. Prisoners would rather kill you than learn your name. Rape is expected, demanded, longed for rather than the long knife in the kidneys. Funny thing, the prison is located in a very pretty town on the eastern tip of the island, a town founded by Ponce de Leon. But the only fountain a man finds there is the fountain of death, fire, or prison stampede. No, I think you should wake up every day, Mr. Younger, and offer thanks to God that I've saved your sorry ass from a place that makes hell look like a carnival. But I warn you, I'll send you to Huey for one last night if you get out of line."

Skip, the comandante got my attention with his threat. Still, even on the first day out, I think of ways I might escape the island and find Rosario. Skip frowns, then smiles as if the comandante might be a man he could work with.

Monitoring the flow of boat traffic in and out of Puerto Plata should be easy, but the comandante warns me against talking a line, so I'm a nimble mute, anonymous, unacknowledged, and unknown to anyone but him.

Like me, many of the skippers who straggle into Puerta arc blown off course and their boats arrive in a snarl of sheets and torn sails. These men, late middle-aged, rich, sunburnt and coupled with babes half their age tricked out in dental floss bikinis, don't know how to "Med moor" their boats with crisscrossed stern lines, spring lines, and an anchor off the bow. They don't know how to cope with the prop surge from the cruise ships.

They don't know exactly how they got here, nor how to get out. I want to ridicule them for their ignorance and fear, but if I had a mirror in my room, I would see I'm more like them than not. Day and night I'm on call to settle disputes between boat owners, to help reset dragging anchors, to handle complaints. Still, I like working in the sun. At least once a day I catch sight of a sailboat beating across the Thorny Path. With my fingers, I trace the pencil-thin slant of a mast, the page of a sail.

At night, I'm locked inside the *comandancia* in a small room with no windows, no books, no coordinates, no sun angles. With sticky air straddling my windpipe, I roll and toss and braid the threads of a dream.

I sit in the first pew at the funeral home chapel as a bald-headed minister of no consequence prattles about the hour of resurrection enclosing all sorrow with new light. Hale's swim coach gives the eulogy and speaks of our prodigy, his record-breaking accomplishments, his miraculous ease in the water. I wince when the coach says the words, *the heart of a champion*. Beside the wreath, there's a photo of Hale in a Speedo.

In death and in life, Hale is presented to the mourners as part boy, part fish, ready for submersion and propulsion. Then, the chapel blurs inside the crackling of candles. The wreath floats off. The great swimmer fades from view. Someone sobs with a quiet yet violent heave. This single cry crests the empty chapel, and the room swells with hot running salt water and I can't escape because the chapel lists off its footing and sinks. I wake with my hands at my throat, my mouth thirsting for air. There's nothing to hear but the boom under my ribcage. Nothing to feel except the sweat of stone walls. If I call out, no one hears, so I sit knee-drawn in the dark and wait for someone to knock and tell me I can walk out into the morning one more time.

After a year, I meet with the comandante. I sense he wants to talk as much as I do. Why else does he come to my little room as if peering into the bones of a wreck?

"What about my boat? What happened that morning?"

The comandante ignores my question while he bites a cigar, then speaks in flat, low, official tones.

"The man working the docks said two women came into the Customs office very early and paid up the dockage fees. The women said they were the new crew for *Stardust*. They showed my man a set of keys to the boat. One woman was blonde, the other Dominican. He saw them load supplies, haul anchor, and sail out of the harbor. They knew exactly what they were doing. He said they were experienced sailors."

"Where were they headed?"

"I can't say."

"You still haven't told me why you let *Stardust* leave?"

"I told you. I wasn't there," the comandante says.

"You mean anyone can come into the Customs office and say they're taking a boat off your hands?"

"If they've got keys to the boat, yes."

"I brought *Stardust* into the DR and cleared Customs in Luperón. Only I can sign out. I'm the skipper. Why did you let that boat go?"

The comandante pulls the cigar from his mouth, puts one hand to his lips, and flicks off a bit of ash. "Maybe," he says, "it was time for her to go."

"There was a woman on board my boat," I say in a pleading tone. "Her name was Rosario Estrella. You know her. She came to see you one night after my first mate jumped ship. I know she's just a whore to you but I wanted her to go with me to St. Thomas. She said she would meet me at the Christ statue. I waited for her that morning. She never came. We were going to leave that morning. Don't you see, the whole thing is a terrible mistake. I was set up. My boat was stolen."

"I do know the girl you speak of. She's not some whore. She's my daughter," the comandante says with his head angled down.

"Rosario's father is dead," I reply, stunned by his confession. "She told me he was killed in a hurricane."

"It's true, I was dead to her for many years," he says. "But after my other daughter was killed in Jamaica, I tried to find

Rosario." He turns to leave my room but then looks back. I tell myself if he keeps talking, I'll have a chance of backing him into a corner where I might gain some small advantage or favor.

The comandante sits down and rests his head on his elbow.

He talks into the room as if I'm not there, mesmerized by the plumes of his own cigar smoke. He seems like a man broken from his church and bent by the blood of his covenants. The looped rings beneath his eyes look swollen with the weight of the earth.

After his young wife died of rum and cigarettes, the comandante says, he can't face raising two girls. What does he have to offer them but his poverty and grief? He left the girls with neighbors and promised he'd return after he made enough money in Santo Domingo. He had no plans for a regular wage-earning job. There was no future in that, he laughs. He entered his cocks in major fights to salt away enough dollars to open his own *gallera*. One opponent, an important government official, put up a job in lieu of $10,000 cash if his cock lost. He guaranteed a comandante position in Puerto Plata. At night's close, one fighting cock was dazed and bloody. The other cock's throat was slit. And the man I know as the comandante returned to the north coast on a white horse. As the new comandante, he pledged to find his two girls and begin again, yet by the time his luck turned, one daughter was dead after a drug-bust shootout, and the other was lost somewhere in the DR.

"I know who killed Jimmy," I say, spitting the words out. The comandante studies me.

"So that was you?" he says, flicking ash and sucking down on his teeth in a mock grin. "Tell me one reason why I shouldn't kill you now?"

"Because your daughter loves me," I say, needing to believe my claim is more true than not. "Some part of her loves me and if she finds out you put a bullet in my head, what little connection you have with her will be gone."

He says nothing. Looks at me like I'm a stone wall in a dim light on a long-suffering avenue where no one ever goes.

"You let me go now and I'll never tell her or anyone else what I saw."

"You must be joking," he says. "Do you think I give a rat's ass what you saw or what you say to anyone? You mean less than spit in the DR."

"I think you care about your daughter. So much has gone wrong between you, you'll do almost anything to bring her back here one day. Too many people have seen me here working on the docks. I've talked to too many sailors. My name's well known. You already have the unsolved deaths of three Americans. Do you really need a fourth? Getting rid of Jimmy wasn't a bad thing. The man was poison for everybody, including you."

"Don't lecture me, Mr. Younger."

I consider lying and telling him I've written a detailed letter to the U.S. Embassy in Santo Domingo revealing everything I know about the drug trafficking between the Turks & Caicos and the DR, but I know he'll see through that ruse. I stick with my love for Rosario and stare him down from nothing even close to a position of strength.

"I don't want to talk anymore about Rosario or your boat. As for Jimmy, he too is a *fin de libro.*"

Closed book, my ass.

There's nothing concluded.

No page has been turned. Over the next few months, the comandante and I only talk about harbor business, the shuffling of boats for dockage, the infrequent discoveries of contraband, the occasional body of a Haitian washed up on the beach. No one knows how the Haitians die and no one seems to care. In the Dominican mythology, Haitians are expendable. When they die, or are found dead, they don't even warrant mention in the newspaper, and I, too, stop questioning their anonymity as my own becomes more wildly self-evident. Nothing registers anymore: not the stale summer heat and thick afternoon rains, not the pulse of merengue blasting from buses, not the stink of boiled molasses pouring from the Brugal factory, not the hookers who wave as they try to catch the eye of cruise ship passengers broken free from their wives.

I linger on Rosario's scent and shape while my mind dredges and sifts particulars. Skip, I know it's a sloppy business, the re-arranging of the past, but what else do I have to do, but try to bring her back so we can discover who the other is? If the comandante is Rosario's father, then it explains why he might want to kill Jimmy, but it doesn't explain why he let Jesse and Rosario leave the harbor on *Stardust*. Nothing tells me whether Rosario was intimidated by Jesse or whether she was in love with her or whether our time together was just another rum invention.

Skip sits up and scans the room, wondering where he is, how he got there, who came with him. He's got nowhere to go, but he wants to get moving. He wants to get beyond this sheet, this bed, this rail, this room, this limbo.

"Have you ever scattered ashes at sea?" he asks, craning his head as if to glimpse the Atlantic just a few skipped stones away.

"Make sure you read the wind right so I don't come back on board. I don't want to end up in somebody's bilge."

"I got it, Skip. The wind will be behind you. I'll see to it."

Strange talking to a living man about the future ash of his body.

Hard for me to picture what we all come to while the chest harbors a breath-soft heave. But not for Skip. He'll be heading out to sea. Ready to wander from this world to the forever unknown. He was always a better sailor than I.

CHAPTER XX

First light and three turkey vultures with red vests talk shop on a sand dune.

No one knows if the hurricane will come in time to iron the flames leaping out of the swamp. Rain and more rain and the smoldering fires still burn. How can that be? I read somewhere the ancients believe the oceans remember the shape of every hull that plies the waters. I feel that too, sitting at night with my father—some powers in us may not die even after our life slips away. How else to explain the comfort of watching him half asleep, half drifting between this life and the deep?

Another day passes and my Mother and I don't speak. We're polishing our talons to become vultures ourselves in our next life. We gesture. We nod. We point. We go out for solo walks on the beach. I can't stop thinking about *Tabula Rasa*, the turquoise Tartan '37 Bob Martin needs to unload fast so he can hold up his end of a divorce. More than half of the boats sold in Florida must be distress sales. The owners jammed up by wives, creditors, lost jobs, or no time to use it, the broken dream of the getaway glide dogging them like a pinched nerve in the neck.

On the way home, at a stoplight, I look at my hands, stronger and more calloused than my father's in his prime, the skin ripped off by hours of wet salt pull, chunks of shriveled flesh now grown back with a thick meaty reserve, even the cavity of my missing finger scabbed over by years of sea work.

Once home, I make the call.

"Mr. Sunman, this is Matt Younger. I'm calling about the pearl."

"Yes."

"You said you knew a collector who would kill for a pearl such as mine."

"Those are your words, not mine."

"I want you to take this collector's first best offer. What do you figure that would be?"

"I don't know. I would think you could realize between $200,000 and $300,000, maybe more if we take our time and think through all the potential buyers."

"I don't have time. Can you do it now?"

"Why the hurry?" he asks quietly, unruffled by my demand.

"There's a boat I want."

"Just like your father," he says, with a delicate tone of consolation and regret.

"How fast can you do it?"

"It might take me two weeks to arrange and finalize the sale."

"I need cash, Mr. Sunman. Not a check."

"Why?"

"I don't trust banks."

"OK, cash it is, minus my commission."

"Make the call," I say.

Just one pearl placed into the hands of one collector and I can shove off from this Younger family gone astray and write a new story on my own blank slate, my *Tabula Rasa*.

Night returns and I leave my mother to her Bible. My father calls out for water. How quickly the wind gathers up the little knot of a life and cuts it loose, but not before another song swims into his throat:

My father was the keeper of the Eddy stone Light,
And he married a mermaid one fine night,
And out of that union there came three,
A fish and a porpoise and the other was me.

"I'm almost done, Skip. Trust me."

"Every woman wears a blouse. Every man's a mouse. Every boat turns south," Skip sings again.

"I went south, Skip, because I couldn't stay north."

"Carry on, son. The candle's burning down."

The only break in my windowless speculations is the one-time visitation of someone I now regard as the unpaid oracle of Puerto Plata.

"Some wounded dog told me you buried a bone down here," Desmond trills one morning.

"Yeah, that'll work as a description," I smile, genuinely happy to see him.

"You need slow-think time in this fast life."

"I've got plenty of that."

"Going nowhere's the best time to travel. A double-minded man, the Bible says, is unstable in his ways. The good news is, you now be of one mind and this is your time to shine."

"I just want to get out of here. I've seen enough."

"No such thing as seeing enough. You got to keep looking out. Look twice before you leap, then leap a little farther. You be Mistah Sailor Man, the one with a compass rose thorned on your wrist. Watch the length of your own lies and see where they circle back. You just lived a love story, top to bottom, get it?"

"Did she love Jesse? Just tell me that."

"She loved lots of people. No, that's not right. She wanted the one big love, the start-from-scratch, garden-of-eden, come-home-to-jesus, kind of love."

"With a man or woman?"

"Her eyes always looking for Eve." I wince when he says this because even now I still believe she loves me and wanted to leave the DR with me and not Jesse.

"But how could she leave with Jesse?"

"Who can say how many quills a person needs to pluck from a porcupine?"

"You worried about her?" I ask.

"Not so much, with Jimmy gone. She might survive Jesse."

"Should I go looking for her?"

"Should, could, would. You do what you got to do, Mistah Sailor Man, and don't ask so many questions no man can answer."

"Thanks, I think."

"No thanks needed," Desmond replies, spinning around and clapping his hands. "But do enjoy. This is your horn of plenty. And remember this one thing, my man, it's not easy getting into this life, not easy to get out, so you just have to wait your turn at the boat launch. Maybe your turn comes at night, maybe at dawn, but either way, the moment is not without wonder for where you've been and what's coming your way."

"I'm not gonna die down here," I say.

"You already have," he says, "but don't worry. Something's cooking for you, Mistah Younger. I can smell the change ahead. Give it two days and you'll see."

Desmond ambles off the docks, carrying his mile-long dreads in the bag by his side, a red stocking cap pulled down to his ears, a pair of key-lime colored sunglasses strapped to his head. He looks very much the traveler from other kingdoms.

Two days later, on Desmond's cue, a black sedan pulls into the parking lot of the *comandancia*. Three men step out. They don't enter the building. They walk toward me on the docks where I'm helping re-secure the anchor lines of a Morgan Out Island '41 ketch named *Arabesque*. She straggled into Puerto Plata a few months back under torn sails and the captain and crew vanished, with no word. Just one more mystery simmering on the back burner of Paradise.

Two of the men wear gray suits. The third man wears a white cotton shirt and black pants. I figure he's the man who wants a word with me.

"Are you Matt Younger?" the shirted man asks.

"The one and only."

"We'd like to talk with you?"

"What's on your mind?"

"Drug trafficking."

"Serious business," I say, "But I'm just the unpaid help here."

"We have reason to think otherwise."

"Since I'm here due to the hospitality of the comandante, we should include him in this discussion, don't you think?"

After months of pounding sunlight with nothing I can make of it but shadows, finally, Skip, I get a sliver of daylight. The four of us walk into the *comandancia*. The comandante is at his desk, sharpening a pencil with a knife.

"Gentlemen, how can I be of service?"

"We'd like to know what Mr. Younger knows about Jimmy Q and Jesse Dove."

"And to whom do I have the pleasure of speaking?"

"I'm Dwight Stone, Customs and Immigration, Turks & Caicos. My two associates are with U.S. Drug Enforcement."

Dwight Stone? Where do I know that name?

"I'm honored," the comandante says.

During this thin exchange of pleasantries, I weigh and measure the risk of telling Dwight Stone all he wants to hear, but then I remember the quick draw of the comandante and how I'm squarely in the middle of a possible crossfire. Dwight Stone shifts his gaze back toward me.

"Do you know who killed Jimmy Q?"

"I don't have a clue," I say, meeting his eyes set on a ridge of sharp cheekbones.

"And Jesse Dove?"

"Last time I saw her she was on her way to Miami to buy me a life raft."

"Really?" says Stone. The two U.S. Drug Enforcement men bolt upright, their coats unbuttoned to reveal shoulder holsters. Their faces are cut from stone. Their eyes work the room at shark speed.

"You were last seen with both of them in Cockburn Harbor."

"That's right. Jesse was my cook. And I made Jimmy's acquaintance at the Salt Shack."

"Were you working for Jimmy?" Dwight presses.

"Hell no," I say. "I ain't no drug mule." The comandante looks more interested in the shape and feel of his lead pencil than in the burn of my interrogation.

"Why did you come here, Mr. Younger?"

"My boat was blown off course."

"Where is it now?"

"*Stardust* sank," I say.

The comandante stands up, holding his pencil as if he's ready to make a blackboard talk.

"The cruise ships that dock here throw off a terrible prop wash. We routinely have trouble with boats dragging anchors. I'm afraid Mr. Younger's boat was an unfortunate victim of this chronic problem of ours. His boat dragged anchor and drifted out to the reef at the mouth of our harbor and broke apart."

"Sank? How convenient," Stone says. "We would have liked to examine it. By the way, what are the charges against you, Mr. Younger? Why are you here?"

"Gambling debts," I say.

"We take bad debt very seriously in the DR," the comandante says, turning his back on the men.

"You have any paperwork on the crime?"

The comandante turns with the hint of a frown tucked into his face.

"This is a very small *comandancia*. I have no staff. We try to keep our paperwork to a minimum."

Dwight Stone looks at me and I consider again what he can offer that the comandante can't. I don't have more than a few seconds, but now his name comes to me. He's the airport Customs official Jesse nailed in exchange for Stone telling Jimmy he had his jet on radar which forced Jimmy to dump his cargo. Dwight Stone is no innocent. He's being squeezed by his two companions to produce something on Jesse and Jimmy because they must know Stone had been seen with her. He's the man running the show right now, but he might not live long enough to get back to the Bahamas.

"We can help you, Mr. Younger. We can bring you back home if you cooperate. We know that Jesse Dove and Jimmy Q were using the DR as a relay point for bringing drugs into the Bahamas. We need to know how they did it. Who helped them."

"If you do the crime, you've got to do the time," I say.

"Thank you, gentlemen for stopping by," the comandante says, "but now I need to talk with Mr. Younger about another one of our boats we nearly lost last night."

The three men get up to leave. They walk past six armed men who lean in the entrance of the *comandancia*.

"No staff, right?" Stone says as the three men leave and return to their car. The comandante tells his men to split up. Three should follow Dwight Stone. Three should stay with him. He returns to his desk, puts his feet up.

"You could be a politician, Mr. Younger. That was very tactful."

"I hate politicians."

"How about a rooster with nine lives?"

"I'm not sure I have more than one life left."

He's opens a drawer and removes a smudged envelope with my name scribbled on the front.

"I've read Rosario's letter to you, Mr. Younger. It's quite touching."

He strikes a match and holds it to the letter. When the blue-green envelop catches flame at the corner, he tosses it into a trash can.

"At least tell me what it says."

"Why?"

"It would be of some consolation."

"Give me something I don't have, and I'll tell you what she said."

It's just him and me face to face like mismatched lovers scraped raw by too much mental friction.

"I killed one of the two men in Santo Domingo. My mechanic, Philip Laforge, killed the other."

He laughs.

"I knew that, Mr. Younger, months ago. What I don't know is who these men worked for."

"Jesse Dove."

"That's the not right answer, Mr. Younger. Those men worked for Jimmy Q."

"You're wrong, comandante."

208

He looks at me with a baleful smile that makes me think I should have used a different word to describe his point of view.

"Jesse was one step ahead of everyone. She conned me all the way back in West Palm Beach. She put Jimmy Q on such a short leash, he would do anything for her. And she set you up to kill Jimmy. I don't think Jimmy's men raped your daughter or turned her into a drug addict. They didn't show her how to turn tricks with vacationing Germans and Canadians. She did all that on her own."

The comandante shakes his head, pinches the top of his nose, looks in a drawer for a dry cigar or an oily bullet.

"Perhaps you're right, Mr. Younger, about Jesse. But Jimmy and Rosario had become an embarrassment to me. I wanted them both gone. I'm happy to have her off my hands. Jesse gave me the push I was looking for."

"Turning over a new leaf, were you?"

He vanishes behind smoke, reappears, slips away again, a dark shape at dead slow speed.

"I had a letter from U.S. Drug Enforcement last week and now a personal visit."

"Too much contact with the outside world?"

"Everything's changing fast, Mr. Younger."

"How so?" I ask, thinking now I can press my advantage.

"U.S. Drug Enforcement will launch low altitude radar balloons in the Turks & Caicos to catch Lear jets. They'll be bringing in faster boats, bigger guns, more undercover men. Jimmy's old pirate world was coming to an end. He just didn't see it coming. In another few years, if you fly over the Turks & Caicos you won't see a fleet of wrecked planes. The islands will be covered with Olympic-sized swimming pools, condos, and starlets in G-string bikinis. Everything will sparkle with the look of a new era. They'll make movies about the drug wars here, but all the pirates will be long dead. I was just doing Jimmy a favor. He would have hated prison life. Don't you think? And Rosario, hell, I couldn't keep her out of trouble, no matter what I tried."

Now, it's my turn to squeeze my head, swallow hard, wish for a cloud of my own cigar smoke.

"You wanted Rosario off the island?"

"Look, I hope she figures out another life for herself, but not here, not with me. She was, what's your American expression, a pain in the ass," he says, the smoky tumble of his voice softening a half shade. I look into his bloodstained brown eyes as he pushes his only surviving daughter away, and I see nothing but a lingering undertow of betrayal pulling his shoulders down. He betrayed Rosario when she was young and he must hope that one day she'll return to the congested harbor of his continuing power and forgive him before he dies.

"Rosario's letter?" I ask, looking in the trash can at the smoldering wreck of her letter.

"It's a long ramble, Mr. Younger. Full of heartache and longing over her mother dying, her father leaving. Tender words about meeting Jesse on a dance floor. How they hatch a plan for leaving the DR. Then, you come ashore. Rosario does what she does best. You fall for her charms. But there's a crack in the bottle, Mr. Younger. My daughter wants a light-skinned child. She wants to stay just long enough in the DR to makes sure it can happen."

"What are you saying?"

"She has a boy, Mr. Younger."

"Mine?"

"Apparently her plan worked." Despite my held breath, I fire questions at the comandante because I have no idea when this session will end.

"What about Jesse and my boat?"

"They haven't fared as well. The boat went up in flames somewhere in Honduras. Jesse has not been seen of since."

"Where's your daughter?"

"She doesn't want you to know. She has the start of another life, Mr. Younger. You don't. Let her go. With this letter," he says, pointing to the trash can, "I would say you are now gone from her long list of unfortunate collisions."

Rosario's letter makes sense, every unread line, and none of it makes sense. In the middle of all this craving, all this death, there lives a child, my child, who I may never see except at great risk to Rosario's hard-won escape from the DR.

"Why did you burn it?"

"She says some things about me I don't wish to read again."

"Mostly true?"

"True enough," he says, standing up and letting me know our meeting has ended.

One week after Dwight Stone's departure, and one year early of my intended three-year incarceration, the comandante buys me a one-way ticket to Miami and arranges for me to get on a plane without photo ID. He even folds a hundred dollar bill inside my ticket.

"This one-way is yours on one condition," he says.

"I never saw anything the night Jimmy died," I reply.

"That's right," he says. "You made it all up. You made up the names Rosario, Jesse, and Jimmy. And you and me, we never met. If for some sorry reason you ever think about coming back here by boat or plane, I'll find a way for you to visit Huey prison for one night only."

"No need," I say.

"*Bueno.*"

"When you see your daughter, tell her I hope she's . . . happy."

"I'll do that," he says, standing at the gate, his eyes hidden behind sunglasses. I lumber through the doors of the jet carrying two black plastic bags filled with dirty clothes, books, and a cheese grater-like musical instrument called a *guira* which I found on the docks after Desmond left. It feels like a decade has slipped away instead of just my thirtieth birthday.

"Where's everybody?" I ask the flight attendant, then remember it's the start of summer and there's little traffic to or from the islands. I slump in my window seat, close my eyes, and listen to my heart pounding the back of my teeth. Why am I going back to Florida where Sam Wells, the owner of *Stardust*, is no doubt still waiting to slap me with a lawsuit?

The simple answer is: I need to make some kind of confession to you because my life ain't working the way it is. I can't live one day in the shadow of the Gulf that swallowed my brother like a minnow. I don't know who to talk to but another sailor who has crossed every ocean and lived to tell it all. I need you, Skip, much more than you need me.

From my window, I see Isabel de Torres cloaked in mist, its thin Christ statue hidden from view. To my right, I see two planes skidded off the tarmac, their fuselage so burnt and entangled, it's impossible to tell where one wreckage begins and another ends. The engines rev and a shiver stirs in my belly as the plane rushes forward. I press my nose against the window as the trunk of the island swims into view. The north end of the island swirls beneath a pall of haze, but southern light breaks through drifting vapors and reflects off the corrugated tin roofs and the fields of green running cane. Instead of a tropical island, the DR could be an iceberg swallowed by a fogbank for all I can figure out from the nursery rhyme of what happened there:

This sailor got beat up.

This sailor made a play for a girl.

This sailor stole a boat.

This sailor died a violent death.

This sailor went to jail.

To the north, I see the Thorny Path, its whitecaps run like stitches through the sleeve of a blue shirt. Beneath that frayed cloth, I see an orchard of ballast stones, scattered pieces of eight, burnished emeralds, mountains of cocaine. All the treasure you could ever want is buried beneath the keels of Spanish ships long gone because they got greedy for a fast return to Queen Isabella, and they didn't chart the reefs of the Thorny Path.

What drew me, Skip, to cross the Thorny Path against the Trades?

Maybe Philip can make sense of two mosquitoes hitched belly-to-belly inside a shard of twenty-million-year-old amber. Or I can hire a paleontologist who can extract blood droplets from cavorting insects and show me how the blood they drink becomes my own and Rosario's, and mixed with the ancient hunger in all of us to be changed by fire. Before I come home for the one talk we've never had, I need to stop and see Philip, my first mate, and see if he can fill in a few more missing pieces.

CHAPTER XXI

I call Skip's doctor and he tells me, "It's time for him to lay his body down."

Most every disease has already thrashed him including colon, prostate, and skin cancers, liver disease, heart disease, macular degeneration, gum disease, tooth loss, hearing loss, and every possible bone, muscle, joint ailment and skin lesions, kidney malfunction, and incontinence. Nothing in his body works, but he's still with me, still listening. Dying turns out to be damn hard work. "It's worse than hauling shingles up on a roof," Skip says and I don't think he's talking about the sliver of melon I slip into his mouth. Dying is a dazzling fever and it gives his face and room a flush that must also have been present at his birth.

"Let's go out for a sail. Just you and me and Hale?"

"That would be sweet." I say, my gut churning with his impossible request.

"We'll leave your mother here. She might not like where we get to."

"I need to tell you the rest of my story."

"You tell a pretty wild story, Hale. Is any of it true?"

"Yes, Skip. It's all true," ignoring that he's called me again by my brother's name.

"Do what you've come to do," Skip says, "But don't ever blab to your kids I didn't listen to you."

One bus from Miami and one cab ride later, I step in front of a glittery pink luxury condominium complex surrounded by giant date palms and white flowering magnolias. I see, through waving fronds, a brisk river traffic of power and sail. It figures that Philip has breezy digs with a sweeping water view. I'd forgotten how inviting Ft. Lauderdale is if you can afford to live on one of the many canals feeding out to the main harbor of cruise ships, freighters, tugs, and the Gulf Stream beyond. This city really is Florida's red-tiled answer to Venice—minus the labyrinth of alleys, arched bridges, heraldic door knockers, and sidewalk cafés. I see the letters P. F. on the nameplate inside the foyer and press the buzzer.

"Philip, it's me, Matt Younger."

A voice crackles over the speaker. "He doesn't live here anymore."

I press the buzzer again. "Do you know where he lives now?"

"See the building manager," the voice says.

I find the manager's name posted in the foyer and press his button.

"Hello, I'm looking for Philip Laforgue."

"Who are you?" a world-weary man's voice asks. "Bill collector?"

"No, nothing like that. My name's Matt Younger. A friend."

I hear a buzzer release on the main door and I walk into a hallway flooded with natural light and scented with jasmine and orange blossom. Through a large picture window at the end of the hall, I see a boat tied to a dock with a skipper at the wheel sipping a tall one. When I turn the corner to find #407, a fat dimpled man in a white, sleeveless T-shirt and suspenders greets me.

"What can I tell you?" the man asks.

"Where's Philip?" I blurt out.

"You hadn't heard?"

"What?"

"He's dead. Killed himself about three months ago."

"How?" I ask, staggered by the news. I prop myself up with one hand on the wall to keep my legs from buckling.

"You a cop?"

"Do I look it?" I ask, my two plastic garbage bags sprawled at my feet.

"No, you look like hell in a hurricane."

"We sailed together. In the islands."

"Can't help you. His attorney friend left a card. Maybe he knows something. He's just a couple of buildings down."

I sit on the Ft. Lauderdale Beach weighing what Benjamin Cohen, an attorney, told me about Philip's last days. Philip returned to find his partner, Derek, very sick. It broke Philip's heart, the attorney said, for his Adonis to become a thin old man dying from pneumonia, a "gay cancer," the doctors called it. They have never seen anything like it. Philip is also diagnosed with the same incurable illness. The coughing, the weight loss, the blood in the urine, all symptoms come on fast. Philip had no intention of wasting away with a live-in nurse spoon-feeding him Jell-O and applesauce. Instead, he shot himself in the heart with the gun he took from *Stardust*, the one registered in my name. When Benjamin Cohen said this, I caught myself on his desk. I told Philip's attorney I was grateful he cleared my name with the Ft. Lauderdale police. "Why did he do it?" I asked the attorney. He gave me a letter written in a finely-drawn script:

Dear Benjamin,

Having run from Derek for so long, I surprised myself at how easily I came to love the spirit behind the wreck. However, in his absence, I've decided not to watch the same vanishing, what I loved, what I went in search of. God-fearing or godless, each of us navigates death in our own boat. So, here's the lay of the land from my watch:

On the night of my 40th birthday, March 15, 1983, I will take my own life. I will use a revolver that belongs to a sailor named Matt Younger. He and I delivered a boat to the Dominican Republic. While I was there, I took his gun. I was seriously hurt as I've told you. I had nothing but time down there, so I built a plastic, lead-lined cradle for the gun and molded it to the inside of my tool box with a blow-torch—so I could carry it with me on the plane. I must say, it was a nifty piece of engineering because I made the butt and barrel of this gun look like just another long-handled socket wrench. I've never used a gun before. I hate loud noises, but I know it will be quick without any chance for error. I do regret my death

215

will be messy for someone else to clean up. Most of all, it could be messy for Matt Younger should he return to Florida.

As a way of making amends, I should like to will to Matt Younger a small token. It's a conch pearl I found when he and I were in Cockburn Harbor. He'll appreciate its beauty. As you know, I spent all of my savings in the last year on Derek who never did have health insurance. Please use the sale of any furniture in my condominium and my yellow Cadillac to help pay for your legal services in carrying out the terms of this letter.

Thanks, in advance, for your help and understanding. By the way, there's no one else you need contact. I have no siblings. My father's dead. My mother still lives in Brittany but is senile, disconnected from memory, and quite happy among her potted ferns.

What did Keats say about Joy's grape? I tasted all of it, but now it's closing time at the museum of love and despair. As for my ashes, if you can have them taken out to the Gulf Stream, where the deep blue water meets the green, that would be my wish.

Yours, Philip Laforgue

In addition to the letter, Philip's attorney gave me the conch pearl and a box with two thick rubber bands looped around it. He asked me to scatter Philip's ashes. There's no way on this earth, I told the attorney, I'm going to ignore this sailor's last request.

The sunburnt blonde in a black-string bikini doesn't want to rent me a Hobie Cat. She slouches in her canvas beach chair and kicks the sand with her indigo-colored toe nails. I guess she doesn't like my stringy, shoulder-length, blonde hair, my bloodshot eyes, my torn clothes, my homeless smell, my two trash bags.

"It's $40 an hour, plus a $150 deposit on a major credit card."

"I don't have a credit card."

"OK, leave a driver's license."

"I don't have one of those either."

"No credit card. No driver's license. Who are you?" she says, flipping her hair over her shoulder.

I want to tell her, I'm a son of a gun. A man on the run. I want to tell her it's none of her fucking business who I am. I just need a boat for a very important delivery. I take a deep breath and say, "I'm the son of a sailor and I know what I'm doing here."

"No card. No boat," she says, flatly.

"This is not about a boat. It's about a memorial."

"For who? Yourself?" the woman asks, her chest heaving just enough to make her breasts catch the eye of another man walking by.

"Listen, I need a boat to go out to the Stream to scatter the remains of a friend."

"We don't let Cats go out that far. I don't want to get in trouble. I could lose my job if I don't collect a deposit," she says, fluffing her hair.

"Wouldn't you want a friend to follow through after your death? Wouldn't you want someone to bend the rules? Help me out here. I came from a long way off to get here."

"How do I even know you can sail one of these? You don't look like you could paddle a bath toy let alone a Hobie Cat in twenty-five knots of air, going ten miles out into the Stream. I'm sorry, but you look like an escaped con or something worse."

"I may not look the part, but trust me, I can sail anything." I convince the woman to let me have the Hobie without a credit card, but then her male boss turns up.

"What's the problem here?" Whatever headway I've made with her is soon lost with him, so I back away. I walk a long way off from the rental stand and wade out into the waves as far as I can go. I say, "May the Stream carry you up past Bermuda and back to the Brittany of your birth. You had a good run and it's not over yet." I open the box and empty Philip's remains into the blue-black curl of a rising wave. I pull out a leather pouch which holds Philip's pink pearl found in Cockburn Harbor. I want to throw it and Rosario's amber shard after the ashes.

"A pearl for a pearl," I say, but then I think, no.

Philip went to a lot of trouble to find this pearl. He wants me to have this globe of fire and use it for some purpose I can't yet detect. I slip the pearl back into its pouch along with Rosario's amber shard. My nightmare voyage, my sea trial, I think, was it only worth throwing away? Maybe some other day, but not now.

After scattering his ashes, not in the Gulf Stream as he wished, but at the water's edge he found so boring, I zigzag across A1A to Crazy Greg's bar for an afternoon buzz.

I've nursed a good intention of not drinking anymore, but I can't bear my own promise. Not now. Not as my brain twinges with the image of Philip cradling my gun against his heart. I climb the stairs into the cool dark of Crazy Greg's, thinking maybe some conch fritters and Corona will serve me better than a tall Jamaican rum. I don't see a bartender so I turn around scanning for a booth. The whole place is noon-day empty or so I think. At the back, I see the face of a man who swims out of the darkness.

I step back and feel my breath unhitching itself from my lungs. I want to downshift and turn my body around, but I keep walking toward the man in the booth who must be Sam Wells or his twin. The need to move forward surges through me like a shorted wire looking for a ground. *Click, clack, hold me back*, I say like I'm rehearsing one of your rhymes, Skip.

Some part of my wasted self wants to rise up out of the brig and come clean with the owner of *Stardust*. After all, I lost a couple years of my life, but he lost his ninety-thousand dollar boat. All he wanted was *Stardust* delivered to St. Thomas, so he could bring his sick wife down to the islands for a vacation and instead he lost his dream rig in a scrambled drug deal he never knew anything about. The man talks to someone sitting across from him. I barge into the little world of the booth, lit only with a curl of smoke, thinking I've got one more hard knot to untie.

"Sam, I'm sorry about your boat, really I am. It's a long story, but if you let me explain . . ."

Sam Wells turns away from the person he's talking to, looks up at me with a broad smile, extends his hand.

218

"Mr. Younger," he says, as if he's half-expecting me for a drink. "You seem to have traveled a long way off course. I never thought I'd see you again. How long's it been, what, three years?" Up close now, his face is much thinner and charged with a twitching set of changing angles. His frame in the spacious booth seems almost lanky like maybe he's shed fifty pounds of fat and replaced it with gristle.

"Mr. Younger, I'd like you to meet my wife," he says, reaching out for the hand of the woman seated across from him. "Carol, this is Matt Younger, a man I hired to deliver *Stardust* to St. Thomas. Remember, I told you how the boat never arrived."

His description of my boat delivery gone awry seems oddly formal like he's describing a minor business deal that flopped, but caused no real financial damage.

I glance over at the woman expecting to see a matronly woman, somewhat sickly in appearance, but instead I see a pretty brunette in a clingy, low-cut yellow dress, her face partly shaded by smoke.

I know this woman.

Carol reaches out to shake my hand.

"It's a pleasure to meet you, Mr. Younger."

I lean over the smoke to look hard into the woman's face. The blonde hair is gone. The tattoos are gone or hidden by make-up, but not the broad shoulders, not the powerful arms, not the kick-start sexual defiance. My eyes itch with the shape of all that she is. The bluster. The force. The craft of her plotting. I wonder which parts of her expensive body Sam Wells lusts after more. Is it her cotillion waist, her jackknifed legs, her collateral tits, or maybe her spitfire brain, its appetite and ingenuity, that keeps his voice in a low, hoarse purr.

"Do you sail, Carol?" I ask.

"Sam just bought a Bermuda 40' in St. Thomas and we plan to take our holidays there, so maybe yes, finally, I will learn how to sail. In time, it should be possible, don't you think, Sam? It would be lovely."

She has lost most of her Florida cracker twang and replaced it with a Yankee blue blood accent delivered in a measured cadence. Yet, even there, Carol gives her self away by saying Bermuda 40' instead of sailboat. As you well know, Skip, a Bermuda 40' is any sailor's wet dream. Carol, better known to you as Jesse, may be sneering at me with the weight of a joke unrevealed, but she just smiles as if looking down on this booth from a great height, undisturbed by the scribbled logbook of distressed ports assigned to my name and hers. I look at both of them again, thinking I must be dreaming them in front of me or they must be dreaming me. For that's how this moment feels in a near empty bar off Las Olas Boulevard in Ft. Lauderdale.

I came over to Sam Wells' booth hoping to cleanse my body with a modest nod to my soul, and I'm thrown back to all I've lost just as I wanted to gain Rosario's favor and make a new start in St. Thomas. Now, it's Carol and Sam who will make a new start there. It's Carol and Sam who, starting in West Palm Beach, listened to my naked fat frying in the pan and found the sound of it to their liking. Now, standing in the midst of another storm I never see coming, I want to collect some additional payment for my troubles. I want to tell someone I know who they are, but the bar is empty except for the three of us. I can report them to the police, but Sam can also report me. As good as I thought I was, Skip, I was no match for the two of them. Not even close. Jesse set me up. Jesse snagged Jimmy Q off his bar stool. Jesse talked the comandante into taking out Jimmy. Jesse sailed off with *Stardust* and the cocaine and Rosario. And Sam Wells bankrolled her from the start. God, for all I know, maybe they really are married. What now, brown cow? Once again, there's a fierce trade wind clutching my throat and I've got nothing to throw back at the wind but a corkscrew smile.

Before I walked into Crazy Greg's bar, maybe they were discussing the worn collar and flip-flops of their next island-hopping victim. Or pouring over the finishing touches of how to use some other stooge to make more money than they can use. Maybe they were fixing to grab more of the cocaine trade Jimmy left behind in the Turks & Caicos. I want to laugh and tell them they're good, very good, yet Philip is dead, Rosario is living on another island with my child, and I can't reach her, and I can't get back the years I spent under the dim light of the comandante's pearl-handled gun. My mouth has gone dry because I've got no way to turn down the smug smiles on these unexpected collaborators and masters of the double-cross reverse.

What you know can't hurt us, she says without words. I can see him making any deal to keep the thrust of her, gathered close. Jesse Dove and Sam Wells slide out of their booth. Jesse straightens her dress, turns back, stubs her cigarette on the end of the table. Wells takes her by the arm. For such a skilled trader in the chaos of human collisions, his touch on her skin seems too gentle.

"Don't worry about *Stardust,*" Wells says. "We got everything of value off of her before she sank, although it took some time to find your hiding spot."

I nod and say, "Bravo."

"Look us up some time in St. Thomas," Jesse says. "*Stardust* is now a black B-40, sleek as a witch, so pretty and fast in any weather. This is a boat to die for."

"What about Rosario?" I say to their backs. "Was she just another puppet?" They pause inside the heat of the only words I can think to hurl.

"Lovely girl, but I've lost of track of her," Jesse says. "My contacts tell me she's living in New York. She's gone, vanished." Jesse scans the room. Something in her eyes chokes back the raw conclusion of what follows. "I can't find her there."

I grab a glass of rum off their table and throw the gold liquid at her feet. She grabs a napkin, lifts her leg onto a chair, and wipes her right ankle. I see again the coral snake I remember, still pretty, still lethal. Jesse walks on in a modest sashay, her heels snapping the floor. Sam lingers, turns back, approaches me with something of an offering.

"We all have our weaknesses once we get to the islands," Sam says.

As I finish my DR tale, the sailboat weathervane with the blue-green patina clicks on the cottage roof. Sleeping or not sleeping, my skipper now aims to reach the tidal gate through which all the waters of the world will surge, turn, reverse and flow again. His eyes flutter, close, then open wide with blood tears.

"I miss Hale," he says.

His words enter me like a glass shard. "I know you do."

"I thought he could swim forever," he whispers.

I swallow hard. "So did I."

"The Gulf took him from us. Not you. It wasn't your fault."

I nod my head, unable to speak.

"The Gulf will bring him back," he whispers. "Are you coming on board? It's about time for all that."

"You've got more in the tank, Skip."

"No matter what you did or didn't do, I don't care about any of that. I'm just glad you made it back home alive."

"I'm here with you, Skip."

"There's a photograph in my desk," he says, his words backwashing down his throat. "I want you to have it. Look at the back. The numbers there."

"What about the numbers?"

He doesn't answer. He can't swallow. He can't find his air.

I reach out with my left hand, the one that's always looked like a claw with the pinkie missing, the one he would never acknowledge given the origin of its pain, and I wrap my damaged hand around his damaged hand, the one he burned as a boy. I squeeze hard. He squeezes back. I take a long look, not knowing what I'm going to say until the words come. "We'll meet again out in the Gulf Stream. I'll be looking for you on the high side, so let's both keep an eye out."

"That's the way it is." he says, his face wet like mine like we've been standing watch inside the teeth of something we don't fully understand. He adds, "Don't worry about me. I'll be here or there. I had the best possible run. The wind at my back. I could ask for more, but why should I get it?"

His breathing comes on shallow and hard. His eyes flicker. He can't find an air pipe. He's drowning in his bed. He reaches up, pulls me close, lets go, sinks back. One gulp, two, three, no more. I slump in the chair, my hands shaking, my teeth chattering.

I stagger into the darkened living room where my mother sits at one end of the sofa with her eyes closed. I don't want her in this house. I want to shake my fist again at the sky because my skipper is gone. He gave me what I wanted. He heard me out my long, dark way, but now I want more. I want to know him again in this new place after the tale is told. I want him back home alive. I won't tell her he's gone.

The mask of my mother's face slants open.

"When you die," she says, "the circle of memory doesn't close. The body remembers the soul while the soul remembers the body. We think we lose everything, but it's not that way."

"How do you know any of this?" I say, pinching the sofa arm.

"Your soul's always looking after you even after your body has failed."

"I don't know what you're talking about."

"Yes, you do."

I want to go back and sit with my father's body.

I start to get up and she grabs my arm. "Sit with me," she says. "All you've been doing is sitting with him, night after night. It's my turn now."

"Hale's death," she says to the darkness holding each of us separate from each other, "is something that nearly killed each of us. Some part of us all wanted to die. No one more than you. I saw it in your eyes but I couldn't help you. Your father and I thought you had put him up to it. The police later told us they'd seen Hale hanging out with dope smugglers. We told them they had to be wrong but they had Hale on camera. They were following him. The boat that came out that night to the freighter was Coast Guard. You were both a hair's breadth away from arrest."

There's no air in my lungs after she says this. I want to hurt her right now, but her husband lies dead in the next room.

"How come you never told me you knew Hale was in trouble?" I shout, digging into my left hand with my right, my head swooning with the thought I might have been spared a decade of dazed and blunted torment if she had offered any refuge.

"I didn't want to believe it. I wanted to believe you were responsible for his death. I didn't think it was possible Hale could get mixed up with dope smuggling. He was on everybody's A team. Then one morning he's gone. I never saw him again. After that fact sank in, I hated you. I hated your father. I hated Florida. I wanted to get away from this miserable state and never return, but your father said, no. He spent decades trying to get to Florida so he could sail year-round. He was not going back to Ohio or anywhere else."

"You wanted to punish me for killing your god," I say, inching back from her on the sofa.

"You were the last one with him."

"I know, but . . ."

"You should have never let him go out there. You could have done something."

"Yeah, you're right, but I didn't, and we've all been paying for my lapse in judgment ever since. And what do we have to show for this payment except we're all fucking broke. Why didn't you ever call a spiritual truce, Mom? Aren't you the enlightened one in this family?"

Tears stain my mother's glasses, but I don't give a damn. Tears you can boil and drink on any voyage.

"It's not old age killing your father," she says, "it's his not knowing what happened to Hale."

"I told him everything. The whole story. Nothing left out. And by the way, our skipper is dead. I was with him when he died." Now, it's my turn to hold the burning sword over her head. She folds her arms around herself. Minutes pass or hours. Neither of us move.

"Shouldn't we call someone?" she finally says.

"He's not going anywhere," I say. "Let's keep talking. This is the best chance we'll ever have, here in the dark, with our skipper still listening in."

"Your father kept us moving so he never had to see himself frozen up inside. He couldn't even sleep unless he'd belted one too many. He couldn't stand to think about Hale dying out in the ocean. He couldn't stand to think how lonely and confused Hale must have felt, so he drank down his pain while you ran off to god knows where, and I tended to my knitting. I might just as well have been knitting a shroud for all of us."

"That's exactly what you did, Mom. You were our shroud-maker."

Before she finishes, I already know where I have to go next.

"Hale wanted out of this life," I say.

"Don't ever say that," she sneers.

"He'd had enough of winning, performing, jumping through hoops. That's not who he was. He was just a confused kid like me. He didn't know what he wanted until it was too late, but I know he was tired of having to prove his greatness."

"I never saw him complain about his gifts," she says, her face rigid with a fierce glow. "I never heard him say he wanted off the swim team. That he didn't like all the attention from those big-name schools. He'd already sent out applications. The whole country was knocking on his door."

"The whole country was killing your son. It was not enough or it was too much, but either way, this life was not giving him what he needed."

"You can't know that," she says.

"The cards always conceal as much as they reveal, isn't that one of your lines, Mom? Isn't that your trick to winning every card game you ever play? Knowing how to read what you can't see? Well, you didn't read the one card you cared most about. But don't feel bad, nobody figured Hale out."

"Stop it, Hale was no card trick. He was my son."

"No, he was the family god."

"Stop it, please."

"No, not yet," I say, hitting the sofa because I can't bring myself to hit her. "Skip wanted to know if I'd ever spread a man's ashes at sea. He's not counting on a spiritual reunion. He only wants to find Hale out there in the godforsaken Gulf Stream."

My mother blinks back tears with no more combat left. She gulps air as if drowning. I do nothing.

"Your grandmother believed we don't have a soul. We *are* soul. And that's who your father is in that bed."

"He's a dead sailor who's not coming back. Can't we agree on anything?"

Now I'm the one who needs air. I leave her on the sofa, walk out to the back porch, and open the sliding door. I wet my finger to see which way the wind's blowing. There's not a puff. I look back at my mother, but she's gone to sit until morning with her skipper. I hear her weeping and I weep too. The two of us now equal in the night rain.

CHAPTER XXII

No Bibles. No eulogies. No flowers. No tender music playing. No promise of the better life to come after the stowaway of the robust worm. Just the *blub, blub, blub* of the idling diesel. I bring the sack of ashes. My mother brings a basket of pink rose petals.

Ten years ago, Skip hired Captain Joe to scatter his ashes. He gave him three hundred bucks as advance payment. He wanted to make sure the job got done. Skip didn't want to spend one extra minute toe-tagged in a refrigerator morgue. I read in Skip's will that he hired Captain Joe to insure *safe conduct*. That's one of those peculiar nautical terms that means, "a written guarantee by a belligerent that a ship will be allowed to proceed in safety on a designated voyage." My father wanted to make sure he hired the right captain to escort his remains safely to a north-running ocean river big enough to spawn its own storms.

Who would that man be? Not me on a bender.

Captain Joe's a handsome, nearly ageless mariner of mixed blood with a full-crown of thick dark hair. Joe and Skip spent time together because Joe was always in need of cash and Skip was always in need of someone who could lift, haul, or repair something he no longer could. Captain Joe has had a string of marriages and an even longer unraveling spool of jobs and repossessed boats sold for next to nothing on the auction block. Skip said Joe was saddled with more debt than the Feds, so he always paid him a tad more than the price they agreed upon.

"I don't know how one man can get so jammed up," Skip said about Joe. "He can fix anything faster than the pope. Smart as a crowbar. He doesn't drink. Doesn't swear. Doesn't get rattled. Good man in a hurricane. But god damn does he have poor taste in women. He'd be better off with his dick in a sling for all the good it's done him."

At the Tiger Point Marina on Egan's Creek in Fernandina Beach, the sun swings as hot and bright as a ball-peen hammer. The air stirs in transition, not clear, not yet muggy. I pull Captain Joe aside and ask him if he's done this before.

"Yeah," he says. "I've been on a run like this before."

"Skip wants me to make sure his ashes don't fly back on board."

"Don't worry." Captain Joe says, wiping down the wheel. "We'll do right by the skipper." I want to ask Joe if he's got any booze on board, but I remember Skip telling me Joe keeps his boats dry as a desert. I'll have to take this last ride sober. My mother and I stand on the aft deck of a thirty-two-foot cruiser looking for a signal from Captain Joe to man the lines and shove off. I want to say something to her, but the words won't come out. He gives me only the slightest nod that he's ready to go. Like Skip, he's used to doing most things by himself. Captain Joe presses the stainless steel lever forward and we leave the dock for the ocean.

There's nothing as thrilling, Skip said, as pulling away from the dock, threading the channel markers, slipping past the break-wall, and finally leaving behind the land for the unknown. He always wanted the unknown ports and islands to outnumber the known ones. So here we are, just where he wants to be, setting out and facing the unclear hour of arrival.

As we round the northern tip of Amelia Island, I walk to the foredeck. To port stands the southern tip of Cumberland Island where Skip loved to dock and eat a ham sandwich and salted hard-boiled egg while Mother walked across the island to go shelling on a great sweep of wild beach. To starboard rises Fort Clinch, a brick pentagonal fortress used as a safe haven for blockade runners during the Civil War. Always look back once before you leave a harbor, he told Hale and me, so you know what the land is going to look like when you return.

Captain Joe signals me back to the poop deck before we reach the entrance swells. It's his show and I mean to give him no trouble. Now, the voyage begins. No one knows exactly where we're going. Everywhere I look, there's almost no heave to the water. This world of storms strong enough to snap steel is now out of breath. I've never before seen the Atlantic smooth enough to freeze a boat's reflection on a summer day.

The Gulf Stream is sixty miles offshore from Amelia Island—too far for Captain Joe. He promises Skip he'll carry his ashes out to the deep running swells, but he asks permission from my mother to pull up short. My mother nods, waves a hand. She says wherever we stop, that's where the Gulf Stream starts. Captain Joe cuts the engine twelve miles out. He says that's a nice round number for a sailor's life, always looking to ride one of the twelve points of sail. It happens to be noon when we stop. Twelve miles out at twelve even. The boat sashays with no anchor down.

Captain Joe tells me to open the transom panel and park myself there. "Take a handful of ashes," he says in a hushed tone like he's trying not to scare off any big fish. "Lay them down on the water—gently, slowly, nothing fancy, no song and dance. We don't want the ashes coming back on board cause they don't belong here anymore with us."

I go down on both knees. I reach into the sack of ashes.

"Matt, I want to say something before you start." Captain Joe takes off his cap and puts it over his heart the way sailors in the Navy are trained to do.

"Thanks, Skip, for being a good friend. For making me laugh about my troubles with money and women. God knows we need more laughter and I'm grateful for you showing me how it's done. I'll miss seeing your long-finned Chevy pull into Tiger Point. I'm glad you were a friend of mine."

My mother pins herself to the stern, her head bowed. I sink my hands into a plastic bag inside a box and hold shards of bone mixed with the silk of ash and lay my father down on the twelve o'clock waters.

The seas don't open for his ashes; just the opposite. The waves that come in bunches lay down smooth enough for footfall, and I find it amusing thinking, even now, Skip won't have to swim and get his head wet. My father will walk weightless toward the Gulf Stream, in league with his own reflection and also released from it. My mother tosses pink and yellow rose petals overboard. That's not quite right. She holds the rose petals over her head and a freshening breeze picks them up and carries them to the water. She never looks at the ashes, never looks at the petals. Never says anything while I reach down into the box of ashes and let them go through the sieve of my fingers.

What did my father call this life? *One salt hour between two eternities.*

I see him there floating over the transom, a puff of smoke cut with pink and yellow petals that flutter, then fall; so many of them has my mother thrown that they gather on the surface of the water and blink in the sun. In that blinking, I remember her telling me about the ten-year-old flower girl at their wedding. They were married outside because Skip said you can't breathe right in a church because you can't open any window.

With the flick of my mother's wrist, I see the petals floating from the basket of a flower girl leading a wedding party to their vows on a knoll overlooking Lake Erie, the mood expectant, ephemeral, irresistible, the view of the Lake good enough to glimpse the shimmer of Green Island.

How strangely comforting, Skip, to know that somewhere on an island to the distant south, there's a pearl of a boy that neither you nor I have ever met, and yet he must resemble one of us in some small way. His skin is golden brown. His eyes, a streak of hazel or indigo. He's strong and swift and lives near the pull of deep current that reaches from Africa to the Americas. His story is unknown yet familiar, for he lives near boats with keels that take easily to the long distance foam. Friend or foe I can't say, but there's a fiery laugh that comes from his throat that will not be easily tamed.

When Captain Joe swings his boat around and aims for shore, Emily holds out her hand to Jack Younger. I can tell my Mother wants to wave, but she doesn't. She wants to say something, but she doesn't. She wants to reach down into the greatest of all ocean rivers, rippling north with enough power to light all the cities of the world and let his body shine back to her from the depth of the chasm, but she doesn't. Then, before the engines pull us out of the harness of the drift, she does offer a wave, a little wave of her fingers toward the curve of petals, a hidden gesture to the way-showing hand of a summer boy from Sandusky, Ohio, on Lake Erie.

"I'm going to stay on," I whisper to my mother. "We can work something out." But even as I offer these few words, I wonder how much of my promise will hold strong and true to the mark.

"Just give me a few days more," she says. "After that you can do what you want."

CHAPTER XXIII

Just two days after we scattered Skip's ashes, my mother sweeps the cottage of his belongings. I would have thought seeing his clothes on hangers and his shoes on the floor might have offered some comfort, but no, she wants me to take everything to Goodwill. I dig out plastic grocery bags and fill them till they bulge. As I carry them to the trunk of Skip's '67 Impala, I see myself only a few weeks before coming to their doorstep with my own trash bags stuffed with dirty clothes.

I work for two days, moving from the guest room to his old single room, stripping sheets, scrubbing chairs and tables, vacuuming carpets, pounding rugs, blasting loose the stain and smell of my father's last days. She sleeps while I work. In his old single room, I sit down at his roll-top desk and try to picture him hunched there reading magazines, writing notes, paying bills.

How did he pay his bills, I wonder, if he didn't keep much cash in the bank?

The desk comes with many drawers like a house with many windows. I open each cubby and remove the contents. In one drawer alone I find business cards, spare change, chocolate candies, loose keys, paper clips, pens, chewing gum, a ruler, a calculator, newspaper clippings, notebooks, photographs of friends long since gone.

In a bottom drawer, I find a photograph of Skip at the helm of the *Pirate's Penny* taken at dusk during the Mentor race on Lake Erie. It's the one he wanted me to have. She's roaring downwind at seven or eight knots, flying a spinnaker. There are three people in the cockpit. Two at the mast. One on the foredeck. All in shadow. Two of these figures at the mast are Hale and me. I would have been twelve. Hale, almost fourteen. Why is this photograph, which first appeared on the front page of the

Sunday *Cleveland Plain Dealer*, not in a frame? Why is it hidden inside a desk drawer? Skip must have loved it. It must have made him want to swoon, so rich is the charge of his boat, the spinnaker perfectly sculpted and filled, the city of Cleveland in the background dwarfed by the size and rake of the mast. On the back, there's a block-lettered stamp, Cleveland Plain Dealer, June 19, 1965. And beneath that stamp, there's a second set of numbers 38-12-4-52-22-15.

I turn the photograph over and look again at the number on the mainsail of the *Pirate's Penny*, 2215. I work backwards from there. How tall was the mast? Fifty-two feet. How deep was her draft? Four feet. How wide was her beam? Twelve feet. How long was she on the waterline? Thirty-eight feet and eight inches. Close enough. 38-12-4-52-22-15 is a number he wanted to remember.

How do you remember a long number if you're a sailor?

You put your hands to work in the wood of dreams. You look down at the deep creases, the scars that won't heal, the nicks and blood bruises, and you let them guide you all the way back to an Amish barn where you built the *Pirate's Penny* in three years of nights and weekends, and you see again how you conceived of her, her length, her width, her depth, her height, and the number on her sail. This is a truth number, cut with blood and memory, a number you can splinter, but you can't sink, a number only he and I and my mother know. It's the number to his safe.

I close the door to Skip's old room, open the closet door, and squat in front of Skip's gray Pioneer safe. My fingers tremble as I cup them to fit the face of the combination dial. I spin through the numbers on the back of the photograph: 38-12-4-52-22-15.

Click. Clack. Cha-Ching.

The safe opens and I peer inside and find a number of manila envelopes with insurance policies, birth and wedding certificates, Social Security cards, and copies of titles to cars and boats long sold. Beneath those are two steel boxes. One brimming with gold coins in plastic sleeves and pouches. The larger second box is packed with cash mostly, in hundred dollar bills.

I count out forty bundles of ten hundreds each and I leave ten bundles behind. I close the safe, spin the dial, return the photograph of the *Pirate's Penny* where I found it. I tell myself maybe she will figure out Skip must have given me the combination and told me to take the money. Maybe. Maybe not. I zip up my duffel, grab a pair of Skip's red leather topsider boat shoes from his closet, and put them on. They fit nicely.

I call Bob Martin. Tell him I have thirty thousand in cash. He doesn't believe me. I tell him all I require is a Bill of Sale. I want to shove off from Tiger Point on the hour. He gets cash I tell him, and in exchange, I want no third degree. Just the keys.

I study Skip's room one more time.

There's nothing more of his I want, but there is the one photograph of our family quartet in Mystic Seaport, taken six months before all our troubles began. It's the picture I saw when I first came home. We've sailed across Lake Erie and across the Erie Canal.

We detour north into Long Island Sound and stop in Mystic on a hot, windy day before we turn south down the Hudson River, past the Statue of Liberty, Sandy Hook, then out past Atlantic City to Norfolk, Virginia, then inside on the Intracoastal Waterway to Charleston, then back out to Jacksonville, and finally into Ft. Lauderdale. We are so strong and tested by the weather that nothing can stop us, but something does that I still can't explain.

I put the picture in my duffel.

I reach under Skip's single bed where I sleep and pull out my duffel where I keep the pearl. I open up the pouch and look again at the gem, feel its weight, admire its river of flames. Thank you, Philip, I say to myself. I put the pearl back in my duffel, zip it up, and turn to leave the room.

I pause at the door, look back again.

This is my father's room. Where he kept his shoes, his sailing photos, his floppy white hat, his chocolate stash, his treasures. This is where he wanted to die instead of in the guest room sealed away from the rest of the cottage. This is where he found his comfort and consolation when he wasn't seeking out the shape of wind over water. This is his pink-flamed conch shell. His place of safekeeping. Where he launched his dreams for the next boat after the very last boat was sold. This single room is his lamination factory for the wound of his long lost son.

I return to the safe, take out the pearl, and put it on top of the Pioneer safe along with the business card from Mr. Sunman. I take a pen from my father's desk and write on the card, "Call Sunman about the pearl."

I tell myself this about the pearl: I can't wait for the auction block, the rich collector, the six-figure sale. I need to get away from the land. I need to get back to the water. I need to try again to make my way again to the south. That direction on the compass rose promises only more risk, more turbulence and uncertain pay, but it's all I know, all that my skipper trained me to do. South is who I am.

I hope my mother recognizes the pearl is meant to be a gift of much greater value than a stack of hundred dollar bills. This pearl was clawed out of the deep. It cost nothing less than Philip's life. Not knowing its worth, I almost threw it back into the sea. He never knew what treasure he had found. Now, it's hers to do with as she pleases. More than its auction price, I hope she looks upon the pearl as a little planet, containing everything our family was. I hope she marvels at its beauty in a world where so little beauty guides us beyond the channel markers unseen. If she sees none of this inside a prized pearl clawed out of the Bahamas, then to hell with making amends. I have a boat to catch at Tiger Point Marina.

I slip out the front door and find Skip's '67 Impala parked in the gravel beside the house. He keeps the keys in the ash tray. I put my duffel in the back seat and then I see her walking toward me. She looks sweat-stained and hard-road traveled at the edge of fields and cities. She pulls from a handbag draped around her neck the photograph she had taken of us by the shoeshine boy in Puerto Plata, the one I wrote my parents' address on: 43 Spanish Moss, Fernandina Beach, Florida. I glance at the photo, then I look up at her. It's the same woman and it's not. Gone is the pretty green dress. Gone are the silver bracelets. Her hair is swept off her face, making her pinched eyes stand out. Her hands no longer dance as they do in the Polaroid, but still it's her, daring to travel the long way into the greater loneliness of not knowing where to find me and risking more exhaustion to come this far from wherever she's been.

Part of me wants to say, "What do you want?"" Another part says, "I don't care what you want." I returned to my home because I had nowhere to go and I had a story to tell my father. Maybe she has a story to tell me that can't wait, but it must.

"Get in," I say.

"Where are we going?"

"You'll see."

Rosario climbs into the front seat.

"I thought American cars had seat belts," she says.

"There are no seatbelts in this car. My father didn't believe in them."

I look at my father's cottage, knowing this is the last time I will see it. It's the last time I will come here. My mother will sell it and go live with her sister in Satellite Beach. In another ten years, someone will tear it down and build a bigger house. I drive away slowly, not wanting to draw attention to myself or the car. Rosario looks out the window wondering what comes next.

"You had a baby?"

She says nothing and I think it's too soon to speed back to the source of a stinging wound, but I can't help it. "Ours?" I add.

"He died."

I want to ask how the baby died and when, but I say nothing because the death of a child that she wanted so badly must be part of a longer story that will take time for her to sort out. Where better to work out pain than on the water that breaks all things and repairs all things with silver spray and stern wake? We met each other at the fingertip border where she longed to escape her island and I longed to arrive, a confluence that immersed us in each other's bodies until there was no telling water from land. Now, we've reversed course. She longs to arrive and I, to leave. What the hell, let the uncharted tacking begin . . .

236

"I hear a siren," she says.

"It's not for us," I say, turning past the cemetery where so many Fernandina shrimpers and sea captains are buried, but not my Skipper. The weight of one more death burns me down.

"Give me one reason why I should trust you about anything."

Rosario looks out the window at the slabs of fading granite.

"I left Jesse. I left everything she promised me."

"That's not enough," I say.

"I know . . ." she says, turning her head to see me straight on.

In another mile, at the entrance of Tiger Point Marina, I see a man walking the gravel shoulder. He looks to have been out in the elements a long time, worn, beaten, but not broken by long distance foot travel. I recognize his broad shoulders, the sure stride and residual sorrow lingering on his face.

Here he is borrowed from the watery distances, a figure of fair weather, his grip on the earth as strong as mine and by the pace of his arms, as keenly intent on departure. Where to, lost traveler? He can't say anymore than I can, but in his wave I hear a curious phrase from Melville, *no more to rise forever*, and I imagine the whaler's words contain the riddle of who my brother is, no more and forever, both rising and falling, both lost and found, long gone and just at the side of the road.

He looks once at me, our eyes reaching out. He offers a tip of his hand off his forehead as if he were thanking me for releasing him from my story. I wave back, reluctantly. I want to pull over and greet him at long last, but a U-haul truck whizzes past and blocks my crossing the road. When the truck passes, the man, my brother, offering a bon voyage nod, is gone again to wherever swimming gods go when they can no longer hug the road.

I turn into Tiger Point Marina and drive to the end of the dock on Egan's Creek where just two days earlier we set out on Captain Joe's boat with Skip's ashes. I leave for a half hour to close the deal with Bob Martin. He gladly takes the cash. Asks no questions. He neatly folds the Bill of Sale and tucks it into an envelope. I take my sweet time because I want to see if Rosario wanders off just like she wandered back into my life. I want to see if she's just another cross-wind ghost dredged from a past I can't always recall. But no, she's still there beside the dock, listening, looking, a figure of remorse, a lost shining behind a stray noon shadow.

"What happens here?" she asks.

"We're picking up our boat," I say.

"I was hoping you'd say that."

That's all I need for her to say. Yet that's not true.

There's also the child, the gone, goodbye, who-were-you? child. In place of words, I taste the brine of another dark cloud, weightless and freighted. When is the right time to press Rosario about this past we share? My wrists sting with an older salt: *Whatever you steal, you lose.* Not that she stole a child from us, but that I never knew how much she needed our sex to work in her favor. Silence from her is like a deep-trolling hook, then a tug, and finally a strike as we pull up beside the dock of the *Tabula Rasa.*

"Sometimes a woman can't bear a child of a certain gender. Sometimes we are suited for a boy or a girl, but not both."

"I've never heard of this," I say, walking toward the *Tabula Rasa,* holding her hand, not fully hearing her words.

"A doctor in Honduras told me I couldn't bear a boy child."

"That's what happened?"

"I don't know. I had a boy, but . . ."

"But?"

"He was never strong. He caught malaria."

I pinch the bridge of my nose, remembering how Skip took malaria in Cuba and nearly died. The blood of my blood nearly sucked down by a mosquito. I pull the troubled piece of amber from my pocket and hold it up in front of her the way she held up the photograph of us. If nothing else, the last thirteen years show me this riddle: my body is littered with shards of rare pathogens that help me to live.

Looking at Rosario, through the thumb-sized window of the two mosquitoes trapped in gold amber, I smile at how her face blooms there, and think, yes, these two time travelers are long dead, but who's to say they can't be resurrected from blue smoke, reassembled out of the fire that consumed the world they once lived in? On this voyage, everyone pays up with their greatest treasure, and then must start again with nothing but the next day, a boat, a little wind, nothing clear enough to write on a postcard.

From inside the *Tabula Rasa*, I hear a series of acrobatic pings.

I leave Rosario on the dock and stick my head down the companionway and catch the ship's clock and bell making itself heard. I didn't know it worked. A crack runs through the glass face and the current time is wrong. The bell's brass rim is blackened with salt patina. Inside the striking of the bell, I hear Skip waking Hale and me from our bunks to take the graveyard watch as we slip past the Cape Fear River in Wilmington, North Carolina and make good time toward Jacksonville. "Three bells and All's Well," he shouts to us where we groan a return greeting, wanting to stay curled in our bunks, half-dreaming, knowing that our lives are about to change once we arrive in Florida, but not knowing how.

"Three bells and All's Well," I say to Rosario.

"What?"

"We have a working ship's bell," I say. "We'll be able to time our watches by the ship's bell."

"I don't know what that means, but it sounds important."

"Yeah, it is," I say, thinking she and I can do this. With a little luck and a ship's bell, and the blackwater rivers well behind us, we can keep our appointed watches and make good time to the south.

"Come on aboard," I say, offering her my hand, "so you can learn your way around."

Rosario smiles weakly, bravely, not knowing where we're going, but go we must, the two of us soon to be given over to the sawbone combers that never stop running. The bell stops and

I scan the marina for a familiar face. When no one returns to see us off, I want to snug the lines. I have no idea whether Rosario and I have the smallest sea bean of a chance of working something out on water any better than we did on land. So much has gone wrong. It would be easy to say only lying wins the high ground, not truth, not loyalty, not understanding, not love. It would be easier still to call each other poison. But I want to hear her story, every single last detour and dead-end.

I want to know what bartering with lost angels and blue-eyed devils she's had to make in order to get this far turned around inside the chaos of her own tilted heart. *I want out and I want in*, but no matter the confusion, I aim to shove off from Tiger Point, motor out the sleeve of Egan's Creek, and, as my brother and father further disperse into the great unnamed pastures of living salt, I will head south once again with Rosario seated cautiously in the cockpit, and lift my hands to the heavens, and give thanks for all the unspeakable sorrows of this life.